THE MIRACLE GIRL

THE
MIRACLE
GIRL

A NOVEL

ANDREW ROE

ALGONQUIN BOOKS OF CHAPEL HILL 2016

Published by
Algonquin Books of Chapel Hill
Post Office Box 2225
Chapel Hill, North Carolina 27515-2225

a division of
Workman Publishing
225 Varick Street
New York, New York 10014

First paperback edition, Algonquin Books of Chapel Hill, March 2016.
Originally published in hardcover by Algonquin Books of Chapel Hill,
April 2015.
Printed in the United States of America.
Published simultaneously in Canada by Thomas Allen & Son Limited.
Design by Anne Winslow.

The following chapters have appeared previously, in slightly different
form, in the following publications: Chapter 2, published as "Lonely Man
Sitting at Bar" in *24 Bar Blues: Two Dozen Tales of Bars, Booze, and the
Blues* (Press 53). Chapter 7, published as "The One You Don't Pick" in
Wigleaf. Chapter 9, published as "Accident" in *The Sun*.

This is a work of fiction. While, as in all fiction, the literary perceptions
and insights are based on experience, all names, characters, places, and
incidents either are products of the author's imagination or are used
fictitiously.

LIBRARY OF CONGRESS CATALOGING-IN-PUBLICATION DATA
Roe, Andrew, [date]
The miracle girl : a novel / by Andrew Roe.—First Edition.
     pages cm
ISBN 978-1-61620-360-3 (HC)
1. Coma—Patients—Family relationships—Fiction.
2. Daughters—Fiction. 3. Miracles—Fiction. 4. Medical fiction.
5. Psychological fiction. I. Title.
PS3618.O3623M57 2015
813'.6—dc23   2014038607

ISBN 978-1-61620-532-4 (PB)

10 9 8 7 6 5 4 3 2 1
First Paperback Edition

For my parents

"I BELIEVE IN EVERYTHING."

—David Ferrie, in Don DeLillo's *Libra*

THE MIRACLE GIRL

VISITORS

THE CROWDS KEEP coming. More and more every day it seems. But in the beginning it was just the random neighbor or stray soul from the surrounding area, drawn by rumor and whisper and desperate wish. Word spread. Somehow they heard about the girl on Shaker Street, the one who almost died—who should have died—but didn't, and now she can't speak or move, she's paralyzed, mute, hooked up to machines and tubes, her body a living statue, but also holy, blessed, a gift from God, a child who heals and gives hope to those in need . . . And it went from there, slowly at first, a mysterious, massing thing with a life of its own. People appearing at the house, awed and urgently curious, polite as churchgoers, something ancient in their eyes.

They find their way, clutching foldable maps and Thomas Guides and handwritten directions, in this, the fall of 1999, the much-publicized final year of the millennium. For reasons known, unknown. Yes, the full-on tragedies and crushing misfortunes, the kind of sorrow you'd expect, as well as the everyday, the shitty little speed bumps of life—the work problems, the marital despair, the doomed conspiracies of the heart. The girl might be able to help. So why not go and see for themselves? They park their cars and walk up to the small one-story house. Arriving singly, or in pairs, or in larger groups—sometimes entire families even, multiple generations seeking relief, holding hands, chanting the names of loved ones. You wouldn't believe the traffic getting here, the freeway a nightmare crawl.

It's like any neglected house in any neglected neighborhood. The yellowed lawns and chain-link fences and toppled children's toys, the latter discarded and forgotten, the plastic leached of color long ago. Trees are sparse, infrequent. The doorbell doesn't work. And if someone else is already inside the house, spending time with the girl, they remain outside and endure the Southern California sun. Shading their eyes, waiting their turn. Because now, sometimes, there's a line, depending on the hour and day of the week (Saturday mornings being the worst). And if that's the case, and the line grows and more visitors arrive, conversations spark, stories are exchanged. It passes the time and reminds them of why they've made this journey. They marvel at how the narratives are the same or different or a little of both, yet all share a common theme: the need to believe, the yearning for something beyond one's self.

"I'm here but I'm not sure why I'm here," someone might say, waiting and looking up, briefly, at the sky swollen with light and heat.

"You'll know once you get inside," another will explain. "That's what they say."

Others know exactly why they've come: personal addictions (substance, sexual); various disorders (physical, psychological, spiritual); parents with cancer or one of the lesser-tiered diseases;

daughters who have lost their sense of smell and taste; sons who have lost their sense of love and kindness; siblings, cousins, nephews, nieces who are simply lost; friends who could not make the trip on their own due to their particular infirmity but desperately require the girl's help, her saintly, sacred intervention, because it's the last hope they have; the times apparently calling for a new way to understand, a new way to be.

Once inside they are greeted by the mother and then led through the living room and down a hallway and into the girl's room. And there she is. They behold her in her perpetual repose, Sleeping Beauty–like, but eyes alarmingly open, unblinking, unmoving, her hair long and dark and freshly shampooed. They hear the hum of machines, the ventilator's insistent suck. They note the aroma of flowers. Stuffed animals everywhere: her bed, shelves, the floor, spilling out of the open closet. With the bed and machines and furniture there isn't much space left, only a narrow path allowing them to get close enough to the girl. They ask if it's all right to touch her. The mother always says yes. And it always surprises them: how warm the girl's skin is. How it is burning. Burning with God.

The time invariably elapses too quickly. They are never ready to leave. *Just another minute, please.* And so they pray harder and mumble faster and the minute expires and they go. On the way out, they linger so they can ask questions: How long ago did it happen? Was she in a lot of pain? Is she in a lot of pain? Does she know we're here? Is there any awareness that, you know, this is happening? The mother can only answer the first question: the accident was nine months ago, another lifetime ago. For the rest, she shrugs, says the doctors don't know for sure, no one knows for sure, but many people think yes, yes she knows, yes she's aware, yes she's with us, it's all unfolding in front of her as if she's watching a movie.

Then they thank her, the mother, repeatedly, trying to say what cannot be said—what else can they do? There are other people waiting and it's time to move on. The day now more vivid, more substantial, in fuller focus. Could it be that the curative has already begun? They exit the house and step back out into the sun, the judgment gone, the light flooding everything and everyone, light that does not cause them to shade their eyes but to open them farther, see clearer, see deeper, light that's alive, light that's viscous, light that connects and fills and sustains, light that reflects (inwardly, outwardly) and seemingly has no end, light that's like a breath, like oxygen, the light, the light, everywhere the light.

PART ONE

MIRACLES AND WONDERS

1

| Karen |

EVERYTHING NOW: A before and after. Time split, a line separating what *was* from what *is*. Actually, two before and afters: the accident itself, and when things started happening with Anabelle. And *things,* Karen knows, is not the right word, not the right word at all; it sounds wrong and wobbly when spoken aloud and even when it's thought of in her mind, but what else to call it? Strange occurrences? Unexplained phenomena? Curious coincidences? Nothing is right. Nothing is adequate. And so: *things.*

She does this often, distinguishing between past and present, and it's what she's doing now as she retreats down the hallway and toward the kitchen after having ushered the first visitor of the day into her daughter's room, a woman who came because of her own daughter, who has cancer and is only eight years old, the same age as Anabelle. Before: visitors were rare. After: they show up almost every day. Before: she hardly spoke to anyone. After: she talks to people all the time. Before: she had a daughter that was fairly normal. After: a daughter that is anything but normal. Before: a husband. After: well . . .

The woman had traveled all the way from Bellingham, Washington, driving straight through, stopping only for gas and coffee and M&Ms, her face manic and oily from the road, one of her earrings having gone AWOL, strands of uncooperative, graying hair escaping a long ponytail, the rapid-fire speech of a standup comedian on a roll. "It isn't right," she told Karen before she hurried into the bedroom. "It just isn't right. A child. Cancer. Those two things, those two words, they don't go together. It doesn't make sense. And yet. The tests. The confirmation is there. She can't lift her left arm now sometimes. This isn't how the world is supposed to be. It shakes you to the core. It isn't right. I'm—I'm sorry. Off I go. Rambling and such. Just ask Terry. Terry, my husband, who's taking care of her while I'm here. Terry'll tell you. How I start in on one thing and then end up on another completely. He's half saint, really, Terry, after all we've been through. But your daughter. I'm sorry. Is it all right to touch her? I don't want to overstep. Or be like inappropriate. How does it usually work? I'm not really religious, see. It just felt like the right thing to do. I knew I had to drive. I knew I had to come."

Before: she didn't know such struggle and sadness could indiscriminately deploy in people's lives. After: she does.

And there in the kitchen is Bryce. With his little-boy wonder and NFL build, like two people in one. He's unloading the dishwasher, stacking plates and dishes on the counter. Not even nine o'clock now, and already it's blazing outside. Inside, it's time to close the windows and blast the air conditioning. It's what she'll do next. But first she needs to sit down. The kitchen table as temporary refuge, as site of intermission and much-needed pause. Bryce turns as she pulls out a chair. The day officially underway.

"Hey there. Our visitor all set then?"

"Just went in. I don't think she's slept in days. She's on a kind of a high. How long is it that a person can go without sleep?"

Bryce joins her at the table, his hair still wet from the shower. He smells like morning.

"I don't know," he says. "Three days? Four? There's coffee if you want. And guess what? I had an idea."

Bryce is always having ideas. He was one of the first to come, from La Mirada, a sweet soul and firm believer in fate, who'd been taking care of his sick mother (cancer, strokes, asthma, depression) until she finally died late last year. He'd been lost after, he told her, in a fog. Then he read about Anabelle online somewhere and came to see her the very same day. And now he helps out, answers the phone, changes Anabelle's sheets, brings groceries and books, cooks meals, cleans. She can't picture all this without him.

"I have a feeling you're going to tell me what that idea is," says Karen.

Bryce smiles. They have banter, definite banter. She's not sure when it started. But one day it was there, in the house with them, like an old friend.

"So there's this little core group of people we have helping out with Anabelle—Dominique, Marnie, Meredith, you, me. And the nurses and PTs and all the delivery and medical supplies people. And I was thinking, just thinking, we needed a name. You know. Something catchy. Something like Anabelle's Angels. We could have T-shirts and a secret handshake. What do you think?"

Now Karen smiles.

"I like it," she says, admiring the table's immaculate gleam and the organized stacks of mail: letters to Anabelle, letters to

Karen, bills, coupons, unheeded solicitations to people who used to live here, names that make her a little sad. "I like it a lot. Especially the secret handshake part."

"And I still want to get that website going," Bryce continues. "I have a friend who can help out with the coding and get us up and running. But first things first: how are you doing? Are you ready for this afternoon? Today's the big day, right? Ready for your close-up?"

"As ready as I'll ever be, I guess. I just don't want to sound like a spaz."

"Maybe we can practice a little. I could ask you some questions and you could practice your answers on me."

"Sure. Thanks, Bryce. That would be great. Thanks for everything."

She almost says more but stops herself.

"And there's coffee," adds Bryce. "I can make some eggs. Just give the word. Man. It's already a hundred out there it seems like. And you know what they're saying about the weather. It's not like it used to be."

"And when you can't count on the weather, then what?"

"All the earthquakes and power outages we've been having, too. On the drive over this morning there was a story on the radio about streaks of light in the sky, meteor showers maybe, out in the desert, near Joshua Tree. At this rate, we might not make it to January."

Inside Anabelle's bedroom the woman from Bellingham begins to weep. This is not uncommon. People cry, they fall to their knees in outright supplication. Some faint. Karen understands and doesn't understand. She's trying, though. They come and they keep coming and they are different after. Changed. What else can she do but open her door? Some days she thinks there are more visitors than the previous day, some days she thinks less, that it's finally dying down. But it never does. This is permanent. This is reality now. She's never used the phrase "life's work"—one of those concepts that she thought applied to lawyers and doctors and teachers but not to her. But it's beginning to feel like that. Like this is what she was meant to do. People were even starting to leave donations.

Before: she didn't expect much to come of her life. After: she's seriously reconsidering.

IT'S HER FIRST real interview and so she's picking cuticles and nibbling on nails as she waits for the *Eyewitness News* van to arrive. They're late. Also: the constant reconsiderations of clothing, hair, lipstick shade, etc. But why is she worrying? This isn't about her. It's about Anabelle. It's about everyone her daughter helps, those who come. Yet people would see her, Karen Vincent, on TV, note her imperfections and general blandness, and what would they think? There have been a few phone conversations with reporters, but never this, never an in-person interview with a camera filming everything, filming her. She worries she's not prepared, not TV worthy.

When the van pulls up she recognizes the reporter immediately. Doesn't know her name, but knows the face, the shower of blonde hair and drastic lips. Two men follow her up the concrete walkway; one, bearded, carries two cameras; another, also bearded, painfully lugs cables and lights and tripods. When they are at the door, waiting to be let inside after having knocked, she hears one of the men complaining about the other man's piss-poor directions: they'd been driving around southeastern Los

Angeles for an hour and who wants to be doing that. *I've never even heard of this town before and I've been living in L.A. for how long?* The van is crowned with one of those large, elaborate satellite dishes, looking as if it could be driven from somewhere else via remote control.

A deep breath and Karen opens the door. Kellee Clifton introduces herself, hands her a business card with the ABC logo. She's tall, athlete tall, has movie-star looks and emanates a strong scent reminiscent of the high-end cosmetics aisle. Karen cannot bring herself to look the aromatic woman in the eye: it's too much, the immense gulf between them. Kellee Clifton does not introduce the two men, who right away set up their equipment and continue their grumbling. "Couch'll do," says one. "Light will be crap with that window," says the other. "But whatever. It's late. We're late. I don't even want to think about the traffic getting back."

The house, the neighborhood: not TV worthy either. And briefly, while Kellee Clifton ducks into the bathroom and the men adjust tripods and test lights and criticize each other's respective skills, she wonders about her interviewer's life, what it's like—the people in her address book, the late-night meals at Beverly Hills restaurants she's never heard of—but she can't picture anything specific (and she's never had a business card either, logo or no logo). Even though Karen has lived all her thirty years within the confines of Los Angeles County, she has traversed those otherworldly westside freeways—the 405, the 101, the northerly reaches of the 5—only a handful of times, and she's never once spotted a celebrity in person or been to a party in the Hollywood Hills. It's all as foreign to her as, well, a foreign country. She's from L.A., but not the bright, glittery place that everyone imagines when they think of L.A. She's never been to that L.A. All she knows is what's east of the 605, inland, ordinary, where people have real jobs and real noses and real lives. No Kellee Cliftons here. El Portal doesn't even have its own freeway exit.

"Ready when you are, Kells," shouts the man handling the cameras, matting down his mass of facial hair. One camera faces the sofa; a second, the empty chair next to it. The other man—is the beard a job requirement? a union regulation?—walks over to Karen, takes her by the elbow, and then guides her toward the couch like she's got Alzheimer's or something. "Why don't you just sit right here, K? Get comfortable. Relax. This won't hurt a bit."

Are they starting? She must appear stunned. Because she is stunned. Kellee Clifton emerges from the bathroom, looking even better, younger, fresher. She must not have kids.

"All right, Mrs. Vincent," she says, taking her place in the chair. "We're going to go ahead and get started. I have some questions for you. We'll sit and talk, just like a normal conversation. And then after that, after some questions and background and back and forth, we'd like to get a few shots of your daughter."

"Anabelle."

"That's right. Anabelle."

"So where do we start?"

"Well, it's always a good idea to start at the beginning. Howard, are we rolling?"

"We are now. Camera one and two."

"So how about that then, for starters?"

"I'm sorry," says Karen. "How about what?"

"The beginning. How did all of this begin? Was it one day, all of a sudden? Or was it gradual, like a buildup, where you don't even realize because it's so slow?"

Kellee Clifton balances her chin with a freshly manicured thumb and forefinger, leaning forward, crossing her long, impressive left leg over her equally impressive right thigh, waiting now, waiting for Karen Vincent to speak.

AND WHILE SHE'S talking, while she's answering questions and explaining how the technical medical term for Anabelle's condition is something called *akinetic mutism,* her mind wanders. Where is John right now? What is he thinking at this very moment? Is he by himself? How is Anabelle doing? Is she wondering where her mom is? What's going through Kellee Clifton's mind as I clear my throat and stumble over this or that word? And the longer Karen looks at her, the blonder this woman's hair gets, the redder and fuller her lips seem. She pictures men dropping at Kellee's feet, devastated, giving themselves to her, entirely, in ways they never thought possible.

How DID IT begin? Simply. With smell, with scent. Roses specifically. One of her best friends, Marnie, was over and helping with Anabelle and asked where are the flowers. But there weren't any flowers. Her daughter's room and the rest of the house was, as usual, free of plant life and greenery, with the exception of a long-ago banished Chia Pet out in the garage somewhere.

"Do you smell that?" Marnie said, sniffing, nostrils a-flare in full bloodhound alertness. "It's so strong. Roses. That's roses. I smelt it out in the living room and now here, too."

"I think you're right." A sniff or two of her own, confirming. "I don't know where it's coming from. Weird. Outside maybe. Or the air freshener from the bathroom. I did have some flowers that someone brought, but that was weeks ago. And just a general bouquet thing. No roses."

They resumed changing Anabelle's nightgown, Karen lifting her daughter's body while Marnie removed the gown and replaced it with another, and Marnie would periodically stop and smell, stuck on it for some reason, at some point mentioning something about roses and the Virgin Mary. And that was that. And it did not seem like a beginning, but isn't that always the case.

This was after Karen had surfaced from her dark period, a time when she did not leave the house and did not let her husband touch her and eventually did not bother with the whole ridiculous, overrated charade of getting dressed and pretending that all was well when it was not, it was horribly unwell. She would remain in her robe for days, weeks, the worn, soothingly familiar terrycloth garment (tattered, baby-blue, the left pocket long gone) one of the last gratifications available to her. When the phone rang she didn't dare lift the suspicious device out of its cradle.

With the exception of Anabelle's room, which remained relatively clean and uncluttered and became a safe haven of sorts (the majority of her time spent there, sitting, reflecting, sleeping in the chair beside her bed, watching the relocated TV), the house slipped into deep disarray, spreading from room to room, like a series of smaller countries succumbing to an invading conqueror. The neglect was vast, impressive. Piles upon piles of mysterious, miscellaneous crap (now where did *that* come from?) appeared and did not go away. There was no place to sit or eat. Hallways had to be navigated like hiking trails. The coffee table in the living room amassed geologic layers of junk mail, flyers, receipts, unpaid bills, paper plates crusted with what once was perhaps melted cheese, missing-children postcards that she couldn't bring herself to throw away. Dust insinuated itself everywhere, seemingly with a newfound vigor, as if knowing that it could thrive in such a tolerant environment. The front- and backyards likewise ignored: rotting foliage, useless soil, grass as yellowed as straw. They couldn't keep up, always behind, always overwhelmed. The curtains were perpetually drawn, the windows always closed, insulating them from everything outside.

As for her mental state, it was similarly cobwebbed and unruly. The only visitors she allowed in were those who had to be there: Anabelle's doctor and physical therapists, the nurses, the specialists, the technicians who checked the machines once a week. And even then she had to work herself up to opening the door, to summoning a housewife smile, to making the minimal amount of socially acceptable conversation so as to give the appearance that she was at least functional, which she was not. And despite the fact that friends and relatives were chipping in and paying bills, plus occasionally leaving behind crisp, recently ATM-retrieved twenty-dollar bills, they were drowning in debt. Medicaid covered some of Anabelle's expenses, but not everything. John's erratic employment wasn't helping matters either, while they kept waiting, waiting, for the settlement from the hospital to come through, relying on the smoke and mirrors of postdated checks and credit cards, frequent balance transfers and skipped house payments. Her closest friends took turns delivering food and *TV Guide,* and tried to be supportive.

She's grieving, she's still in shock, she's getting used to how it's going to be from now on. Many kept using the phrase "transition phase."

But the situation dragged well beyond what commonly constitutes a phase—ten, fifteen pounds heavier, multiple lapsed magazine subscriptions, John having left by then. She couldn't picture the future, all the care and bills and sacrifice ahead. She wondered if everyone else had been right—that she should have put Anabelle in an institution. Maybe the burden and responsibility was too much, she'd quite possibly overestimated her capacity as a person. Maybe she couldn't do this after all.

This all led up to the day when she was sitting in Anabelle's room (where else would she be?), tending to her daughter and humming an Eric Clapton song, the really sad one about his kid who died, and she could have sworn a tear gently squeezed itself from her daughter's long-dry ducts, a lone pinhead of water that dissolved just as soon as it was released. Yes, most definitely, something had been emitted: a tear. But it wasn't a tear with origins in Anabelle's own pain and silent suffering—and this she instinctively knew, the way only mothers can know such things; instead it was a manifestation of her daughter's sadness about how she, her mother, had been spiraling. This realization was like getting the wind knocked out of you; suddenly, breathing was not an option. For pretty much three days straight she fought her way back, by organizing and scrubbing and cleaning and boxing and trying to set everything right. There was still a lot to do, but at least she was doing something and shedding the numb of the past months—she began, slowly, steadily, to take her life back, to emerge from the profound gloom that had held her heart hostage.

And so it was around this time, too, that they noticed the rose smell, which lingered and was still in the air when Marnie called to check in a couple of days later. Karen just then getting back into the habit of answering the phone. About fifty-fifty: 50 percent of the time answering, 50 percent not answering.

"It's still there, huh. And you say she's never had any bed sores."

"No, never."

"That's just not possible, not with all the time she's in that bed. Have any other strange things happened in the house recently, anything out of the ordinary?"

"What do you mean 'strange things'?"

On her next visit Marnie showed up with a multilayered casserole and a twelve-inch porcelain representation of the mother of Christ. "A little something for the room, I hope you don't mind," said Marnie, who Karen knew was on the religious side but didn't throw it in your face like some people. Karen wasn't sure of the exact brand of faith, though she assumed Catholic because her kids went to a Catholic school. Maybe such a gift was a little bold, a little forward. But Karen didn't think much about it, the statue, which Marnie purposely placed out of the way, on a small desk in the corner of the room, no big deal, why not. Marnie stayed for *Court TV* and a Hot Pocket and left.

A couple of days went by. She thought she felt an earthquake once, but there was nothing on the news, so guess not. They watched TV, mother and daughter, just like any other mother and daughter, except she had to do things like change the bag that held her daughter's urine, among other intimate ministrations. The house was coming along. She could stand to look at herself in the mirror for more than two seconds.

Marnie stopped by again, and she deposited another casserole in the freezer and popped open a Diet Coke. They passed the can back and forth like a couple of winos. But rather than a park bench or something, here they were relaxing in Anabelle's sacrosanct room discussing the density of bones and how muscles and tendons degenerate if not regularly used. Karen left to go to the bathroom. When she returned, Marnie was looking at the statue, intensely, like it was an eye chart she was having trouble reading: There was something there, buried in all those random letters. She reached out. Cautiously.

"Did you see this?" Marnie asked, reaching farther and then touching the statue.

"See what?"

"This."

Marnie held up the evidence, a fingertip: damp.

"Tears," she said.

Not long after that, Meredith Stroman, a friend from the days when they both worked in day care (severely underpaid teaching assistants at Tot Time), made her weekly coupon drop-off and told her how she'd just been to the doctor's and that sorry if she seems a little out of sorts but in all likelihood, well, how else to put this: There was a statistically significant chance she had leukemia. Karen asked: "What's statistically significant?" And Meredith said: "That's what the doctors said. Statistically significant. I think it's doctor code for we're not entirely sure one way or the other but we just want to cover our asses." Then Meredith asked if she could be alone with Anabelle for a while if that was OK. Of course it was OK. As Meredith described it later, she placed her fingertips first on the girl's forehead, then her cheeks, then her pale, doll-like hands. And then, without realizing it,

Meredith was in the middle of an impromptu prayer to God, asking for Anabelle's help in defeating the sickness blooming inside her. Two weeks later the doctors were backtracking. The evidence of leukemia had vanished. They were hard-pressed for a viable explanation. "I already have my explanation," Meredith told them. Marnie liked to point out that the day Meredith prayed to Anabelle, June 24, also happened to be the birthday of John the Baptist.

Then came more statues (and photographs, and paintings, and other various likenesses of Mary, Jesus, the heavy hitters), as well as more tears, more "signs," and then more friends, and friends of friends, and friends of Marnie's, and friends of Meredith's, all of them asking for time alone with Anabelle. Karen swept up in it all, but trying to maintain an open mind and not arrive at a conclusion one way or another, not yet anyway, to let this thing (again that inadequate word) develop naturally and on its own and not explain it all away, with neither the rationality of science nor the intangibles of religion. No easy task, what with Marnie and Meredith giddy like schoolgirls, saying miracle this, miracle that, what else could it be? But there was one part of it she had to concede to: that, if nothing else, it was clear that her life was becoming seriously disrupted, and that her former seclusion had officially ended. From now on her daughter would have to be shared with the world.

Karen also got her first taste of belief, the power of it, the electric charge of it. And perhaps that's what she's come to appreciate the most. How these people are so devout, so sure. They believe enough for her and everyone else. And how if you believe in something enough, you become free—free from all that otherwise clouds and clutters your thoughts, that takes you away

from your truest true self. The purity of purpose. Sooner or later
their certainty will become her certainty, right? The osmosis
thing. It's just a matter of time. Eventually these past years of
drift and doubt will make sense. Like an old Polaroid picture
slowly coming into focus. That's her. Taking shape out of the
darkness. Materializing into something clear and distinct. She'd
been there all along.

"So let me get this straight. You just let people in?"
Of course. Of course I do, she wants to tell Kellee Clifton. She
opens her door and lets them in, all of them, the whole world if
necessary. How can she refuse when there is such obvious need,
such a raw desire for it to be true?

But instead she replies with a simple yes. Plus she's tired from
all the chatting and describing, not used to talking about herself
like this. It was exhausting. Had it already been a half hour?
How long do interviews typically last? Was "Kellee Clifton"
Kellee Clifton's real name?

The men move the equipment into Anabelle's room. They're
done with the interview, apparently. The door again—there's a
knock. The doorbell hasn't worked in years. Karen apologizes
to Kellee Clifton, excuses herself. It's someone from before. Last
month sometime. She came for her sister who had a rare blood
disease, too many red blood cells or something, which causes
headaches and potentially fatal blood clots. Now: remission,
cured. Thank you bless you thank you. The doctors say they've
never seen anything like it. Amazing. Unheard of. An aberration
that defies medical explanation.

"I wanted you to know," she tells Karen, sounding out of
breath, like she'd run all the way from wherever she came to

deliver the news as soon as possible. "I wanted to tell you in person."

The woman has been holding on to Karen's hands since the door opened, and it appears she has no intention of letting go. She rocks back and forth, swaying with wonder and joy, dressed like she works in a bank—blouse, scarf, skirt, heels. Then she places both of her hands on Karen's face, as if confirming something, and begins to cry.

Kellee Clifton has waited as long as she can. She makes her move.

"Excuse me there, hi. Kellee Clifton. Channel Seven *Eyewitness News*. We're here doing a story. About the miracle girl. Would it be all right if I asked you a few questions?"

GETTING LATE, THE last of the visitors gone, the sun and heat in slow decline, the day finally exhaling to a close—and Karen can barely stand. Her feet ache; her eyes burn; her stomach snarls (yes, she'd missed lunch again). Because when is there time for food? She runs the dishwasher and grabs an almost-empty box of cereal from the top of the refrigerator and then joins Dominique, her niece, who regularly stops by after school (yes, one of Anabelle's Angels, for sure), and who's now in the living room, slouched on the sofa in teenage recline, but without the attitude that's associated with such a pose. She's just tired, too.

Karen puts one hand on Dom's knee, offers her some crumbly bits of Life with the other.

"It's late," says Karen. "Why don't you go ahead and get going."

Dom springs up, just what she wanted to hear.

"Get some rest, Aunt Karen," she says as she gathers her backpack and perfumy magazines she didn't have time to read, Aunt Karen noticing how her niece's awkward and gangly body isn't so awkward and gangly anymore: sixteen and budding into a new exterior with which to greet the world. A transition that Anabelle will never know. Such thoughts—what Anabelle has been deprived of, how she will not experience the most basic joys and rites of passage and everyday occurrences—now part of her daily mind churn.

"You look tireder than usual," chides Dom. "Like you could melt away there into the sofa. Did you forget to eat again? I know I sound like I'm nagging like my mom, but *you got to eat,*" employing the stereotypical Italian accent.

"You're right. You do sound like your mom. And like Bryce. I eat."

"That's debatable."

Dominique is at that age when everything's debatable, relative. The time when you're disinclined to believe in anything too much.

"Did you hear we're getting a new area code?" her niece asks.

"Again? I can't keep up."

"Only now I can't remember. Six? Six-four-something? But if you dial the old one you'll still get through." Stopping to reapply lip gloss. Then, still puckered, she says, "I think that's the most people ever in one day."

"I think so, too."

"I keep on thinking, all right, it's going to start like letting up and then it doesn't."

"I don't know, Dom. Maybe it's not going to let up. Maybe this is normal now."

Karen notices a new piercing: Dom's left nostril, which now

matches her right, two silver studs, each addition no doubt driving Dom's mother crazy.

"How's your mom doing?" Karen asks.

"She says hi. I forgot to tell you earlier. She said she'll try
to stop by soon. Work's been crazy-busy for her. She's got this
new boss. A real jerk. It's stressing her out. She started smoking
again. You know Mom."

Tammy is Karen's older sister, her only sister, her only sibling.
She lives a few towns over, in Norwalk, but her visits are infrequent. Growing up, they were six years apart, always at very different places in their lives. Tammy's suspicious of all the attention
surrounding Anabelle, strongly voicing the opinion—echoing
that of their mother, who fortunately lives in Colorado—that
this isn't right, that Karen shouldn't be opening up her house
and life like this. So usually it's Dom who comes, two, three
times a week.

"Tell your mom whenever she can make it is fine, I understand," says Karen, as she walks Dom to the door, where her
niece suddenly hugs her, something Dom normally doesn't do,
and it feels like a moment, a recognition of something—perhaps
it's Dom trying to tell her that she wishes her mom did more,
too, wasn't so distant and disapproving. Tammy had never liked
John either.

Dom's parked down the block (are the neighbors pissed about
the extra traffic and cars? are they wondering what's happening
in there?), so Karen watches her cross the street and hurry down
the sidewalk to her car. Lights are going on in houses, just minor
illumination at this point in the early October evening. Outside
the sky reluctantly turns red and purple and all sleek, the colors of anatomy textbook diagrams, but the heat—the hellish

heat—does not relent and there's no sign of a breeze. The forecast for tomorrow: more of the same.

Still munching cereal, Karen retires to her daughter's room. At last it's just the two of them. And there she is. Her baby girl. Her baby Belle. Look: her curled, restless fingers. Her bony limbs. Her long, dark, combed-out hair. Her tender shoulders and delicate ultra-white neck. Her mouth open, for now, forever, appearing as if it's being forcefully pried ajar by an unseen pair of hands. Her eyes seeming both alive and dead at the same time.

And the nightly ritual begins. Heart rate: check. Ventilator: check. Catheter: check. Feeding tube: check. Singing Anabelle's favorite song ("You Are My Sunshine"): check. Damp cloth to the forehead, applying ChapStick to her lips, filling out the chart that the nurse will check at tomorrow morning's weekly visit. Karen collapses on the side of the bed. Anabelle as still as a photograph. Karen can study her daughter's face for hours, whole worlds there, levels of subtlety and hint that the inexperienced eye will miss. And sometimes she'll wonder as she stares: *What do you see? What do you think? What do you feel? Do you know that I'm sitting here next to you, that I'm your mother? Do you know what happened and why all these people come to our home? Of course you do. How could you not. I am your mother. It's OK. You're safe now. You can tell me anything. Hello? I'm listening. I'm always listening even though I don't always hear. But I try.*

Karen turns on the TV, habit, then goes about performing additional nighttime sacraments: a quick sponge bath (face, neck, arms, elbows, armpits); removing stray hairs or eyelashes or flakes of skin or any other miscellaneous bodily accretions; reading aloud the notes and cards that have been left during the day (along with the candles, the candy, the flowers, the stuffed animals, the photographs of the sick and the dead); and then fin-ishes the last of the Life, wetting and dipping her fingertips in the cereal dust to salvage all the nourishment she can. How many lives had Anabelle affected today? How many souls touched, mended? She watches the news, and there's her friend Kellee Clifton, interviewing a distraught woman whose husband had kidnapped their two children and fled to his native Iran. Then, because she can't be bothered to change the channel, she sits through a new dating show where the contestants are younger, meaner, more forthcoming with the details of their sexual ap-petites. Again: more that her daughter will never experience, though in this particular case she doesn't mind so much.

The chair that now serves as her bed has become more or less contoured to her more or less plus-sized body. It's almost com-fortable. She covers herself with a blanket and closes her eyes, the TV still going (something about lawyers now), knowing that sleep is not an immediate possibility. But eventually she will fall asleep. Eventually she will dream. And the dream will most likely be the familiar one, the one that floats above all the rest: the dream where Anabelle talks and walks and runs and is a normal regular girl. No more miracles, no more akinetic mutism, no more machines. The thing, though, is this: she can never tell in the dream if Anabelle has lost her power, or whatever you want to call it. If the sacrifice has been reversed. That is the question: Is being normal the cost of being miraculous?

She will sleep but she will wake every two hours or so, the stunted slumber of the new parent, only she's not so new any-more, it won't get any better. Checking Anabelle, checking her-self, checking the numbers of the digital clock (they never change when you look, never), the green digits glowing futuristically in the darkness. Always the hum of the machines. That underwater sensation of having slept but not enough, it's never enough. The day ahead awaits. Then she will get up around five-thirty or six. She will turn on the lights, move around the house, brew the coffee, signs of activity, of the day beginning anew, people arriving so they can have their time with Anabelle, who's still her daughter but also something else entirely, and more and more Karen knows that it's the right thing, what she's doing and how she's proceeding, and how could she deny anyone what she has to offer.

When Kellee Clifton had asked about her husband, there was a very long pause.

"Is he still in the picture?"

Kellee Clifton and the bearded camera guys waited. Karen stared at the lights shining on her and tried not to look at the camera, tried to keep her voice from cracking.

"I don't know," she said.

THE STORY AIRS two days later, featured on the 5, 6, and 11 p.m. Channel 7 newscasts. A week after that, it gets picked up nationally, running on the ABC Sunday evening news, the very last segment, that final slot that's kept free of politics or violence or scandal and that's reserved for the good, old-fashioned uplifting human-interest story. The calls start almost immediately. The phone rings and rings, and she answers it 100 percent of the time. CNN, MSNBC, *USA Today*. What to tell all these people? Editors, reporters, fact-checkers, assistants to somebody. It's hard to believe they're calling for her, Karen Elizabeth Vincent, asking for her comments, setting up times for more interviews.

Before: as anonymous as anyone else she knew. After: someone that is quoted and supposed to have something to say.

One of the callers, a smoker-voiced man from *The Boston Globe,* tells her: "It's interesting . . . We seem to be hearing more and more about this stuff. Maybe it's because of Y2K, the new millennium and all that hullabaloo. The hype becomes the reality. Like a self-fulfilling prophecy kind of deal . . . Or maybe—I don't know. Maybe we need miracles more than we thought."

"Maybe," she agrees, not knowing what else she could possibly say.

2

| John |

IT'S ONE OF those bars where there are only two kinds of music on the jukebox: country *and* western. The best of Waylon, Willie, Merle, Johnny, Hank. Men—and it's always men in bars like this, no Patsy or Loretta or Dolly allowed—identifiable without a surname, the true gods, who have been to the clichéd and well-traveled edge and found their way back. And don't even think of making the suggestion of possibly maybe broadening some musical horizons with a token smattering of, say, classic rock or a tasteful soul compilation: That's not what this place—technically the Wishing Well but known to its dedicated regulars solely by the truncated "the Well"—is about. Here, there's nothing but reliable songs of lament and loss (and of course drinking) that fit right in with the clientele's collective state of mind. And that suits him fine tonight. That's why he chose the Well. Tonight he's up for plenty of authentic lamenting and losing. And drinking. So why not have the appropriate soundtrack?

Because he's already laid a pretty significant foundation with a few vodka tonics, John Vincent takes a moment to reflect on his current intoxication level and contemplate where he hopes to go from here. He stands in front of the jukebox, his unshaven face lit by its sci-fi-like glow. Breaking hearts, broken hearts, cheating hearts. Such a resilient organ, he concludes, and stares up at the mounted heads of various slain creatures—deer, bear, jackalope—which glower above the bar, their dead eyes still very much alive, reminding him, he hates to admit, of his daughter.

It is well after nine, the hopeful Friday night crowd dispersed throughout the classically shoebox-shaped room, the ratio of men to women predictably uneven, the prowling patrons well on their way to good and proper lubrication. After two unsuccessful attempts, he catches the eye of the bartender—shaved head, Satanic goatee, tank top that's purposefully too small, arms like cut logs, basically a man who could pull trains with his teeth and bench-press a Toyota—and orders another. He takes the last empty stool. The bartender doesn't like him. Just doesn't. He can tell. When vodka tonic number three finally arrives, he leaves an even bigger tip than last time.

His only other previous visit to the Well? That would be the time he was dragged here by Janice, a fellow TempPeople sufferer, one of the first people he met after he landed in Nevada, both of them pretending to be busy for two weeks at a real estate office. It was Janice's birthday and a group of coworkers were going out to celebrate and Janice wouldn't take no for an answer. Janice Gabriela Moonstone Verdugo—she of the Hopi jewelry and bioelectric shield and energy balancing. Called herself a "cultural creative," told him there was a website if he was interested. He wasn't. And even if he was, he didn't have an Internet account yet, this latest revolution bypassing him completely, one more example of his lifelong inability to discern what's important from what's not.

A wave of applause ripples through the bar. A play, a score, a triumph, something. He gazes up for guidance, away from the watery world of his cocktail and his musings. There are several TVs, all tuned to different stations, games, commercials; he doesn't know which one to focus on. Whatever it is, was, he's missed it. Too late, too late, once again. So he returns to his drink and that night with Janice, after the other folks from the office had left and it was just the two of them, sitting at one of the Well's booths, where she proclaimed she wasn't a drinker, that alcohol polluted the spirit and deadened the life force (as did microwaves, televisions, and Republicans), but she powered down another rum and Coke, followed by a shot of Jäger and a Kahlúa and cream. She cried about her kid, her supposedly genius son who lived back East and was being brainwashed by her ex-husband, the shit-fuck, which was the exact hyphenated noun she used. Janice: who deep down he suspected didn't believe in everything she said she believed in, not as fervently at least, but it was better than the way she had been living before (he didn't know all of the details, but he knew enough), so who's to say, whatever gets you through the night.

But now he's here again, locked in, marking territory, imagining himself as a painting: "Lonely Man Sitting at Bar." The music could be louder. He wants to feel it more, physically, in his chest. He decides to switch to beer. This is not a decision that's made lightly. Multiple attempts to catch the bartender's eye and finally he's good, he's beered, he's set for another fifteen minutes, maybe longer. To his right, a young man drinking solo; to his left, an old man drinking, also solo. The bartender slaps his change on the surface of the bar, a nasty, incriminating sound, singling him out somehow, it seems to John, and momentarily he considers changing tactics and snubbing the tip this time, teach the guy a lesson, but he relents, slides back the two quarters. The beer tastes warmish and flat. The label tells him he's drinking "The Champagne of Beers." Living the high life, all right.

Let's stay focused, he reminds himself as he takes another sip of his beer. Remember that you have a purpose. To observe the significance of the day, the date. Trying to remember and trying to forget. Mostly to forget. Which is usually the point of going to a bar like the Well. This is important, what he's doing. He has a plan, limited and unoriginal though it may be, and for now he's enjoying the satisfaction of having a tangible goal that can be accomplished: drink, wallow, memorialize, then obliterate; then pay for it the next day, perhaps longer if he does it right. He can't get too distracted.

WHY IS IT that some men are inclined to chat when urinating in public bathrooms while others prefer to be stoic and silent about the whole damn thing? John had always been firmly in the latter camp, preferring to pee and savor the moment to himself, sans interaction with his pissing peers. It was don't-talk-to-me time: a brief respite from the world's ongoing whirl. But for some guys it's an invitation to socialize. They can't help themselves.

"You believe that shit?"

This from the beer-gutted gent occupying the urinal next to him, who stands there with his legs spread wide, a wise and time-honored tactic when a certain level of alcohol has been consumed. John (wisely) spreads his legs a little more, assumes the manly pose, just to be sure.

"Guy says—guy like you, guy like me. A regular guy. Says his wife's pregnant. Out of the blue. Pregnant, preggers. Can't be his, though. Can't have any. One of those low-sperm-count deals, he says, he tells me, the guy. Unless it's some kind of miracle and his boys finally made it through. Possible, right? Immaculate reception. Stranger things have happened, suppose. She says no, no way. There's nobody else. It's yours, yours, yours, baby. But fool me once. You know. Don't fuck with me twice. And he's staying with her. He's *staying*. Me? I'm outta there."

It's time for John to chime in or be considered unfriendly, a dick, if he does not reciprocate.

"Harsh," he says without looking up, over.

His companion doesn't say anything else, doesn't flush or wash his hands either. Just leaves. John zips up and moves over to the sink. The mirror above is dotted and streaked with who knows what, the shed crud of previous generations of drinkers and pissers. It also has a big gigantic crack. When he looks at himself, the crack slices right through his neck, which gives the not-so-subtle effect of him looking like he's been decapitated.

And why is it that some men leave and others stay? Why is he so far from home on a Friday night in the middle of the desert? Why why why? he wonders.

More than anything else, it's about the simple failures of love, which of course are not so simple.

NEXT HE COMMANDEERS a seat recently vacated by another old man, this one practically skeletal, with minimal teeth and an oxygen tank, a sight just as depressing as it sounds. Yes, he knew the day would be rough and he was right. Why couldn't there be a delete key for this day on the calendar—press a button and it vanishes. Isn't that how it works in these technological times of ours? But this is not something that can be so easily erased. He cannot, like Janice, revisualize, recontextualize. He's too fucking literal. What happened, happened. And what he remembers most, the grainy home-movie footage that played in his head more than anything else now, is not the big scene with Karen (curled in a ball on the living room floor, rocking like a child, not speaking but yelling in tongues), or even the days, the weeks—shit, the months, years—leading up to his departure, but after, once he had made up his mind and was in the car and fully realized what he was doing: following a guilty tradition of male abandonment. The long, silent, radio-less drive. He didn't know where to go. He knew only that he was leaving, that it was happening. That was six months ago. Six months ago tonight. He left on Thursday, April 22, 1999, five days after his thirty-first birthday, four months after the accident.

Happy anniversary, asshole.

So here he is, marooned and indistinct, among the Well's nightly flock of followers. This particular stool wobbles. You have to be completely still or it feels like you're about to tip over, fall into the void below. The bartender brings him another beer, just as warm, just as flat. Had he ordered it? Not sure. Then the bartender hovers there, arms crossed, like a cop who knows something you don't, some vital fact about you that popped up on the routine computer check, a mistake from years ago that continues to haunt you. How long does it take to have a clean record, to be free of the past? He'd like to know. Janice Verdugo would like to know. The bartender still hovering, weird. What? he wants to ask. A gesture, a line seems to be called for. John raises his bottle. How about a toast? Does he know any toasts?

"Here's to swimming with bow-legged women," he says.

The bartender is not amused. Doesn't get it.

"That's a quote. I'm quoting. Quint. From *Jaws*. You never seen *Jaws*?"

Apparently not. The bartender shakes his head, like saying *sad,* a dude quoting lines from a movie, it's come to that, and returns to the other end of the bar, his preferred geography. John deciding he most definitely will not be tipping on this round and possibly the next. The jukebox's current selection fades to a tear-stained end—a cheery little ditty called, he's pretty sure, "He Stopped Loving Her Today."

You leave a family once. But then you leave them every day after that, too. There is always the leaving. It never goes away.

DISAPPEARING IN LOS Angeles is relatively easy. It's certainly big enough, capable of sufficient anonymity. But he thought he needed something more, a greater exile, and so he left the area, having vaguely decided to travel east and then take it from there, with no real plan or purpose other than putting space and mileage between him and his recent past. And besides, as a lifelong Southern Californian who'd only been out of the state two or three times and never farther east than the Hoover Dam, he got sort of swept up with the idea of finally experiencing some of the rest of the country. It would be an adventure, he tried to convince himself. His own private version of *Easy Rider* except without the motorcycles, the acid trip, and Dennis Hopper. Getting down to essences. Living off the land. Meeting

Indians. He would turn a bad situation into something positive, and continue to try to tame the guilt that was now part of his blood.

But nothing much happened. Mostly he drove a lot. Sweated, too. Listened to the same cassettes over and over. The revelations he'd hoped for were a no-show. The speedometer spun and he squinted like a lost explorer into the approaching horizon. Dust swirled, settled over everything: his car, his backseat, in his ears, a layer of lingering remorse. Tourists always seemed to be asking him for directions, at which he had to laugh. The sky was open and blue and oftentimes disturbingly cloudless, a thing that could swallow you whole and you'd never know the difference. And there was no land to live off, at least none that he could find, at least not for free. So he settled for KOAs and Motels 6, 8, 9, and 12. The only Indians he saw drove pickup trucks and talked on cell phones. Apparently there were no more essences to be had.

He yawned through a string of jobs that didn't require paperwork or references. Phoenix. Albuquerque. Missoula, Montana. In Savior Lake, Idaho (good name, that), he watched a woman choke on her Grand Slam, coughing up flecked remnants of scrambled egg and diced ham, her face ghosted with death after. About three months passed, which felt like three years. He swore he saw a new wrinkle or line branching around his eyes every time he glanced up at the rearview mirror, something he tried to avoid doing, not only because of his unsettling reflection, but also because there was a lot of bad voodoo back there, and what else is there to do when you're driving eight, ten hours straight and "Hotel California" just isn't cutting it anymore. It became pretty obvious that he wasn't taking to the vagabond lifestyle; it looked better in the movies. He craved the familiar. He wanted to sleep in, rent a movie, have a pizza delivered. He wasn't, he concluded, much of a traveler.

By then he was up in Oregon (a stint driving a truck for an antiques dealer, a two-week construction gig outside Portland). In addition to the more spiritual I'm-not-a-traveling-soul insight, he also had the financial epiphany that he needed to stay put in one place for a while and save up some cash for himself and to send home. And that was when he had the thought: Go to Vegas. He said it out loud, like the words needed to be uttered in order for it to happen, for the sentence to come true: "Go to Vegas." Not Vegas itself, but Henderson. Cheaper to live. Growing economy. Lots of jobs and opportunities. No state income tax. Right next to the light and awe of Vegas. And it wasn't like he had a lot of other ideas. Plus he had a friend who'd recently moved to Henderson from Downey and who'd split up with his girlfriend, so he had a place to stay rent-free for a while.

He worked his way west toward the Oregon coast, then down Highway 101 and into Northern California, passing through rainy towns he'd never heard of: Crescent City, Orick, Fortuna, Garberville, Leggett, all in Humboldt County, which he saluted by firing up the soggy remains of an ancient joint he exhumed from the back of the ashtray. The highway twisted, the trees tangled their way up the hills and beyond. Redwoods, he assumed. There was so much between the Oregon border and San Francisco. He never knew. Yes, these were definitely places where you could disappear, especially up there. That was when it struck him. He was the type of person who really could disappear. No one would know. No one would make the necessary phone calls. No one would post flyers with his gruesome

school yearbook photo. No one would mount the media campaign. There wouldn't be any ribbons or buttons or press confer-
ences. He'd just vanish—simply, without documentation. And
who would miss him? He had no brothers or sisters. His father
had died young, a heart attack at the age of forty-nine, the year
after John graduated from high school. Long before that he'd
left John's mother, who never recovered and back then worked
nights in a mattress factory, so John was often alone as a boy
and later as a teenager, his mother in the end moving back to
Michigan, where she was from. John's only real connection to
anything, anyone, had been his wife and daughter. And now
those ties were severed, too.

When he finally hit Los Angeles and it was early morning
and the sun began rising and there wasn't much traffic, he sped
up, powering east, moving faster like there was someone behind
him, in pursuit. He thought of one of the few quotable things his
father had ever said: Whatever you wind up doing to yourself in
this life, just don't let the past bite your ass.

THEN HE LOOKS up, hoping the TV will throw him a
rope, save him from something he can't name. He looks up, up.
The bar lights dimmer, darker now. But which TV? So many
TVs, so many options. Welcome to America. At last he goes
with the TV that's closest, proximity winning out. It's not sports.
It's not a commercial. It's a movie he's seen before, but it's been
years (high school?), and he can't remember the title, the plot,
anything. And there, next to him, is the old man with the oxygen
tank. Except the oxygen tank is gone, missing. He's wearing a
blue Walmart vest. Smoking. Eyes moist and glazed and full of

untold regret. He's standing, technically swaying, but not for long, because he's falling, falling forward, his face landing smack on the bar, bone meeting lacquered wood, and the terrible, thudding sound causes John's shoulders to wince and rise, the old man's old face twisted and ruined, grimacing, all gums inside his mouth, a pink nightmare, and John grabs him by the shirt so he doesn't crumple to the ground and hurt himself even more.

This all brings the bartender over, arms waving, and he's even surlier now, yelling, "Fuck, Wendell, fuck. Not again."

AFTER HIS FRIEND'S place, he found an apartment a couple of blocks away, a generic one-bedroom, month to month, parking space not included. There were Howard Hughes periods when he didn't get out all that much. No frills, no extras. Read the same Stephen King paperback three times. He frequently reminded himself that it was probably about time he did some sit-ups before it got seriously out of hand. Most meals were smuggled in from the outside and consumed over the kitchen sink for maximum efficiency. The curtains didn't close all the way, allowing in a thin strip of unwelcome light. He didn't talk to his neighbors and they didn't talk to him, both parties sensing the mutual need for discretion.

He burned through most of the cash he'd saved up, did the job search thing, answered ads he was underqualified for and overqualified for, one day landing in the offices of TempPeople, the manager, Phil, saying they look for only the best and brightest without cracking a smile. He was offered the job right then and there, started the next day. And so now every few weeks he's sent somewhere else, a new office, a new system and new names to learn and then forget, where he files and answers phones and faxes and collates and stacks and does whatever he's told, one time driving to Walgreen's to pick up a home pregnancy test for a secretary. Nights, he came home and sometimes didn't bother turning on the lights, sitting in the dark until he remembered who he was and what he did. Every other day or so he picked up the phone to check and make sure it was still working. Mail arrived for Current Resident. It was a life. Every Saturday he put money into an envelope and sent it off to his wife, no return address, no note, just the cash.

THE BARTENDER NOW saying that's it, he's had enough, he's going to call the cops once and for all, and the old man begging *please don't please please don't,* practically crying, also saying *they'll fire me they find out and where'll I be then?* The bartender picking up the phone and dialing.

"Wait," says John, who's managed to transfer the old man, Wendell, to his stool. "Don't call. I'll take care of him. I'll get him out of here. I'll take him home. I need to call a cab anyway. I'll drop him off on my way."

The bartender stops dialing.

"You're volunteering to take care of this broken-down bag of bones?"

"Yes," John says, without understanding why.

"Fine," says the bartender, putting down the phone. "Get him out of here. Get him the fuck out of here and out of my sight and the next time you come back you're drinking on the house."

John hauls the old man outside to wait for the cab. Leans him like a rolled carpet against a rusted newspaper dispenser rack

(*Las Vegas Weekly*) and hopes for the best. The desert air—thick, oppressive, ever vigilant—assaults, even at this late hour; he'll never get used to the weather here, never. Music and voices spill out of the Well. A few smokers have congregated on the sidewalk, watching their practiced plumes rise into the air while complaining about the lack of a professional sports team in Nevada.

"I'm Wendell," the old man says, only it comes out more like "Iwenal." Wendell extends a chapped-to-hell hand, waits for John to shake it. And once John does, the old man doesn't let go, latches on to John like an anchor, the last fellow human being on the planet.

"Where do you live, Wendell? I've got a cab coming. Just tell me where you live and I'll drop you off, help you get situated."

"I'm a greeter."

"What?"

"Greeter. That's what I do. It's my job. You come in the store. You walk in. I say hello, how are you. Maybe you see me, maybe you don't. But I greet. I need to greet. It's what I do."

"Didn't you have an oxygen tank earlier?"

"Sold it," says Wendell, the left side of his face growing redder by the minute, only three teeth total, it looks like. "Needed cigarettes. Now they're gone, too. Everything gone."

The cab pulls up, and John manages to insert Wendell inside the vehicle, his body heavier than expected, still some weight and heft to him despite the stick-figure frame.

"How's your face feeling?" John asks after he tells the cab driver where Wendell lives.

"What face?"

"Your face. From when it hit the bar."

Wendell, collapsed and limp against the half-open car window, the alcohol and Marlboros seeping off of him like a force field, feels his cheeks, his defeated chin, as if feeling his face for the first time, a new discovery after all these years.

"Still there," he concedes. "Never much of a face to begin with. Ha ha. You make do with what you have. Or not. I'm old. Hell knows, I'm old. But probably not as old as you think. Hey, are you one of Bobby's friends? Is that it? You tell him, you see Bobby, you tell him I said hi. You tell him I understand. I understand. I'd probably be the same way I was in his place. You tell him I'm doing OK. You tell him he don't need to worry none."

John's head spins: from the booze, from the barreling cab, from the mission he's apparently on.

When they get to Wendell's, the cab driver says no way, he's not going to help, you're on your own bub, this ain't a charity service, which means John's working solo now, lugging Wendell out of the cab and onto the sidewalk and up a short flight of stairs. The apartment complex's architectural distinction defined by concrete and gates. Because John's drunk, too, it takes a good ten minutes to make it all the way to Wendell's apartment on the third floor. John starts trying out the different keys on Wendell's key ring. And it's then, with Wendell leaning against him, his eyes now closed, that the old man violently pukes. A volcanic spew. Which covers the front of John's shirt and pants. Sure. Of course. Why not. This is part of it, this is part of his well-deserved penance, this is what he must endure because of what he did.

Wendell opens his eyes, surveys what was once inside and is

now outside. Barely any damage to his Walmart vest, just a little dribble of fluid. Then he looks over at John, narrows his failing gaze, like he's trying to place him from somewhere in his past: one of the many faces that have come and gone, and are now lost.

"I'm a greeter," Wendell says. "Next time you see my Bobby, you tell him I'm OK. You tell him I'm a greeter and I'm doing OK. You tell him I'm not fuckeroo'd yet."

THE HANGOVER FROM the Well lasts a good two days, the entire weekend spent on the couch and in significant pain. Impressive. Mission accomplished. And the smell from Wendell's vomit? It's the first thing that registers (his nostrils twitching at the memory) as he awakes this morning, Monday, and silences the chirping alarm. And so the day begins: shower, shave, breakfast while dressing and getting ready for work.

His current TempPeople assignment is at a company that prints DVD covers for porn flicks. The people who work there (mostly women) don't look like porn people, they are middle-aged, overweight, tired, very un-porn. He works in the warehouse, filling orders, inserting covers into plastic jewel cases, boxing up stacks and stacks of packaged pornography and calling UPS for the 3 p.m. pickup. The person who usually has this job got a DUI and lost his driver's license for three months, and because of the inadequate Clark County bus system, he couldn't make it to work. The company wanted to keep him on (he's a good employee, he shows up), so John is here, temping. The guy's name is Alfonso, and John has to wear a shirt with an embroidered patch that says ALFONSO because, as one of the tired women pointed out, why should they go to all the trouble of ordering JOHN shirts when John would only be here for three months? Didn't make sense.

When he arrives at Dazzle Productions for the day, he heads right to the break room, where two of the women (Tisha and Sharon, or maybe Sherry?) are sitting at one of the tables and talking about a story they heard on the news this morning, something about a mother microwaving a baby. Birthday streamers and signs hang here and there, leftover from a party that occurred weeks ago; no one had bothered to take the decorations down. That burnt coffee smell common to all break rooms.

"It's John," announces Tisha, pouring a generous stream of powdered creamer into her coffee. "California John. Quiet John. Good morning, Quiet California John."

"Morning."

"The next time you go back to California, John, can you tell all those people there, all those fine California people, tell them there are enough of them over here already. We're good. We got enough folks. Can you do that? A favor for me and the rest of Nevada?"

"Sure."

Tisha turns back to the other woman (Sandy?). "Now where was this? Florida? It sounds like a Florida thing."

"Florida. Or Arkansas. One of those two."

Then it's back to him: "You got kids, Quiet John?"

He usually tries to avoid the kid question whenever it comes up. Or he lies to keep things simple. But here, in this situation, with these tired women, he decides to say yes, admit the fact of his complicated parenthood.

"Just one, yeah."

"One don't hardly count," says Tisha, who has like twenty kids and walks with a cane.

"How do you think a parent, a mother," she continues, "puts one of her own, a little baby, in a microwave like it's popcorn or something. I don't get it. You get it, John?"

"No I don't."

The other woman (yes, it's Sandy, he's pretty sure now) takes a bite of a Frisbee-sized Danish. Mouth full, she says, "It's too much. You hear something like that so early in the day, it's too much. I just want to drink my coffee and eat my highly caloric pastry, thank you very much."

John shrugs his way out of the break room (the world, the crazy world we live in, what can you do?), walks down the hall toward the men's bathroom, where he'll avoid his face in the mirror and put on his ALFONSO shirt. He'll go into the warehouse. He'll breathe the plastic-y smell of all those DVD cases. He'll start filling his orders. The work will take over. The time will pass. And he'll think of Wendell's sad old-man apartment, empty and anonymous, the way he laid him down on the sofa, how Wendell thanked him and then closed his eyes and it seemed final, like those eyes would never open again, and John walked back to the cab and threw up himself, the contents of his own stomach winding up in the gutter and sidewalk.

And he'll think of the past, too, and what he's done. Because this is what you do when you're living with the fallout from a decision that you can still taste in your mouth and see when you close your eyes. He'll think of going back, as he always does, and he'll also wonder if too much time has passed. Each day banishing him further. Yes, he'd freaked, he'd flinched, he'd fucked up. Plain and simple. Part of a long lineage of guys, men, dudes, fucking up. And now, here he is in the desert, living sparse and seeking silences, he's beginning the process of working his way back—day by day, week by week, month by month—and to become someone who would never do such a thing again, would never even think such a thing, a man who can stand seeing himself in the mirror and not look away.

3

| Anabelle |

THE MAN WAS there, and so was the woman. But the man wasn't her father, and the woman wasn't her mother. They were someone else. Sometimes she'd pretend. They were just the man and the woman. Blank. Blank as the blank whiteboards at school after you come back from a vacation and there's no smear or ghost letters. They didn't know her. She didn't know them. Sometimes she'd pretend.

Sometimes, too, she'd go all day without speaking. It was like a game. She'd decide in the morning. Then do it. Or not do it. Not speak. As the woman sat her down and combed out her long, long, long hair in the mornings, she'd decide. At school, if Mrs. Stinson called on her or asked her how her additions and subtractions were going, she pointed to her throat. "Are you sick, dear? Does your throat hurt?" And she nodded. She nodded yes or no, or, to say *I don't know,* lifted her shoulders and eyebrows as high as they could go and made an I-don't-know-type face. She realized that most of the time you didn't need to talk.

Your body could do the talking for you. It was a powerful thing, not speaking. People noticed it more than speaking.

And when she did speak, she'd sometimes make up her own language and say the new words aloud, whispering them to herself. Instead of living on Shaker Street she lived on *Flizpertid* Street. Dog was *zloom*. Cat was *swilterfuzz*. Every word that she thought of she gave it another name. It was easy, making up the names. They just came to her. She didn't even have to try. The dry-yuck taste of her hair when she put it in her mouth and chewed and they told her no.

When she had enough words memorized, she tried out her new language on the man and woman. "What are you doing? Speaking in tongues?" And she didn't know what that meant. So she stuck out her tongue. They laughed. The man and woman thought that was funny and it was nice to hear them laugh.

She played. She played spy. She tiptoed and made no sounds whatsoever. Everything got louder when she did this. Like someone had turned up the volume. The quieter you were, the more you heard, the more you noticed. She listened when she wasn't supposed to. She heard things, the man and the woman having conversations, talking when they thought she was asleep.

"I mean I know I'm no expert. But. It seems like she, sometimes, she just doesn't seem right to me. Something's a little off, you know? She's just a little . . . off. I look at other kids and then I look at her. It's not the same. She's not like other kids. Just to compare. The periods of not talking. And then when she does . . . Those voices and words that she uses. It's like she's another person when she's in these, what, states."

Different. Off. Not right. Not like other kids.

"She's fine, John. She's six. She's a little girl. How many times have we been over this? I was the same way. Shy like that. Always observing, always absorbing. Always in my own little world, according to my mom. 'You were a deep thinker from early on, always thinking.' Don't worry. I work with kids and kids go through phases. She's figuring things out."

She played and she sat on the sidewalk in front of their house, which wasn't really their house, it was someone else's. She did this for hours and hours, rocking, concentrating, watching the people and the cars and the sky. She looked at the sky and searched for planes. Sometimes you could see them, sometimes you couldn't. It depended on the sky. How ucky it was. If there was too much uck, you couldn't see them. But if there wasn't, you could see them. Planes passing overhead like dreams. There were people inside the planes even though it didn't seem like that was possible. But there were. There were people in there who, inside that plane that looked like it was going really really slow but was actually going really really fast—people who lived in houses and ate peanut butter and had pets and burped and farted and slept and drove to the market on Saturdays and cried when someone died and went away. She imagined them all as friendly, the kind of people you'd like to invite for a sleepover. Although she, herself, didn't have sleepovers.

When it got dark, she was told to come inside, usually by the woman. The man didn't say a lot. Often he looked like he was about to say something but then he didn't.

There was a story about when she was born. Right after. Right after she came out of the woman, the man said something. He asked a question. He asked: "Is it a boy?"

She was many things. She felt this, knew this. But she was not a boy, would never be a boy. What did the man think every time he looked at her? Did he wish she was something else?

But sometimes the man would pick her up, tickle her, play with her and her dolls, pretending to be a prince or dinosaur or giraffe. And he became another man, one that she liked better and wished would be around more. The woman seemed to like this other man better also, and when he was around, she was another woman, too. Those times, she didn't go out on the sidewalk as much.

Alone in her room, quiet and dark, when the lights were out and it was taking a while for her to fall asleep, and the sounds and the swish of life seemed very far away: that's when they came to her even faster, clearer, more formed. The words. Bed was *nitzobob*. Blanket was *adnomorkin*. Plane was *dragflowestumack*. She made up the words and that made everything new, it made everything hers. The man and woman were not her father and mother. They were someone else. She closed her eyes and then opened them and the world would be one way. Then she closed and opened them again and the world would be another way. Opening, closing. It was like magic. One day something would happen. One day everything would change.

4

Nathaniel | Mavis & Marcus | Linda | Donald

THESE THINGS CAN be explained: the weeping icons, the bleeding statues, the healing of disease, the aberrations of sun and sky and light, the apparitions of Jesus and Mary and Springsteen. Because the answers are there. It's only a matter of knowing how to look, how to see beyond the glow and the primitive need to believe. But wanting to believe doesn't make it true. Truth is what makes it true. Was that a quote from somewhere?

This is what Nathaniel Zoline wants to say when his mother asks him what's new as they browse the laminated, jumbo-sized Red Lobster menus, full of seafood specials and kids' meals and exotic cocktails he'll never order. The occasion: his father's sixty-eighth birthday, a midweek evening out after a day of teaching Linnaeus and binomial nomenclature to bored teenagers, Nathaniel making the drive from Daly City down to San Jose when he'd rather be home, researching, writing, living his true life.

But instead he says what he always says when similarly queried by his mother: "Fine, good. Work is good, things are good. Moving right along. Can't complain."

What's on his mind, though, is the recent increase in reports of the miraculous, the strange, the millennial. Because when he's not teaching biology to sophomores, he's working on his website and sporadically published newsletter, *The Smiling Skeptic.* And lately it's all about the girl in the coma in L.A. That's why he doesn't want to be here. He wants to be online so he can see what the day's search results yield, and he wants to start his article about the girl, about false hope, about the blind embrace of faith.

"And what about in the female department?" his mother asks, not willing to give up quite yet. "Are you seeing anybody? Anything, anyone on the horizon? Any possibilities I should know about?"

"Joan," says his father.

Their waitress, Janelle, is taking orders at the booth across from them. They're next. A table would have been better (more space, more freedom, not so trapped), but his mother likes booths, always insists even if it means waiting longer to eat.

"Well if I don't ask we don't hear anything," his mother says. "We don't know what's going on and I'd like to know. I'd like to know what's going on in my one and only son's life. I think that's fair, Edward. So I have to ask."

There was someone once. A fellow teacher. Younger. She was a long-term sub for an English teacher who had cancer. The cancer went away and then so did the young teacher who was the long-term sub. He'd thought maybe. If there had been more time.

They order and eat their shrimp salads and lobster-fest specials. The meal concludes with dribbles of conversation,

which is fine by him—updates on old neighbors who have died
or are dying, the slew of medications required to keep his father halfway healthy, the cashier at Sears who'd overcharged
them and they had to return to the store for only $1.50, and
they probably spent more on the gas driving back there, but
it's the principle of the thing, you know? There's dessert, too, a
brownie fudge sundae with a lone candle. They all share. Nathaniel's father handles the bill. They say good-bye in the parking lot. His mother has been using the same perfume for thirty
years.

"What about that Janelle?" she tries one last time. "She
seemed like a nice girl. Why don't you go back in and ask her
out? I didn't see a ring. Waitresses are sturdy people. That might
be good for you."

"Joan," says his father.

There's fog on the drive home once he hits the 280, thicker
and whiter the closer he gets to San Francisco, but he's not going
that far, only to Daly City, an unremarkable, largely unknown
suburb just below the famous, glittering city, remaining in the
fast lane the entire time despite the weather. First thing back
at his apartment, he powers on his computer and attempts to
jump online, the pain of the parental chain-restaurant meal just
starting to recede; he really should upgrade and graduate from
dialup to DSL; he spends way too much time like this, waiting
to connect.

Today he'd told his students, "Someone once said, 'God created, Linnaeus ordered.'" But they didn't blink. Not until he
added, "That is, if you believe God created." He liked a good
quote. He'd also quoted Linnaeus himself: "In natural science
the principles of truth ought to be confirmed by observation."

He'd paused then, letting that sink in. Nathaniel was a believer in the principles of truth.

While waiting he makes the short walk to the kitchen and retrieves a Mountain Dew. Then back in his computer chair, hunkering down for another long, bleary-eyed night spent scrolling and reading and writing, clicking hopefully, eternally, on links that half the time are dead or disappointing or something he's already read, conducting keyword searches ("miracle," "healing," "vision," "stigmata"), compiling the evidence, investigating leads, and sending off e-mails all over the world (Latvia, the Philippines, Texas), updating his site with the most recent news, which, he fervently believes, has led to a slight yet substantial increase in traffic and spurred his vigilance even further.

Finally, yes, he's online. He checks his e-mail, reads about a poll saying 96 percent of Americans believe in God and digests another millennial/miraculous story (a church statue that supposedly emitted a bright, beautiful light through its eyes, infusing onlookers with the warmth of the divine and the desire to lead better, more productive lives) in which a Modesto, California, Diocese official was quoted as saying: "I think people are mindful of their calendars these days and of what they're seeing on TV and in the papers. There's a kind of mild hysteria brewing." This is the time he looks forward to most. This sacred time online with what—something like 200 billion–plus documents at his disposal. Like a cop on his beat, patrolling the streets. But not for menace. For mystery. The mystery of belief.

After doing his usual searches, he not surprisingly turns up a couple of new stories about the girl. She's the talk of the message boards and newsgroups and mailing lists he covertly subscribes to (under the alias truebelievernate316) via a Hotmail e-mail address created specifically for this purpose. There are entire websites devoted to her, including the Official Anabelle Vincent Site, prominent among Nathaniel's bookmarked online destinations. He knows the site's loud background colors, the amateurish HTML design well. On one page you can post your own prayers and messages of hope, and Nathaniel can spend hours, entire evenings, devouring these mournful, rambling, typo-filled, syntactically challenged dispatches. Some offer their testimonies of the girl's healing power and first-hand accounts of visits to her house. Others lament they can't make the trip to Southern California to see Anabelle, but give thanks for cyberspace and how her gifts and shining spirit can be shared like this. He copies and pastes the better examples for his files. Moves on eventually.

He opens a new Microsoft Word document.

These things can be explained, he types.

The words he's been craving to write all day. To place in the world. And they're out there now, documented, taking up space, weight. It feels good.

And how can they be explained? Take the weeping statue phenomenon. There's always the possibility that it's plain old simple condensation. More likely, though, is a flat-out hoax. Fill an eyedropper with water or Wesson oil or real tears and voilà— instant weeping effigy. Bleeding can be manipulated as well. For example, one of his favorite case studies: the so-called "Miracle of Saint-Marthe," which happened near Montreal, Canada, in 1985. A statue of the Virgin Mary, belonging to a railroad worker by the name of Jean-Guy Beauregard, appeared to be weeping. Then, after it was taken to another home at the request of Beauregard's landlord (the crowds, predictably, were getting out of control), the statue began to bleed. Then other nearby statues and crucifixes in the house also started to do the same. Thousands upon thousands showed up, waiting in the cold (it was December) to view the miracle. When the statue was taken in for testing, it was concluded that the "blood"—which Beauregard later admitted was his—also contained pork and beef fat. So whenever the temperature would increase, even a little, the substance would liquefy and run, and there you have your magical bleeding.

Los Angeles isn't that far away from Daly City, only an hour's flight south, barely time enough to run the drink cart down the aisle. The Smiling Skeptic might just have to see this miracle girl for himself.

Nathaniel continues typing, sips his Mountain Dew, gains momentum, the right words coming at the right time, beautiful when that happens. Tomorrow there will be more Linnaeus, more naming of species, more yawns from pimply boys and faraway girls. But for now he's in the chair, writing, wondering how long he can hold out, how far he can go in one sitting. 12:37 a.m. Still and quiet. Like a church. No lights on, nothing but the blurry shine of the screen, the way he likes it, bathing in the computer monitor's rectangular radiance and nothing else.

*　*　*

"They still there?" Mavis Morris asks her husband, Marcus, who for the past hour has been checking the window, pinching the mini blinds open and closed with a well-honed disapproval like the nosey neighbor that he is. He's been spying (across the street and over one house, to the left) in growing disbelief—the spectacle continues. He doesn't even bother answering his wife's question this time, you're married this long and all it takes is a look, a significant enough arching of the eyebrows. The dopes, standing in the sun and in front of the white-turned-gray house and on down the block who knows how far, trying to convince themselves that they'll find whatever it is they think they're looking for in the room of that comatose little girl who he remembers sitting by herself on the sidewalk and who should just be left alone, is Marcus's take, not that anyone besides his wife is asking. It's getting ridiculous. But what can you do once people start believing something? Marcus returns to the couch—site of naps and meals, late-afternoon periodical reading, and of course TV viewing—where Mavis finishes chewing a forkful of pasty mashed potatoes. Instant. What do you expect?

"All those people," she starts in again. "I'm trying to understand."

"I don't understand anything anymore," says Marcus, his final verdict, hoping that will be that, but probably not.

The TV going, a game show, a new one that's actually a remake of an old one. Laughter, applause. People with nametags and bad haircuts are winning cash and prizes and pretty respectable parting gifts, none of that Turtlewax bullshit but cruises and decent-looking jewelry and gift certificates to stores where you'd really consider buying something. They made it look so easy, the contestants. How your life can change. With the spin of a wheel. With answering a question about Greek drama. Game shows are a form of religious devotion in the Morris household, and they're dedicated parishioners. They plan out their meals and errands and doctor appointments according to the various time slots of their favorites. And not only that: they buy their lottery tickets every Sunday, send in contest entries whenever they arrive in the mail, have the phone numbers of local radio stations on speed dial. Their name and address grace countless mailing lists and computer databases. Luck: it has to come your way eventually.

"I mean tragedy strikes, that's gonna affect you," Mavis needing to get this off her chest, apparently. "And then what, she never leaves the house, we never see a thing, there's all this whisper-talk about what's going on in there and is the poor girl dead, like the mother's some kind of reprobate. And maybe she is, I'm not saying one way or the other. That's not my place. And now this. CNN across the street."

No comment from Marcus. Instead he takes his own reluctant bite of mashed potatoes, the cheap taste, the cardboard blandness once again filling his mouth. Now they've got people camping out. Sleeping right there on the sidewalk, in the front yard. He gets up in the morning, walks out to pick up the paper, the sun already carving out its space in the sky for the day, and they're there, rubbing dreams from their eyes and sharing boxes of donuts and tuning their portable radios. Crazies. He thinks of things: Spraying them with the goddamned hose, for instance. Telling them to get a life. Delivering a speech they'll never forget and that will cause them to rethink everything. If you want to believe in something, believe in yourself. Believe in the randomness of the universe and how you are a speck. Deal.

"How long can it last? That's what I want to know. How long do these things last?"

If Marcus knows he isn't saying. He concentrates on his food. Switches over to the pork chops, slightly burnt, just the right amount, just enough to give a little extra crisp and crunch as you bite. He's very particular about his food, how his clothes are washed, the way his sheets are tucked. He's a picky motherfucker and he knows it. His mother used to say he was too fussy—fussy like a girl. Which probably didn't help matters, psychologically. But we've all got our quirks and preferences. Take his wife. She doesn't seem to care much for the new version of *Hollywood Squares*. But he does. And yet they still get along just the same. They watch *Hollywood Squares* and then he puts up with her PBS nature crap. Compromise being the key to any successful relationship. As a connoisseur of daytime television ever since his early retirement last year, he knows that much. And seventeen years you have to consider a success, though, sure, it could always be a little better. There's always room for improvement. This he knows from daytime TV as well.

"Why is it always white folks with this kind of stuff? White folks and Latins. Why is it you never hear about black folks seeing Jesus in their shower curtains?"

Good point, Marcus concedes, cutting into his second pork chop, which invariably never tastes as good as the first. Good, satisfying. But not as good, as satisfying. You lose that first bloom of flavor, the way it takes over your mouth, trickles underneath your tongue. The first pleasures are the purest.

"I don't know, Marcus. I know it's strange. I know in some ways it probably isn't right. But maybe we should pay us a visit. You know, to be neighborly, sure, but to check it out, see what all the commotion is. I don't think we even officially met the woman all these years. Or the husband. And maybe she, the little girl, could help. Could help us with our . . . problem. We could just visit and see."

Marcus stops in mid-chew. On the TV there's a man jumping up and down, not getting much air, mostly knee flexes actually. The superiorly dressed host is maneuvering to shake his hand and offer hostly congratulations, but the man remains too transfixed by the exaltation of his win. A crazed white man from Florida who's something called a crisis management consultant and just won ten grand for a half hour's work. Marcus loves his game shows, but he has to admit: every time he sees someone win big like this, especially white people from Florida, a little part of him dies, too. He'd like to be a contestant himself one day—who wouldn't. He'd like to be hopeful and on TV and electric with suddenly realized potential, like you were maybe a different person—greater, vaster—from what you'd thought all these years.

"Now why would we want to go and do a damn fool thing like that?"

* * *

You think you know the body but you don't. Not really. Not the body that's falsely advertised on billboards and magazine covers and fitness equipment infomercials. But the body as it truly is. Finite and unforgiving. The body as memory. The body as mystery. The body as final truth. It's what we gain and what we leave behind. And yet for the most part it remains unappreciated and unconsidered, especially among the healthy, who do not have to confront the body and its inevitable failings.

But Linda Santiago, certified physical therapist, divorced mother of two, recently liberated from her Sisyphus-like student loans, tax-paying and coupon-clipping citizen of Anaheim, California, confronts the body on a daily basis. Every day she excavates the body's endless intricacies and delicate wonders. Every day she commands skin and muscles and limbs and tendons— where to pressurize, where to pull back, breathe, talk instead of tuck. She knows the body the way a painter knows color.

It's what she interacts with, what she touches—yes, physically touches, actual intimate human-to-human contact, silent witness to eczema and cysts and all variances of blemish and imperfection and much worse—week in, week out. The body, according to Linda's own personal philosophy, is a map of who we are, where we have been. And if you touch it and heal it properly, with the appropriate care and respect and honed expertise, then you can follow that map right into the person's heart. It's why she's a P.T. It's why she's doing this—which, at the moment, is working with Mr. David Trujillo, pressing his spindly legs toward his chest, as far as they will go, the old man lying on a mat spread out on his living room floor, his body brittle and light as a child's, yet he's trying, he's making the effort to stop the onset of decay. A lot of her geris suffer from depression, too. They don't want to do their exercises. They don't want to do anything.

Later on today, there's also a session with the little girl, one of her newer clients, the one who's been on the news and causing such a fuss.

"Good, Mr. Trujillo," Linda encourages, "good. Keep it up. We're almost done for the day. You'll be trying out for the Olympics pretty soon, you keep going like this. You sure you're eighty-three?"

Mr. Trujillo smiles. Or rather he smiles as best he can, more like his jaw shifting slightly, because of the stroke, his second, far more severe than the first, a common enough pattern. He lives in Anaheim too, near Disneyland, and on those rare clear days you can even glimpse the snowy Matterhorn from his driveway. He's one of her favorite clients, most of whom are geris—all these poor folks getting older and older and their bodies letting them down. The agency she works for has a stat they like to throw around, about how many people are old and in need of care and therapy and how that number is likely to continue to grow in the new century. It's what makes their business viable, her manager, Kyle, says. But Linda doesn't think of her job that way. It's just helping people. It's helping the body, which helps the mind and so on.

"Done with the leg stretches, Mr. Trujillo. You are on fire this morning. Let's move on over to your chair and do your leg lifts and then we'll be finished and you'll have to miss me till next time."

Mr. Trujillo uses a walker and can no longer feed himself or go to the bathroom by himself without messy consequences; his wife, Esther, a woman as large and powerful as her husband is small and weak, cares for him and his every need; they have been married for far longer than Linda has been alive, longer than her own mother has been alive in fact, such permanence as rare as sincerity these days. Linda now helps him stand, guiding his frame gently and respectfully, and situates him in the chair, his favorite recliner, she's learned, where he sits and reads and thinks and naps. Then she kneels and attaches the ankle weights on Mr. Trujillo's legs and holds out her hand, indicating how high he should lift, three reps of ten for each leg (if all goes well). The body, Linda thinks as her client prepares for the regimen with a deep breath (just like she's instructed him), tells stories. The body speaks. And she listens. She always listens to what the body has to say. And these things, these thoughts: she keeps them to herself. Not even Victor knows about them; he'd probably laugh; those kind of deeper textures are beyond him, and he's the first to admit it.

"Ready when you are, my friend," Linda says, and Mr. Trujillo takes the cue and obediently lifts his left leg toward her out-stretched hand, concentrating like he's working on a math problem, sending thoughts and signals and requests to a body that's no longer listening very well.

Victor: Who hadn't stayed the night last night (sometimes he did, sometimes he didn't, you could never predict) when she'd really wanted him to, badly, like a whiny second grader; she'd wanted the sheets to have the heat of two, not one, one was not enough to induce the kind of sleep—the contented sleep of contented couples living contented lives—that she longed for. It was a simple matter of saying it: *Please stay*. But she knew how he was, who he was, you didn't need to be Miss Cleo to divine that faraway mood further insulating him the longer he remained, and there you had it once again: the distance of the male species, his desire to be gone, away, somewhere, anywhere but here. And even if he had agreed to stay, it would have been reluctantly, it would have been because he was doing his duty, serving his time so he could say no and be free another time, Victor half living/half not living there—something like that—one of those relationships you fall into because you are lonesome and rent too many movies and can only complain so much about the lack of prospective dating material without putting yourself out there every now and then, but one that surprises you, too, and becomes more than you initially thought. So she didn't say anything. Although she pouted, which didn't work, and massaged his shoulders as luxuriously as shoulders can be massaged, which also didn't work, and which was then followed by a last ditch two-fingered circling of the tender terrain between pubis and belly button. Nothing. His body was not listening. Which she internalized as a failure of her own. It had been a year now and

she, the expert of touch and contact and believer in the holiness
of the flesh, had not been able to make his body listen.

Best, though, to focus on the here and now, today. There's
work to be done, other bodies that require her more immediate
attention. After Mr. Trujillo (and she now has him switch to the
other leg, telling him that they're on the home stretch), there's
Alejandro, a paraplegic in Whittier, shot in the back, completely
arbitrary, he'd been walking down the street on his way to pick
up a prescription for an aunt (high blood pressure) and a car just
pulled up, and then it would be the girl. The Miracle Girl, they
were calling her. The one in the coma. Except it wasn't a coma
exactly, as she found out on her first visit to the house, which was
out in some nowhere area she'd never been to or heard of, and
when she arrived half an hour late the mother said not to worry
about it, everyone got lost the first time and even after that, too.

"No, it's not a coma," explained the mother, whose name was
Karen and who had the permanently tired and half-stunned, half-
sainted look of most caregivers. "Although that's what everyone
says, coma, because it's easier that way. We all know *coma*. But
it's actually something rare that's called akinetic mutism. Which
basically means she can't speak or move."

"Akinetic mutism, huh? Sounds like my ex-husband."

Karen liked that one; they laughed, exchanged girly-girl smiles,
setting both women a little more at ease; as much as Linda was
sizing up the girl and the situation, so, too, was the mother sizing
up her. The incense, the army of miniature Jesuses and Marys,
reminding Linda of her long-lost Catholic schoolgirl days. She
approached the bed and breezed her fingers across the girl's arm,
neck, forehead. So pale, so white. Like you could press a finger
to her skin and leave a mark forever.

"Just getting to know each other," she told Karen, who liked that one, too.

"Sometimes I squeeze her hand and I think maybe she's squeezing back," said Karen. "Sometimes it's there, the feeling, just the slightest sense, and sometimes it's not. Or I can't be sure. It's hard to tell."

The girl's eyes were open, seemingly seeing everything, which was pretty freaky. It would take a while to get used to that. Otherwise it was like she was asleep. Unaware. Or so it appeared. The mother said that according to the doctors there was no way to be sure if she knew what was going on around her. But the girl looked so remote, so sadly still and lifeless, that Linda seriously doubted whether she was capable of understanding much of anything, let alone the situation, the growing whirlwind around her. They went over more of the details and arranged a schedule: twice a week, Tuesday and Thursday afternoons. Linda's last available slots now filled.

She checks back in with Mr. Trujillo: beads of sweat have gathered on his forehead, she notices, his mouth grown even more crooked, his lips visibly dry. So little requiring so much exertion. He's a trooper, though, determined as hell. One of her geris: he won't cut his fingernails, won't brush his teeth. It happens.

"That's six," she tells Mr. Trujillo. "More than halfway done. It's all downhill from here, *tigre*. Four more to go."

The little girl, then, was definitely a change of pace. Her previous P.T. had lasted only a month. "It's turning into a freak show over there," warned Linda's predecessor when she called to have the girl's file faxed over to the office. "It wasn't so bad when I started, you know, a few people stopping by from time to time and asking real polite if they could come in and see her and maybe leave some flowers or say a prayer if that wasn't too much impositioning. But now since the TV, why you've got folks parading through the house all day long like it was the mall the day after Christmas. Quoting John this, Luke Skywalker that. Passing out right there in the poor girl's room, some of them. Every time I was there there was something new: the girl appeared in someone's dream and then that person was no longer sick. There was this little blotchy thing on her neck, poor thing, probably just a regular old rash or some such, and they say, 'Oh, the girl, she's taking on the what, the side effects of the chemo this man was getting who visited and had cancer.' One day they're all standing around saying how the Virgin Mary appeared in the clouds over the house. So I go outside in the backyard and it's just clouds, regular old clouds like always, and I said, 'That's clouds. You never seen clouds before?' People see what they want to see, is what it is I guess." And even the mother cautioned her: "It's not for everyone, Mrs. Santiago, that's for sure. It can be too much for some people. Why don't you come out to the house and see for yourself and then we'll take it from there."

Linda agreed to the preliminary visit, more to pacify the mother than anything else. She didn't care about all the hubbub going on, the *chismosas* who claimed the girl conversed with God. She specializes in domestics and you had to expect the unexpected, though granted this was no ordinary client, and plus the commute wouldn't be any picnic either. Still, when you got down to it, it was just another patient that required healing, another challenge for the curative magic in her fingertips. Already she's started to think about what it will be like to get the girl's body to listen. It might take time, sure, but eventually they will reach the point where they'll be able to converse without words. Together they will master the silent language of the body. Of this she has no doubt.

Mr. Trujillo has stopped his leg lifts, waiting for her to notice, Linda still thinking about the little girl, when Mrs. Trujillo walks into the living room. It's nine forty-five, the time when they finish. Their house is warm, cozy, filled with knickknacks and photos of children and grandchildren and a fierce, full love that nothing—not strokes, not death—could ever destroy. What would it be like to have that kind of love? Would it simply make her heart explode? Would it render her as speechless and motionless as the little girl?

"How'd he do?" Mrs. Trujillo asks, wiping her hands on her apron. Always cleaning, washing, something.

"He did great," says Linda, standing and packing the ankle weights into her backpack, gathering up her jacket and Mr. Trujillo's file. The day is moving, one body down and two to go.

* * *

One morning, in the forty-sixth year of the Westerfeld's marriage, not long after Donald Westerfeld had retired from a successful career as a civil engineer, and right before the annual descent of the hectic and draining but also somehow rejuvenating holidays (four grandkids now, and counting), Patricia Westerfeld woke up briefly and then went back to sleep. This was unusual—unusual because Patricia awoke each morning at the same time with alarm-clock efficiency, always bubbly and ready for the day right from the get-go, Donald being the groggy, slow-moving spouse in the morning. He got out of bed and let his wife sleep. Turns out, though, that this was a sign, a beginning.

Patricia soldiered through Christmas, relegated to a supporting role for the first time in family history, the kids and Donald picking up the slack and letting her rest and camp out on the sofa. *I'm just really really tired,* she kept saying, *but I'll be fine, I'll be all right, I just need to rest.* And so she slumbered like a hibernating momma bear and profusely and repeatedly apologized and no one complained about the food or the poorly wrapped presents. After the kids and grandkids left and New Year's came and went (no Dick Clark, no champagne) and it was 1999, Patricia continued to rest. Donald played solitaire on the computer, watched TV alone. Later he'd tell her about the shows she'd missed, doing his best to summarize and reconstruct and tell a compelling story, which he'd never been particularly good at. She said she was feeling a little better and he shouldn't worry so much. And she did seem better: slept less, had enough energy to go on a hike and visit some friends in Santa Monica. But then she reverted back, had even less energy, required even more sleep. *We should go in,* he finally said, fearing that too much time was passing. *I don't know,* she said, *it might be nothing, I just need to sleep more, that's what happens when you get old, Donald, we can wait until my annual checkup in May.* He said, *I think we should go in just to be sure.*

They went in. Questions, tests. Waiting. Blood work and scans and specialists. Referrals were made, appointments scheduled and rescheduled to accommodate the many doctors involved. More waiting. It could be this, it could be that. Donald surprised at the uncertainty and the time wasted as they waited. They cancelled bridge dates and a trip to Scottsdale, reconsidered the Mediterranean cruise planned for later in the year. They hit the Internet. Did countless searches, absorbed the results, tried not to get too frightened. Diseases you'd never heard of, obscure conditions that ravaged the body and mind. Then more tests. They went in again.

And now, today, they huddle together in yet another doctor's office, waiting for the new oncologist, supposedly a genius, highly sought after and known as the "Miracle Man" for the high ratio of his patients who made it into remission. Donald holds Patricia's hands, which are cold and dry. Multiple magazines offer potential distraction, but they don't bite. They are beyond the solace of celebrities and sports and recipes for butternut squash soup. They stare at framed pictures of the ocean and charts of the human body, all the organs and bones and so on that will fail you if you live long enough.

The genius doctor enters and starts talking, no polite preamble. Donald hears the first few words and then everything else falls away; he's seeing the doctor's lips and mouth move but nothing more registers. The doctor's young—too young, Donald thinks, to be delivering this kind of news. Over the years he'd imagined this scene many times before (sometimes it was him, sometimes it was Patricia), but always the doctor was old, wise, salt-and-pepper-bearded, prominently balding, vaguely reminiscent of the actor Pernell Roberts, not from his *Bonanza* days but from *Trapper John, M.D.*, where he played, surprise, a doctor. Donald wonders: Does anyone know who Pernell Roberts is anymore? Patricia's hands seem to turn even colder, blood rushing away while it can, anticipating what is to come.

Lung cancer. *Lung cancer.* Fucking *lung cancer.* She's never smoked. Not once. How does this happen? This was not right. This was not how it was supposed to be.

The doctor's voice returns and now Donald hears about stages and surgeries and statistics. It was possible to try A, or B, or maybe even C, and new treatments can always emerge, but that was about it, due to the late stage, how advanced and pronounced things were, it's farther along than we'd ideally like, meaning our options are unfortunately limited, if it had been earlier, if there'd been earlier detection, well, we'd be having a different conversation, and as the doctor—who's clean-shaven, has a full head of boyish Adonis hair—recites all this he also flips through Patricia's chart and keeps scribbling notes and tapping his foot, seemingly in two places at once in his head despite the gravity of the subject matter, his eyes careful to avoid theirs, as if eye contact would force him to admit modern medicine has its limitations like anything else. They needed to schedule a follow-up visit once they'd made some decisions. There would be no miracles here.

Five minutes. Five minutes and it's all over, they're done, they're taking the elevator down and then walking through the parking lot, searching for the Lexus that was Donald's retirement present to himself. Now it looks like a stupid car, like a stupid thing that doesn't mean anything. *This,* Donald burns, thinking of the grim prognosis, *this* means something. He opens the door for Patricia, guides her in, buckles her seatbelt as if she's a child. She remains silent for the entire drive back, the day appropriately overcast and gloom-skied along the coast, clogged stop-and-go on Pacific Coast Highway, the traffic breaking after they escape downtown Laguna Beach and head into the canyon, where they've lived for decades, raised a family, made a life, a very good life, Patricia always saying how they've been so blessed, so lucky, so lucky, all these years.

At home they don't know what to do. Everything had changed, and yet here they are, in their house, the same house they left only a few hours ago.

"It's lunchtime," he says. "Would you like something to eat?"

Before leaving for the doctor's appointment in the morning they'd forgotten to turn off the coffee maker, the house now smelling burnt and vulnerable.

"No," she says. "No thanks. I'm fine. I'm not sure what I want to do."

"You sure? I could make you a sandwich."

"No. I think I just want to sit. Let's sit."

They retreat to the sofa in the living room. The curtains still drawn. Light leaks in from outside. He feels the weight of the moment and doesn't know what to say or do. He feels it, the moment, in the temples of his forehead and deep in his chest, a sensation he remembers from when he asked Patricia to marry him, from when each of their children was born. He looks down at the coffee table and sees the newspaper he read yesterday. It's a different object now. Transformed. The same pictures and words, yes, but they had been altered between the time they left and when they got back. He glances around the walls, the room, the hallway leading to the downstairs den where he sometimes napped and read *U.S. News and World Report* and biographies of dead presidents. He thinks of the backyard outside and the white gate and beyond that their peek-a-boo view (quoting the real estate agent who sold them the house) of the Pacific Ocean. This is where they live. This is their home. And yet it's all different now. The carpet— it's a color he no longer knew the name of.

"We should call Tim and Amanda," says Patricia.

He nods. Yes. They would have to tell their children. Another dread. They would be telling countless friends and family and neighbors over the coming days. The grim task of communication awaited them.

"Definitely," he says. "But later, OK?"

"OK," she says. "Later then."

So they sit and wait and after a while, because he doesn't know what else to do, he turns on the TV. They watch one show and then another, all afternoon, until it gets dark, the screen glowing before them, a forgiving radiance that neither wants to end.

"It's getting late," she says, her voice sounding tired and drugged and ancient, already half gone.

"Are you hungry yet?"

"No."

The local news coming up next: something about Clinton, terrorists, the Lakers, a little girl up in L.A. who was paralyzed in an accident and now was supposedly performing miracles, people lining up outside her house.

And he wants to reach over and touch Patricia's face, her arm, to see if that would be different, too, her skin, her lips, also transformed, but he can't bring himself to do it, not yet, he wants to touch and verify but he also doesn't want to frighten or alarm, it's another important moment, one that he knows he will relive many, many times and he doesn't want to do anything wrong or make her jump or disturb her, but then he realizes she's fallen asleep, his wife, Patricia Marie Kennard Westerfeld, girl and then woman of his dreams, all these years, all this history and significance, as well as the future ahead, which is now no longer a future, and he just sits there and gives up and does not give up and believes and does not believe and listens to her breathe and it's a beautiful sound and a resilient sound and it's hard to imagine that such a thing would ever cease from happening, that it would be gone from this earth and from him, and fairly soon, according to the doctor who was too young, who did not look anything like Pernell Roberts. Donald doesn't want to move. It's very late. They could try A, B, or C. He listens to the house settle, an old, familiar, soothing creaking now rendered new and alarming.

5

| Karen |

AND SHE'S OUT—OUT of the house, out into the world, away
from 147 Shaker Street and its many layers of drama and in-
volvement and responsibility, the trips out now more and more
infrequent as the number of visitors has increased in the wake
of her interview with Kellee Clifton (three weeks ago), so much
to be done, so much to be done, and plus, too, as more people
arrive and so desperately want/need what her daughter has,
she finds herself becoming increasingly protective of Anabelle,
hesitant to be away from her, fearful that the visitors will suck
her dry, leave her empty, depleted, changed yet again. But Bryce
and Dom insisted she go. They told her that it'd been too long,
weeks, whatever, and that she needed to come up for air, breathe.
"Go, go, you're gone," said Bryce, who's now at the house just
as often as her niece. "Come back before five o'clock and I won't
let you back in the house. Don't write. Don't call. See ya." Had
it really been that long? She didn't want to leave Anabelle, didn't
want other people to have to deal with the new hustle and bustle.
Sleep was now further minimized to only three or four hours a

night. Always on the phone or talking to a visitor or tracking down a nurse last minute or figuring out what the time difference in Australia or Laos was, because people from there had left messages and she really, truly tried to get back to everyone. Always something. Including, of course, the caring for her daughter, the constant work and worry. There's no time for herself, so it's hard to know how long it's been since she's left the house, hard to sort out one thing from the other. The result? She's driving up and down El Portal Boulevard like a teenager on Saturday night and doesn't know where to go or what to do.

El Portal Boulevard cuts through the city of the same name, dividing the southeastern Los Angeles suburb in half: above the boulevard and below the boulevard. The former has the hills and the money, while the latter is flat and has the Food Outlet. Karen has lived below the boulevard in El Portal her entire life: it's where she grew up; it's where she went to high school; it's where she met and fell in love with John; and it's where she became a parent. Most of her friends have left (college, jobs, relationships, life), and so had her mother (Fort Collins, Colorado) and her father (Yuma, Arizona, living with his second wife and their many cats), but Karen has always felt an allegiance to the place where she's from, even if there isn't much there, even if it's the kind of city that gets left off those maps the local TV weathermen show every night.

Since she doesn't have a destination in mind yet, and since she's tired of aimlessly driving and hearing the same Prince song on multiple radio stations ("1999," of course), she decides she might as well be useful and get some shopping done. So she hangs a U-turn and heads to Costco, two towns over and near the recently renovated Prado Mall. The sky is both metal gray and bright yellow at the same time. She passes a bank with a sign that alternates the time and temp: 9:42, already 94 degrees. Another scorcher. The electric bill is going to be a bitch this month, the air-conditioning running around the clock.

It's a weekday, a Tuesday, but the Costco parking lot is packed. Karen manages to find an orphaned shopping cart and, once inside, navigates the aisles and the shoppers and the darting kids. Costco always overwhelmed her, all that space and the endless items for purchase. It's usually best to have a list, but she does not have a list, this is a dangerous unplanned visit, and so she wanders from section to section. She buys cookies and snacks and an assortment of juices (apple, grape, kiwi, mango) for the visitors. Plus paper cups and plates and napkins and more. The cart quickly fills. She realizes she's hungry and so she says yes to every sample item offered to her, the people wearing their doctorly white jackets and latex gloves and smiling, smiling, smiling. Suddenly it seems very important to have a vast quantity of oatmeal.

Near the canned-goods aisle, a woman stops her.

"Hey, it's you," the woman says.

Karen thinks it might be someone from high school. She scans the woman's face—round, tired, ordinary—for recognition but comes up empty. They're roughly the same age. Could have played softball together. Gone to summer camp. Talked about boys and braces and Robert Plant's jeans.

"You're the mom," the woman clarifies, and then Karen understands.

"Yes, it's me, I guess."

"I've seen you and your daughter on TV. The Miracle Girl. Wow. And you're the mom of the Miracle Girl. And you're here, at Costco, you're here, too. Wow. Could I get your autograph?"

Karen scribbles her name on the back of a receipt, moves on. The experience dazes her, makes her head spin like she's just been on a pukey carnival ride. Weird. How do celebrities do it? Do you get used to it? Do you ever like it? People knowing you and yet not knowing you. She puts on her sunglasses and escapes to one of the lengthy checkout lines, every cart in front of her filled and brimming with bulk merchandise, as well as last-minute candy for Halloween—she hadn't thought of buying candy herself, but it's too late now; there's no way she's getting out of line. The cashier has one of those patchy hippie beards that John had unsuccessfully tried to grow, both she and Anabelle complaining of the scratchiness of his insufficient whiskers. And in fact John had applied (also unsuccessfully) for a job here once. There was a time when he applied just about everywhere.

When it's her turn she makes the usual small talk (the long line, the weather) with the cashier. If he recognizes her, he doesn't show it. And then everything begins to shake. There's that initial quiet as the fact of the earthquake sinks in, then there's a building panic as people think they better make a run for it and bolt outside, because outside is safer, inside a huge, cavernous warehouse store is not safe and could be quite fatal and fucked up, and last words/thoughts are hastily composed, loved ones considered, obituaries visualized, but then before it progresses any farther than that it's over, the shaking ceases, and there's a collective relief and everyone can breathe again, earthquakes like little mortality checks for Southern Californians. This all lasts a mere six seconds.

"That's the third one in what—a month?" says the cashier.

"I don't know," says Karen. "Something like that. There's been a lot."

"And that was the biggest one yet, I think. Five-point-seven at least. Maybe five-eight. What do you think it means, all these earthquakes we're having?"

Karen doesn't know what to say. She looks up at the ceiling, seeking out a crack or hole or something to indicate potential structural damage, and wonders what would happen if it all came down, before she then realizes she needs to get back home as soon as possible, because there'd been an earthquake there, too.

ON THE DRIVE home, she passes the mall, which takes her back, which always takes her back. On the radio they're saying it was centered somewhere out in the desert, no reports of damage or injuries yet, more updates coming soon.

THE PHONE WAS always ringing. That whole six months or so with John before the accident, the noise didn't let up, erupting through the house no matter the day, the hour, its harsh, cheap, electronic cackle accusing her somehow.

She wasn't working then. Wasn't even really a consideration, it had gotten so bad, her bluesy spirits and feeling of sinking deeper into a nameless despair, often unable to sustain a single, simple thought. And plus the phone was never for her. The voices all sounding guilty of something, a crime yet to be committed. Ninety-nine-point-nine percent male, their names hard to spell, their manners and general phone etiquette wanting. Speaking in hushed secret-agent tones, as if a person was sleeping next to them, as if there was someone nearby whose attention the caller did not want to arouse, much like the way John spoke when he was on the phone. After a while she didn't want to know who was calling, and so she refused to take messages, then to pick up at all, which John filibustered about because the answering machine was either broken or intermittently reliable at best, and how did it look, he said, to have people calling with no machine, no one answering, just the ringing and ringing, like he'd given them a bum number, and no one answering meant they wouldn't be able to pay the mortgage this month, and they needed the money. Another thing about the phone was that it only rang when John wasn't there. When he was there, the phone did not ring. Well, at least not as much, but not as much by a significant margin. When he was there, he was the one who made the calls. He dialed, he had conversations, he left messages, then he left the house. It was only when she was alone, that is with Anabelle, the two of them, that the phone rang.

At some point he bought a pager. Then besides the phone ringing there was the pager going off and beeping. He clipped it on his belt like a doctor. Or no. He didn't wear a belt. So he must have fastened it to his jeans. His beloved Levi's, which he'd buy three at a time (and they had to be Levi's, not Lee's or some wannabe pretender brand; and they had to be 501s, the cardboard shrink-to-fit kind), then wash them over and over until the stiffness and dark blueness faded away, the denim lightening and softening. Only then were they worthy of entering his limited wardrobe rotation. Jeans and T-shirts almost exclusively. The jeans piled in their closet, the T-shirts taking up two drawers plus overflow, some dating back to high school and qualifying as archeological artifacts, some from relatively recent concerts by bands on their third or fourth final farewell tour. The first time she saw him he must have been wearing jeans and a T-shirt. It's just the odds. Which prompted the question: how does a woman fall in love with a man wearing jeans and T-shirt? How is such a thing possible?

Life was a real cabaret. And there were episodes, as they came to be called, like she was on a TV show. They varied in intensity and severity. The mall episode had been one of the worst, one of the worst public ones (the private ones sometimes just as bad, if not more horrible in their own way), the memory of which has stuck permanently in her brain, snapping in place Lego-like, along with the phone ringing and the other irrational fixations from those days, a reminder of how close she had been, how little it takes to fall and perhaps never find your way back.

All morning she had been deliberating about making the trip to the mall. Now that she was spending all this time at home she was realizing how easy it is to get obsessed, obsessive—completely, totally. That was the danger. Every little thing had the potential to mutate into a costumed epic period drama. So one simple decision that had germinated while forcing down her reheated-from-yesterday morning coffee—hey, maybe I should swing by the mall real quick sometime today and pick up whatever it is I've been meaning to pick up—had dragged through *Judge Judy* and a *Home Improvement* rerun, a draining play session with Anabelle, the sofa contemplation of sit-ups and more coffee, the search for a masculine tool of some kind in the black hole of the garage (turns out it wasn't there, loaned to a friend of John's and gone for good), and into the initial preparations for lunch as she flipped on the old portable black-and-white in the kitchen that, if nothing else, made you appreciate color all the more. And still nothing had been decided. See, there was so much to consider. Until your life slowed down to practically nothing, to a stagnant hum, there was no way you could know how one trip, one decision, could be so complicated and take up so much mental and physical energy. But it did.

Not helping matters much was the fact that she'd spent the previous night in the bathtub, in her robe, and now her back hurt. She'd been in the tub smoking and crying and after a while she didn't see the point of leaving. So she slept there. It wasn't the first time. Anabelle more than once waking to discover her mother curled inside the porcelain like a punished pet. But her wavering about whether or not to go to the mall involved more than sleep deprivation. Increasingly she had developed a full-blown, probably diagnosable anxiety about leaving the house, and it was getting difficult to conceal, John starting to make comments, grumbling about being the one who had to run out for milk or eggs or whatever they were lacking—there was always something, their privations numerous and diverse. Actually, she had been thinking about the trip to the mall for the past week. It had become a major preoccupation, a multiday serialized internal soap opera with ups and downs, tensions and climaxes, resolutions and further plot complications. Deciding, postponing. Rationalizing. Re-rationalizing. Re-*re*-rationalizing. Thinking tomorrow. Thinking why not combine a trip to the mall with a trip to the market. Two birds, etc. But then concluding that no, that would be too much. Better one trip one day. Spread it out, equalize. So do the mall today, or tomorrow, and then do the market the following day or on the weekend. Although if you go on the weekend it will be more crowded, meaning that waiting until Monday was probably best, but since Monday was a transitional day, a bridge from the weekend to the week proper, Tuesday was more likely. So you see.

The phone was ringing again. John wasn't home, of course. He was there less and less, even though he wasn't working. Not technically. Not according to the government. He was freelancing, he liked to joke. This after he got laid off from his job installing doors and windows, and after his unemployment ran out, John often explaining, "It's temporary, Karen, just temporary until something else comes along. How else are we going to pay our bills?" His friend Tommy Arroyo had moved to Humboldt and had a cheap, steady supply. The packages arrived in the mail, the baggies nestled in coffee grounds because Tommy had seen it done like that in a movie. John called a few friends and some former coworkers, wanting to keep it mellow and controlled, just a little extra income to get them through a rough patch, but the friends had friends, and so did the former coworkers, and plus there was a sudden shortage of marijuana in the greater Southern California area due to some recent seizures and arrests and bad weather in Mexico that had significantly curtailed the year's crop. So the phone rang and rang, and since she wasn't working, basically incapacitated at this point, who was she to say anything? John always coming and going. Driving with his sunglasses and color-coded Ziploc baggies and Anabelle's car seat in the back, making deliveries to apartments and bars and, once, the parking lot at Dodger Stadium. She didn't pick up the phone because picking up the phone not only would entail hearing the voices she didn't want to hear but would also entail a conversation of some sort, no matter how rudimentary. So she let it ring. She yelled at Anabelle, "Don't pick up. Don't you dare pick up that goddamn phone." Sometimes Anabelle did that. Answered the phone and said nothing. Waiting for something, someone to come on the line and clarify the situation, provide information, hint at what she was supposed to do next.

And then Karen was there. The mall. It had happened. She

was in the world once more. Obeying traffic laws, using her turn signal. She was there with her daughter and they had driven the so-and-so miles and found a parking space. She had come for something, only she couldn't remember what. She had told Anabelle what the thing was but now she couldn't remember, and neither could Anabelle, or maybe she knew and wasn't telling, which was entirely possible. They were hopeless, mother and daughter. The mall was crowded even though it wasn't the holidays or the weekend or the summer. She didn't know where matters stood calendar-wise, but maybe it was the first of the month, which would explain all the shoppers. There were young mothers everywhere—young mothers who looked like they didn't want to be young mothers, or mothers at any age for that matter, their children circling them, like baby birds clamoring to be fed. There was music, or Muzak, part of the universal mall background drone that you don't really think about until you force yourself to listen. Which was what she did. The sounds, the people, the mall maps and signs, all pushing her toward the early stages of overload, engulfing her slowly like a lapping wave covering the sand, spreading its wetness and damp. It was a Beatles song. The one about looking at all the lonely people. "Eleanor Rigby." Was that song from before or after the Beatles started taking drugs? She didn't know. John would know. John knew all kinds of useless trivia like that, yet had trouble remembering their anniversary.

Anabelle was probably sniffling. It seemed like she was always sick, always sniffling. She was probably also hungry, since they hadn't eaten anything (the beginnings of lunch abandoned on the kitchen counter) before coming to the mall, which was musty with the smell of burnt pizza cheese and expired chow mein, but she would have to wait, they both would, because they were on a budget, and that budget did not include extravagant trips to the Food Court. Karen, intuiting that dizziness was looming, here we go again, beelined to the first bench she saw, while Anabelle took the opportunity to go over and inspect the hazardous-looking play structure in the middle of the mall, an area that became Santa's Village or Villa or something during the holidays, starting around like Labor Day. Although the mall served its purpose, barely, it was a shitty mall, utilized only by those who lived nearby and conspicuously missing a multiplex and a Radio Shack.

Seated around her were mostly young mothers, slouched like the teenagers the majority of them were, but also two or three old men sitting and waiting for their old wives. You had the bookend evidence of the young and the old. Where you've been and where you're going. One man clutched a walker, his left hand trembling uncontrollably, a possessed appendage, a restless, wasted thing. Mouth open, apparently for good. He looked completely ravaged and used up. An oxygen tank next to the walker. Everything a betrayal at this point, even, thought Karen, the continuing absence of his wife, if he did in fact have one and was not alone. Passing the Tots O' Fun play area was a lone teenage boy, a practiced menace in his walk, his pants slung low enough that they would seem to impede motion but did not, with a black T-shirt that said ACTS OF AGRESSION. That's all. No band or sports-company affiliation. Just this plain, unadorned message, which baffled her. What kind of aggression? What kind of acts?

Karen watched Anabelle approach another little girl and then run away. What was that all about? Her daughter the enigma.

Tinkerbell in her own magical land. Which worried John more than her, but still, she worried, too. Several kids were crying, though at different pitches and levels of alarm. It was all building toward something. The longer she sat there, the greater the force of her heart lashing against her chest. The dizziness had not subsided but actually intensified. Breathing becoming problematic. Bad idea, going to the mall. Should have known better, given recent history. Because now standing up was not an option and wouldn't be for some time. Another bad decision in a lifetime of many. More and more on the rare occurrences when she voyaged outside the house, she found herself on this precipice: of black freefall, of dark plunge, of your body no longer you.

The volume dial clicked higher, louder. And not just the overly melancholic violins of the cheesified Lennon-McCartney. But the babble of shoppers, the primal anguish of children. Too, from somewhere, the static-y murmur that was her life. Everything outside her—the mall, the shoppers, the Muzak—and inside her— the phone, the bills, John, the parental fuckups—was vivid and amplified, pretty much equally. No longer was there a shield, a membrane to protect, to insulate the inside from the outside. It was all the same. All one rising pool of panic. Yes, overload. It was official.

She heard one of the mothers yelling for her child to get over here, to quit screwing around, and she felt a shifting, a give, and it was then quite possible that she was the one yelling, except that now, right now, a couple of seconds after the yelling had ceased, her mouth seemed to be clamped shut and incapable of speech and she was maybe biting her tongue but her tongue had been numb for the longest time and so she couldn't be sure, the clamping then spreading from her mouth to her chest to her arms to basically everywhere, circulating like a chill. She could not move. This was now official as well. Although apparently she was shivering. Shaking like the old man's hand, except her whole body.

It had happened before, this seizing terror, this compulsion to be somewhere else, to disappear, poof, like magic. The setting for the previous incident: a market. The cereal aisle specifically, amid a splash of colors and cartoon mascots and endless bounty. However, she had been able to pull herself together and snap out of it in time by reciting the familiar and soothing names and brands stacked all around her—Nabisco, Post, General Mills, Raisin Bran, Kix, Frosted Flakes, Lucky Charms. Well, that wasn't going to happen here. No cereal boxes and multinational companies to anchor her to the receding world. And the people around her, the throng of strangers—they knew what was coming as much as she did. They knew everything—her embarrassingly shallow thoughts, her eroding marriage, her peculiar daughter, her suspect mothering skills, her fear of leaving the house, the tiny wound in her heart that she could not name and that could not properly heal. She tried to stand but there were no legs with which to stand. She tried to breathe but there were no lungs with which to breathe. A line had been crossed, a scary, scary fucking line, one that had not been crossed before. This was all new territory. Her exile to this alternate, unreachable frequency never this remote, never this extreme. Why here? Why the mall? The nausea was causing a rank fluid to assemble in the back of her throat.

At some point she slumped from the bench to the ground, not sure if this was a conscious choice or a chemical or biological command her body could not ignore. She didn't know how long it took before someone noticed her, but finally someone did. People approached her like an injured animal (she was fetal by then, was what she was told later). Somebody said "seizure." Somebody said "9-1-1." Somebody said, "Does anybody know her, who she is?" The old man with the walker and oxygen tank leaned down, heroically, as best as he could, and placed the mask over her mouth, so gently, so carefully, it was as if the act were some kind of religious rite. *Breathe,* he said. And she did. She inhaled the rush of oxygen along with the old man's stale, mortal stench, which lingered on the plastic device. He didn't remove the mask for the longest time. She breathed.

And then they were touching her and she did not want to be touched. Polite, respectful touching, the kind you'd expect in such a situation (testing her forehead for fever, unbuttoning a top button to assist the passage of air), but touching nonetheless. Stop, please, she wanted to tell them. Please don't touch me. But because she could not move or speak, she could do nothing, just lay there and be touched. They lifted her into a wheelchair once a security guard arrived with it, and this was perhaps the greatest cruelty of all, the hoisting of her body, the dead, useless weight, the burden of her physical being in the arms of complete strangers.

The security guard wheeled her through the mall, Anabelle following and trying to keep up. The whole time she had remained in the play area, gawking with the rest of the children and onlookers. The guard took them down a corridor, then down an elevator, and into a large room, the mall security room. When Karen recovered the power of language, she managed to convince the security guard not to call for an ambulance, which would cost money and which she assumed she'd have to pay for, not the mall. But he did insist on having someone pick her up. She dialed home but John, predictably, was not there.

The security guard said to just wait, relax some, try again in a few.

"Can I get you anything?" he asked.

"Water maybe."

The security guard shuffled over to the kitchen area and washed out a coffee mug. He was newly emancipated from his teens, bad skin, worse teeth. It said SECURITY all over him: his cap, his shirt, his jacket, as if repetition of the word would help foster intimidation. It did not.

"You sure you gonna be all right?"

"I'm fine. Really."

He handed her the water: warmish, metallic, residued with Palmolive. But she was grateful for any liquid so long as it made it down her throat. She sipped, swallowed, looked around. TVs all over the place, like a sports bar gone mad. Except the screens were in black and white, and showed people shopping in stores, sifting through merchandise, staring off into space, holding un-cooperative children, and yes, looking guilty. Simply because they were being filmed. The black and white adding another layer to their shame.

"You one of those epileptics?"

"No. Not that I know of."

"I have a cousin who's one. But you'd never know, as long as he takes his meds."

All this time Anabelle watching her. Watching like only a child can watch a parent. That mixture of wonder and disappoint-ment and hurt, in the eyes, the face. Absorbing the particulars of yet another scar on her delicate psyche. Her daughter who so easily bruised—seize her too hard on the arm and the darkness appears almost immediately, but more than that, too. You could bruise her with words, a look, a gesture. And now this, the trauma of seeing her mother helpless, sprawled on the mall floor like a passed-out drunk. Anabelle was a witness to it all, and that couldn't be healthy. Who knows how harmful and how permanent the memory would be?

On one of the screens a pregnant-looking shopper held a blouse aloft for inspection. The security guard nodded like a solemn keeper of societal secrets, of hidden knowledge not available to the average civilian.

"Most people don't get to see this," he said, a little wistful, or at least as wistful as a twenty-year-old mall security guard can get.

"I'm sorry?" Karen still thinking of her daughter, the girl's marked future.

"You know, the pulse. Behind the scenes. This is where it all happens. You'd be surprised at what goes down at your typical average everyday mall."

She kept calling and still there was no answer. Eventually, though, after about an hour, the security guard let her go. She gathered her purse and her daughter and drove home, the time in transit passing like a jump cut in a movie: suddenly you were someplace else, time and space obliterated. She sent Anabelle to her room and then crashed on the sofa. The cushions contoured to her regularly reclining figure. She slept way too much, she knew. But really: is twelve hours too much? Whatever the body requires, right? The mall ordeal had completely exhausted her. Tired in the bones, behind the eyes. But just as she settled in, covered herself with a blanket, closed her eyes . . . the phone was ringing. The phone was ringing and John wasn't there. Of course.

She thought she'd better answer it, since she'd given the security guard her phone number and maybe he was calling to check up on her or something.

"Hello. John there?" a would-be felonious voice inquired.

"John?" she said. The name was becoming more and more unfamiliar. Elusive. A word and not a person. A concept and not a husband. Her husband.

"There's no John here," she informed the voice.

It was, technically, the truth.

THE FIRST THING she sees after returning from Costco is the fire truck in the street. The second thing she sees is the ambulance in the driveway. And the third thing she sees is Bryce running toward her, waving his hands, panic painted on his face, as she parks her car across the street, in front of the black couple's house, the one with the blinds always closed. Then she's out of the car and running herself, Bryce keeping pace next to her, explaining, "After the earthquake the power went out. Briefly, but it went out. Everything was still shaking and we had some trouble getting the backup generators going, and there was some scary few seconds there, and so we called 911, but right then, pretty much right after, the power came back on and everything kicked back in. And so the ambulance came even though it probably didn't need to. She's fine. Anabelle's fine. They're checking her vitals. And I called Dr. Patel, just to be sure. He's on his way, too. I'm so sorry, Karen. I would've called. You should really get a cell phone. I didn't know where you were. I would've called."

People are scattered about the front yard, visitors and neighbors, fifteen or twenty or so, milling around in the continuing chaos, not knowing what to do, if they should stay or go.

Inside Karen rushes past the gauntlet of firefighters and para-medics lining the hallway. They make way for her and she enters Anabelle's room, Bryce right behind her. The air in there is op-pressive from all the bodies and activity, and Karen can't remem-ber the last time she ran like that—like death itself was trying to light a fire under her ass.

Anabelle has an oxygen mask on her face. There are more IVs and tubes and blinking gadgets than usual. Did she look different? Did it seem like she's in pain? Had her body moved some, the smallest of increments, noticeable to no one but her because she was the only one who could possibly notice such unnoticeable things? Why had she been so foolish and left? Did the earthquake mean anything? Was it a sign? Yes and no, Karen thinks. Yes and no to everything.

One of the paramedics bends over Anabelle, readies an injec-tion. His hair is slicked back, like a talk-show host's. A large dragon tattoo snarls across one of his forearms.

"I shouldn't have left," Karen says. "How is she?"

"She's breathing and stable," answers the paramedic, who looks right out of high school, barely an adult, and here he is with her daughter's life in his hands. "We're monitoring. This will help with any potential blood clots, just in case."

He gives Anabelle the shot. And Karen swears, *swears,* some-thing changes in her daughter's eyes, the slightest, subtlest micro-movement to indicate *pain,* to simply say a little-girl *ouch* and *Mommy, where were you?*

"She's going to be fine, Karen," says Bryce. "She's going to be fine. It was just a little scare."

Once the paramedic has moved back, Karen steps up and reaches out and rubs her daughter's arm. God. Goddamn. She picks up Anabelle's hand, places it to her lips. The skin smells like sweat, feels like Silly Putty. And if Karen wasn't crying before, she sure is now.

"I should have learned by now," she says. "I shouldn't have left her. I can't ever leave her."

6

| John |

THE IDEA, THEN, was to become a monk, and if not that, then at least be able to classify himself as monklike. John often pictured men with robes and beards who went without sex or alcohol or cable TV. That's what he aspired to. Living bare. Living without. And so: as he sleep-stumbles out of bed and squeezes into his apartment's tiny kitchen to officially start his day, he thinks that, other than his night at the Well last week, he's done pretty OK monk-wise, ever since he left home. He's even lost about fifteen pounds, so there's less of him. But didn't monks chant? He didn't think he could go that far, chanting, though his empty cabinets and refrigerator certainly attest to his regimen of restriction. Breakfast consists of plain oatmeal, sans brown sugar or maple syrup, and reheated coffee, black. No sexy, excessive extras, just the essentials. He's about to turn on the TV but then he remembers the monks again, and so he doesn't. One more deprivation. A good way to inaugurate the day—his last at Dazzle Productions.

Yes, he's not where he wants to be, but he's getting closer, it's a work in progress, and as he swabs deodorant and dresses, he thinks how he's out there, really out there, floating, unconnected, uninsured, unknown. And now there is only time. There are no calls to make, no letters to write. Friends, his mother, the little family he has—they don't know how to reach him or where he is. He's honed himself down to the simplest existence possible, the most minimal interactions with the world. Of the money he makes, he keeps the bare minimum for rent and food and socks, sends Karen the rest. It is his penance and also his choice. People on milk cartons aren't the only ones who can disappear.

Sometimes he speaks his name aloud (in the shower, while driving to work, when standing in line at the market making his meager purchases) to remind himself of who he is and what he has lost.

No ONE AT work mentions that it's his last day, not even the chatty, pastry-loving ladies in the break room. He powers through the morning, filling orders and loading trucks with freshly minted porn, his *Alphonso* shirt thoroughly soaked with sweat by nine-thirty. It wasn't long after he started his stint at Dazzle Productions that he realized there was probably one person (a guy of course) who came up with all the titles for porn flicks. And the guy was in a rut. Too much reliance on puns and alliteration and take-offs on regular movies—*When Harry Fucked Sally, Romancing the Bone,* and so on. One of the "perks" of working here was that you could bring home all the DVDs you wanted. But monks did not watch porn. Besides, he didn't have a DVD player.

At lunch time the break room is brimming with people and conversations and so he escapes outside to the parking lot, staying only briefly because of the heat, the blacktop baking and the sky rimmed with thinnish clouds; Nevada heat was not the same as California heat. He hears a buzzing—power lines, insects, something. The invisible, unknown humming of the world. Almost one o'clock. Halfway there. He uses the sleeve of his shirt to temporarily wipe away the sweat on his forehead and then he returns to the warehouse for the afternoon crawl. There's a lull, during which Devon, one of the warehouse guys, delivers yet another rambling monologue on his favorite topic ("Y2K, it's coming, Flip. Are you ready? You best be. We're talking no ATMs, no cash, people freaking, power failures, food and water shortages, airplanes crashing, the whole grid holding everything together going down, looting, cars turned over, fires, all of it. And it's coming. Like those billboards say: 'If you hear a trumpet, grab the wheel.' That's what I'll be doing. If I'm driving, I mean. Otherwise, I'll be hunkered down at my house with the door locked, with my gun and batteries and canned goods . . ."), and then for an hour or so it gets busy, the orders accelerate, time accelerates, and John settles into that thought-erasing rhythm, that nameless zone where there is only work and nothing else and your mind is clear and alive and purposeful. The temperature outside is 103 degrees. They have giant fans inside the warehouse running all day long but they do little good. When things slow down, he starts to think again. And he thinks: it's not good to think. Devon brings another order to fill and tells him, "Aren't you having fun yet, Flip? You're looking glum, chum. You should be smiling ear to ear. You're working in the entertainment industry, son. You're looking at titties and ass all day long, *pro-fes-shun-nal* titties and ass, mind you, and getting paid for it and you're not smiling. Look at me. I'm smiling. Happy as a clam. I tell my wife: 'I look at women all day long but I still come home to you, honey.' She likes that. That makes her smile."

By 5:05, he's already changed his clothes and turned in his soggy shirt. Alphonso no more. Alphonso has left the building. No one says good-bye, good luck. For everyone else it's just another day at DP, after all. And he's not going to linger, he's in a hurry because he wants to make it to the TempPeople offices before 5:30 so he can get his check so he can cash it first thing tomorrow morning and send off money to Karen in the mail. By 5:10 he's inside his car and driving on Lake Mead Parkway and he knows he'll never see any of those people again, and by 5:25 he's walking into Phil Wagman's office, inquiring about his next assignment once the check (the final amount always disappointing) is in his hand. But instead of answering right away Phil leans back in his Captain Kirk chair, and John's afraid there's going to be dialogue, a discussion of some kind, when all he wants is to get out of there and return to his hovel and eat the carne asada burrito he'll pick up on the way home and then fall asleep.

"John, why don't you sit down?" asks Phil, who's one of those guys who shaves his head but really shouldn't due to incongruent skull shape and multiple moles and blackheads, which otherwise would have been hidden if he had hair. "Take a load off. Relax. It's Friday. We both survived another week."

John reluctantly sits and can't help but look at the large eight-by-ten framed family portrait that dominates not only Phil's desk but the entire room. Done at one of those mall photo places. A nature-y, fall-harvest background. Trees and a wooden fence. There's Phil, Mrs. Phil, Phil Junior. Matching shirts. Smiling.

Beaming. They all seem as one, one package, one unit, unable to exist without the other.

"Are you sure," Phil begins in a concerned, fatherly tone, even though they're about the same age, "are you sure you want to start right up with another job again? I could get someone else. You've been going pretty hard, going from gig to gig without any time off. You're entitled. You're due."

Phil must not have had time to shave his head this morning, because there's more stubble than usual, a prickly eruption across his scalp.

"No thanks," says John. "I'm good. I'm ready to go. I can do weekends, too. Weekends would be fine."

Phil catches John looking at the photo. It's an opening. Then Phil smiles the same smile that's in the picture: caring, confident, professional.

"You have a family, John?"

Uh-oh.

"I do," John admits. "Back in California."

"Back in California? California isn't that far."

"It feels far."

"And they're there and . . . you're here?"

John nods, regrets the furtive glance at the picture, which obviously wasn't so furtive.

"That's right," John confirms, noncommittal as possible. "We're living apart."

"I see. Well, I hope it all works out . . . the way it's supposed to work out."

"Me, too."

"If you'd like to take some time off, though, to take care of some of the family stuff, that would be fine. You could take the week, drive out if you'd like."

"No thanks. I need the money. I'm ready to start on Monday."

"I've got something. It's another warehouse assignment, for about a month."

"I'll take it."

"And something else came in this morning, for customer service, which could work out after that, if you're interested."

"I'm interested."

Phil hands him the file with all the info for the warehouse job.

A month, John thinks. That would take him through November. He's good for another month.

It's another solitary Friday night at Desert Piss—that's what everyone calls John's apartment complex (true name: Desert Mist Plaza) and for good reason: It's the type of place where nobody wants to live but there really isn't much choice. The bogus little creek running through the main courtyard had dried up long ago, the pool brimmed with sludge and empties (one morning a motorcycle wound up there, and it was weeks before someone removed it), and herds of ratty barefoot kids roamed around like untamed wild beasts—John had never been so frightened of children. The adults weren't much better; the constant yelling, the boozy swaggers, and how they'd throw heavy objects—stereo speakers, crock pots, George Foreman grills—off their balconies, John narrowly escaping a flying chip-and-dip plate the day after he'd moved in. TVs blared constantly.

Even though John's been living here for months he still occasionally gets lost in Desert Piss (which is large, sprawling, and actually a series of four connected apartment complexes, each the same in terms of layout and minimalist construction and skeletal landscaping), and this is what happens tonight as he takes a wrong turn after dumping his garbage, failing, then, at this one simple task. Once again he finds himself wandering through Desert Piss's network of cracked sidewalks and neglected paths, trying to decipher the perplexing system for numbering apartments and units (the unit he just passed, for example, stops at 133 and the next one picks up at 247, while the apartments themselves are sometimes designated by a letter, sometimes by another number). And it isn't long after he resigns himself to an extra fifteen minutes of travel time back to his apartment that he sees a little girl wandering around, crying, it looks like, over by the entrance to what's supposed to be the rec room, which merely contains a ping-pong table with no net and an assortment of Nixon-era board games with most of the pieces missing. It's probably close to midnight. He doesn't recognize the girl, not surprising given the vast number of children that live in the complex and that are, also not surprisingly, spawned here. Yet unlike those kids, this girl seems, well, kidlike; she's softer, gentler; not so reform-school-looking and hardened and prematurely aged; and she may even still enjoy Disney animated features and trips to the zoo. He wants badly to be back in the womb of his apartment, alone and confined and indistinct, but he can't just walk past this little girl, can he? That would constitute yet another moral failing on his part. From what he can discern here in the darkness she's about the age Anabelle was at the time of the accident. Six, seven. Every kid he comes across nowadays seems to be right around the same age as Anabelle at the time of the accident.

"Hello there," he volunteers. "Are you lost?"

"Yeah," the girl sighs, sniffles. "I was looking for the soda machine. But when I put my money in nothing came out. I pressed the button but it didn't work."

"Does your mom live here?"

"No."

"Does your dad live here?"

"No. My dad lives in Hollywood. Not Hollywood, California, which is what everyone thinks when you say it. Hollywood, *Florida*. He has another daughter but she's not my sister. She's my stepsister. She has cottage-cheese breath."

"Uh-huh. Then who are you here with?"

"My mom."

"Your mom's here?"

"Yeah."

"She's visiting someone? She knows someone who lives here?"

"Yeah." Sighing again.

"Well let's see if we can find her."

"But you better be careful. I have pink eye."

"Thanks for the warning."

So together they search for the girl's mother, venturing down another path, the little girl reaching out for his hand—the girl's hand warm, alive, needy. Despite the late hour, most of the apartments show signs of life, emitting dim lights or the periodic lightning flashes of televisions, along with the accompanying sound of gunfire, screeching tires, fevered yelling. There's the usual Friday night assortment of beer bottles lining the pool, some of which had fallen in, bobbing in the black water like tiny, useless buoys.

Any fears about being lost vanish now that she has a companion. The girl's name, he soon finds out, is Rachel. He also soon finds out about her life, more than he's comfortable hearing about, details involving her mother's body and boyfriends, the shape and color of her poop (both hers and her mother's), things like that. She's one of those kids so willing to divulge information and ask personal questions that you begin to wonder what's behind this rabid intimacy.

"How long did you say you've been out here?"

"A pretty real long time. Are you married?"

"Yes, but—" and he stops himself.

"But what?"

"We're . . . estranged."

"What's estranged?"

Didn't he just have this conversation with Phil? She pronounces the word—*estranged*—like it's something from another language, another country far beyond her geographic or cultural knowledge.

"It means, basically, that the two people are still married, technically, all right, but they don't, uh, live together anymore. For various reasons. They decide that it's best to be apart. For a while at least. So it could be temporary, it could be permanent. It's hard to say. It's . . . complicated."

That word again: complicated. John feels a compulsion to explain further, to confess to someone, and so what if the confessee happens to be six years old. But he doesn't.

"My mom and dad don't live together," Rachel responds. This was at least the third time she had informed him of this fact. Jesus, who stays married these days? What are the latest statistics?

"Do you have kids?" Rachel asks.

"Yes I do."

"How many?"

"Just one."

"Boy or girl?"

"Girl."

"What were you like when you were a kid?"

"Oh I don't know. I was probably like you."

"But I'm a girl, silly." She finds this very funny. How stupid can he be? Pretty stupid, apparently. "What did you do? What stuff?"

"The usual I suppose: riding bikes, going to school, looking forward to summer vacation, watching movies."

The question kind of throws him. Sure, he'd done all the things he mentioned (who hadn't), but what else? What had he really been like at seven? Ten? Twelve? His memory had never been good, and all those murky years suddenly seem even murkier, sealed away, unattainable. Mostly he remembers being by himself, how ghostly his mother was, how his father had him every other weekend and would take him to a bowling-alley bar in Whittier, John's clothes smelling of beer and cigarettes after. One thing he'd never done was confide in total strangers.

They roam for a good fifteen minutes, John asking if this or that looked familiar. Nothing did. They pass a cigarette-smoking woman, who eyes them suspiciously, and a group of swaggering teenagers, who ignore them completely. Finally the girl gravitates toward a ground-floor corner apartment with the door partly open. She points.

John asks, "You think your mom's in there?"

"Uh-huh."

But she wants him to check first. The door is open a quarter of the way and the lights are on. Peering in, though, he can't see anybody, just a sagging sofa and a large TV, plus the same oatmeal-colored carpet and yellowing walls that defined the décor of his apartment. So he knocks, careful not to open the door any farther than it already is. But nothing. No response.

"You sure?" John asks. "You sure this is the right apartment?"

"Pretty sure."

"Pretty sure or really sure?"

"Really pretty sure."

John and the girl step inside. The apartment exhibits the familiar disarray of men who live without women and do so unapologetically, like it's a dare to see how far they can take it. The place reeks of greasy fries and spilt beer and other unidentifiable odors. Limited seating options. Left out on a TV tray next to an empty liter of Diet Dr Pepper are a couple of pipes, and not pipes of the pot-smoking variety. This is a whole other level, thinks John, who God knows enjoys his bud but has always been hesitant, even afraid, to graduate to harder drugs.

"Can you watch TV with me for a while?" Rachel asks.

They settle on the sofa—one of those couches that seem to immediately swallow you upon sitting, and once you're down, you're down; you're planted and you don't think you'll ever be able to hoist yourself up—and John stares straight ahead and sees his life before him. Not in a flash. It's actually there. His life. There. There on the TV. His daughter. His wife. His house. He looks over at Rachel, who's watching, too. He blinks, rubs his eyes, shakes his head—all the clichéd things you do when you can't believe your eyes. And he most definitely can't believe his eyes. He manages to remove himself from the sofa (though it's not easy, as expected) so he can turn up the volume. And he continues to stand because he cannot sit.

From the outside the house looks the same, still in need of a paint job and a new roof and reminding him of the Saab-driving realtor who sold it to them and had the nerve to call it a "fixer-upper" (the down payment culled together from various family members, a dead aunt's will, and John and Karen's combined savings), and next they zoom in on the front door and concrete porch where he used to sit at night, alone, and drink beer and watch the streetlights and wonder how long he could hold out and how long it took for love to become something else entirely. Entering the rooms and hallways he knows so well. The reporter person says something about this being *the house where it all began, located in a little-known area of Los Angeles, so near the capital of glitz and glamour and yet so far, where dreams have more to do with survival than stardom.* Then there is Karen, emphatic bags framing her eyes but emanating an undeniable look of exhilaration, of inner glow escaping outward. She's talking about Anabelle, how the accident happened, the fucked-up details and all that happened after, how there was a time when she was afraid to leave the house, it got so bad. Then there is his daughter, Belle, laid out in bed like always, like a prematurely prepared corpse, her face as white and blank and unknowable as snow, the open fish mouth and long Rapunzel hair. Her room filled with machines and stuffed animals and people. And even though he's witnessing the reality of her, his daughter, on TV, right now (comatose, paralyzed, mute, eternally confined to her special bed, with guardrails and wheels and a high-tech remote, which had cost like a grand and put them further in debt), he's also thinking of her as a normal, carefree, gurgling child when she was first learning to walk and talk and was mesmerized by his mustache ("mush-ash," she called it, one of her all-time favorite words, and which is how he still thinks of it, "mush-ash"). *Whether or not little Anabelle knows what's happening around her remains as much of a mystery as her reputed ability to heal the sick and comfort those in need of spiritual guidance.*

Now they are interviewing people. People he doesn't know. People standing in line in front of the house, waiting to enter, it appears. Midwestern faces, sunburned faces, haunted faces. Apparently they have come from all over to spend time with the girl who makes statues weep and people whole. The little miracle girl who's *a bright and shining star.* A woman and her daughter, who've been waiting for hours and have driven all the way from Texas to offer a prayer for an ailing uncle in need of a miracle (specifically: an organ donor, liver), break down and cry, it's just too much. And there's more about his daughter, the rapidly expanding legend: reports of skin discolorations in her hands and feet, of sudden bleeding without explanation. (John trying to comprehend, process, but not doing a very good job of it.) The Catholic Archdiocese has begun an official investigation but is hesitant to make any comments at this early stage, a young movie-star handsome priest only willing to go on the record as saying that the old cliché is true: the Lord works in mysterious ways. Father Jim something. Tanned and gym-fit. He didn't look like a priest. Not like any priest he'd ever seen anyway, which was mostly the TV variety. Back to Karen, who's now in the kitchen and who's wearing makeup and has her hair pulled back, something she rarely did. *I'm as surprised, as mystified as anyone. Who could have imagined. Not in my wildest dreams.*

I can't explain it myself. I really can't. But I know what I see. People come here and then they're different when they leave. Maybe what they pray for happens and maybe it doesn't, but they're different. Anabelle touches them. She brings them peace. The reporter starts to wrap it up, appearing in the front yard with the long line of people behind her for effect, closing with a bit about *hope—something that we could all use a little more of these days.*

Does this all mean he's dying? Is he dead? And what he just witnessed was some kind of final fuck-you flash before The End? Something for him to think about for all eternity? His last punishment perhaps?

Walking backward. Sitting down. The sofa creaking mightily. Fuck. Shit. The girl, Rachel, asleep now, snoring. Stunned isn't strong enough of a word—no word is strong enough a word. A word needs to be invented for this, for what he saw, what he's feeling. It's like there's bad electricity in his brain. Snap, crackle, pop. He rubs his eyes some more, trying to remember if there'd been any mention of him. Was there? He can't be sure. It was like watching a dream, a home movie that he'd been edited out of. He can't be sure of anything. Someone playing Jedi mind games with him. This isn't the life you're looking for. He wants to press the rewind button, confirm that it was real, that he saw what he saw.

"Who the fuck're you?"

A man has appeared, prison-guard scowl smeared across his face. Shirtless. Disheveled and dazed, like he'd just had sex, or, more likely, and judging by his open-mouthed breathing and lightly sweated brow, has been having sex, present tense.

"I'm a neighbor, I live here," John explains. "I was walking, taking out my trash, and I found her, this girl. She was lost and wandering around the complex. She said she thought her mom might be here. The door was open, so we came in."

The man squints in incomprehension, scratches his Santaesque belly.

"Kid," he shouts. "Wake up."

Then from behind him: out floats a thin, wobbly, distracted woman, no more than twenty-five, hair wet and clinging to her reddened cheeks, and cinching a terrycloth robe that's way too big and probably the man's.

"Rachel?" the woman says, reaching for a cigarette in the robe's pocket. "What's wrong with Rachel?"

John nudges Rachel so she'll wake up and explain everything. He expects a film crew from *Cops* to bust in at any second.

"This guy here," the man accuses, "sitting on my fucking couch, making himself at home and watching TV, he says she was wandering around outside. Says he found her and brought her back. This is the kind of shit I'm talking about, Alexis. Too many complications. Too many things I don't want to be worrying about."

"Rachel," the mother says, her voice medicated and slow, checking her pockets for a lighter now that there's a cigarette in her mouth. "How'd you go and get yourself out there? Come here."

Rachel, groggy but now awake, obeys, and as she walks past him John has the sudden urge to reach out and put a hand on her shoulder and prevent her from going to the mother. He has the rash and ridiculous thought of taking the girl with him, of rescuing her.

"The door was open," Rachel says. "I was tired of the noises."

Rachel and her mother disappear into a back room. John looks at the TV again, wondering if there might be anything else on the screen that could blow his mind.

"You can get going now, neighbor," the man says. "You've done your good fucking deed for the day."

The door slams behind him. And once again John steers through the maze of Desert Piss, this time thinking he may never find his apartment, he could be walking and wandering all night, yet more penance, his mind still replaying the story he'd seen on TV, all the people at his house, the expressions on their faces, the porch, Karen (who had definitely lost weight), Anabelle's room exploding with statues, stuffed animals, balloons. All this happening without him. But what does he expect? He's the one who left.

Turning a corner he almost collides with a fellow late-night refugee, another guy who's shirtless, as well as barefoot, basketball-type shorts dragging down past his knees, the night heat relentless even at this hour. John apologizes: "Sorry, man, sorry, I wasn't paying attention, my fault, my fault, totally my fault."

"You all right?" the guy asks, sounding genuinely concerned. "You look like you seen a ghost."

Ghosts—that's for sure.

How the past haunts the present. Shapes it. This he knows. This he knows more than he knows anything else.

7

| Anabelle |

Two DAYS AGO seemed like two years. Was it? Was it last week when Rudy Cisneros rubbed a booger on her back, or last month? Was it this year or last year when she was sick with chicken pox and she was in bed so much her back and legs ached and her mother sat on her bed and sang songs and told her stories about princes and castles and magical spells that turned you into something else? Things kept getting blurrier and blurrier and she wasn't sure why, why the difference. Her mind was funny that way: it couldn't sort the difference. It used to. But not now. Something had changed. She could tell. It wasn't so much about what came first and what happened last. It was about the feeling, the memory of what happened. No longer going from dot to dot but everything going in one big circle, looping around and around and around.

Sometimes she knew when the phone would ring before it actually rang, and sometimes, too, she could make the phone ring. Just by staring. Just by concentrating hard enough, long enough. All her thoughts narrowing down to this one core thing: *ring phone, ring.* And then it would. Ring. Her mother would answer, or her father would answer, and then she would smile, marvel at how she could think something into the world like that.

Before you knew it, it was Christmas time again and they forgot to put up the lights outside.

They had some things, not many, but no pets. Time went by.

She wondered: What would happen if she had to pick one over the other? If someone showed up at their door one day and said to her: "You have to pick one. Your mother or your father. And you must pick now. And then I'm going to take the other one, the one you don't pick, away. Forever. You will never see this person again, for as long as you live."

She wondered about this a lot, what it would be like, how she would act, and when she imagined the details this someone at the door was tall and skeletony and wore a long black overcoat that almost touched the ground. And this someone had a hat and sunglasses. You couldn't see anything but nose and mouth and hints of veiny earlobes. The voice sounded like a machine. It was not like any voice she'd ever heard in her life, not in movies, not anywhere.

"So who do you pick?" the someone said, waiting.

The choice was not hard. She didn't have to hem and haw like you do when you pick dessert at a restaurant. She didn't have to pretend. Because she'd thought of this moment many, many times. She'd thought of what it would be like and who she would choose. And now it had come, this moment, now it had finally arrived like the first day of summer vacation, it might be a dream or not a dream, she wasn't sure, but it was as real as anything else.

She watched her father leave, and was not surprised, was not relieved or happy or anything like that, but felt the weight of this decision crash upon her like a big giant wave, how it would change everything after, how it was something you couldn't ever get back, and she didn't move, she fought the power and pull of the wave and dug in deep and held her ground and didn't fall over, remained standing in the doorway, and she reached for her mother who was crying and crying and would be crying for some time, until they closed the door and went inside and sat down on the sofa and began to talk about their new lives, just the two of them, and what that would be like in the days, weeks, years ahead.

Then she was sleeping again. Then she was awake. Time went by. Rudy Cisneros's booger was the biggest, grossest in the whole entire history of boogers. She started walking, her legs solid and firm and thick, like tree trunks. They were good legs. Strong legs. They would never let her down. She kept walking and walking, and she knew she would do this until she was so tired she would just lie down and rest wherever she ended up: the sidewalk, the street, a parking lot, someone else's driveway, her school, Disneyland, the beach. But that would come later. But now: The sun was high in the sky and it was beautiful and she stared at its brightness and kept walking.

8

Welcome to the Official
Anabelle Vincent Web Site

We hope you enjoy your visit. Here you will find information about Anabelle Vincent aka **"The Miracle Girl."**

In 1998, seven year old Anabelle Vincent was in a very serious car accident. She almost died. The accident left her a bedridden invalid with practically no hope of recovery. But while her body might be frail and stilled, her voice silenced and unable to communicate, she offers hope to those who need it most. She is a very special little girl and miracles surround her.

Today little Anabelle is the focus of international media attention, her story having appeared in many newspapers and TV shows. Everyday people line up outside Anabelle's house in southern California to see her and to pray to her. Wonderous things happen in her bedroom, where she is cared for around the clock by her loving mother Karen and a small group of family, friends, and volunteers. (***NOTE: Because of the large numbers of visitors it is now being requested by the family that people signup for visits in advance. You can signup for the Waiting List by <u>CLICKING HERE</u>. Thank You!!!***)

—If you would like to read articles about Anabelle, <u>CLICK HERE</u>

—If you would like to see Photos of Anabelle, <u>CLICK HERE</u>

—If you would like to sign the Guestbook and share an experience you had with Anabelle or offer a thought, a prayer, or give feedback about this site, <u>CLICK HERE</u>.

—If you are interested in making a donation to the newly-created Anabelle Vincent Fund, <u>CLICK HERE</u>

—If you would like to send Email to the Webmaster, <u>CLICK HERE</u>

Last updated November 17th 1999.

676,381 visitors since this site was created.

Miracles do not happen in contradiction to nature, but only in contradiction to that which is known to us of nature.

~ Saint Augustine ~

9

| Karen and John |

IT WAS A car accident, of course, the most common of contemporary tragedies. And there was no way she could reasonably blame him (the other driver's fault, totally, as confirmed by multiple eyewitnesses, not to mention a silver-haired judge and an insurance company), but sometimes she did, blame him, later, when exhaustion and doubt got the best of her. He had been the one driving while she stayed at home. He had been the one in control, supposedly, of the vehicle, her car, the crap Festiva, because his was in the shop. He was the one who'd decided, after several discussions that eventually escalated into a half-hearted argument, that they needed a new VCR even though they couldn't afford it and their current one only occasionally caused videotapes to jitter and jump and distort. He was the one who, on that seemingly inconsequential December day in 1998, opted for the mall rather than BestBuy, which was a little closer and probably even a little cheaper. He was the one who'd spaced on getting gas the previous day and then had to stop at a gas station, which meant the trip took an extra five minutes and required a slight detour from the usual home-to-mall route. Had he not spaced on getting gas the previous day, they wouldn't have been crossing that particular intersection at that particular time and thus would have avoided the accident and the path of one Matthew Ronald Kimbrough (blood-alcohol level well above the legal limit). And, she thought, he had been the one who'd chosen to make the trip in the late afternoon as opposed to the morning, on Saturday instead of Sunday, because on Sunday there was a game of some kind, and no, he couldn't tape it because that was another problem with the goddamn, piece-of-shit VCR, which just proved his point even more, he said. And she'd learned that these things—these simple, apparently random things that do not appear to mean anything at the time—have their repercussions; they add up and fuck you and shape your future whether you realize it or not. And why hadn't he been able to avoid the other car? All crashes are avoidable, aren't they? His driving skills, when she really thought about it in the aftermath of the accident, had always been somewhat suspect. He was one of those one-handed, cool-guy Southern California drivers who barely grasp the wheel and concentrate more on the scenery and the radio station than the road and the death and horror and destruction looming everywhere. So she wondered: Had there been a brief lapse there, a moment when a bikinied billboard or a Led Zeppelin song he hadn't heard in years had taken precedence over the safety of Anabelle, their seven-year-old child, their world? Had such carelessness been the real culprit, despite the overwhelming evidence against Matthew Ronald Kimbrough, who'd wept repeatedly in court and didn't have a child of his own and said he could only imagine what it must be like, and he was sorry, sorry, a thousand times sorry,

Your Honor, adding that the one positive to come out of this whole mess was that he'd found God, whereas before his life was sans God and pretty much unfocussed and empty, and sure, like everyone else he'd always been skeptical when he heard of people finding religion in jail, but now he understood; he understood how guilt brings you to God. And then there was the fact that he, her husband, was merely sprinkled with cuts and a few bruises and also a sprained wrist, but nothing that required a hospital stay: in and out of the emergency room, while their daughter fought for life.

* * *

John blamed himself as well. Naturally. He was the questionable parent, always had been. This was how the casting of their marriage went—she the vigilant, suffering mother who had the final say on everything; he the reluctant father who, after they found out Karen was pregnant, had suggested that maybe they weren't ready and shouldn't have a baby just yet and as a result felt forever guilty for having committed some basic parental transgression that would never be forgiven. The accident, then, confirming what was already well documented. He hadn't seen the other car creep out, then accelerate toward them, into them. Hadn't seen. Their seatbelts were on, secure. So he was covered there. And he was sober. Completely and utterly sober. Still, it was his fault. No matter what the law and the judge and jury had said; no matter how much the settlement had been; no matter how much the doctors and the hospital had fucked up. And it was all so sudden, like a sucker punch that staggers you. He was driving and Anabelle was there in the backseat, and then the tires and the unrepentant roar of metal against metal. He reacted as best he could, turned sharply to the left, locking it up like in a video game, skidding uncontrollably, but there wasn't enough time. It was too late. Nothing had ever happened so quickly, with such fierce, brute force, so true and final. Immediately he knew it was bad. It was just a question of how bad. The car was flopped around backassward and he'd lost all sense of direction. Where were they? He was OK, basically. His head was a thunderstorm of guitar feedback and his heart a riot in his chest, but not so bad considering. The passenger side of the car, however, had crumpled in on itself like an aluminum can. His daughter was bloody and squashed. That was the word exactly: *squashed*. The silence afterward chilled him. Such fury, then such quiet—which was worse? He started screaming. For how long he didn't know. What he was saying he didn't know either. It was just a primal howl, pure lament. They dragged him from the car (still screaming, he was later told), but they had to wait for the Jaws of Life for Anabelle, and he kept hearing that—*the Jaws of Life, the Jaws of Life*—and it didn't really register, what they were talking about; it was that device you saw on the news that they use to pry people out of cars, and it usually meant death, not life. He dropped to the sidewalk. It was happening and it wasn't happening. Maybe he was more injured than he thought. His wrist throbbed. The left one. The one he'd been driving with, holding the steering wheel. Where was his right hand when it happened? The car that hit them had apparently then rammed another car and then another, though neither as bad as his. There was a man on his knees. The man was saying something. Cops and fire trucks arrived. People hovered stupidly. They seemed afraid to talk to him. *He must be the father,* someone was saying, and it was his inclination to deny this, to tell them no, he was not the father; he was not worthy of such a title, the way his father hadn't been, and the way his father's father hadn't been, shitty parenting having been passed down from generation to generation, and how can you break a chain like that once it gets going? Waiting, waiting. The concrete warm from the sun. Telling the paramedics not to worry about him. But his daughter. The last time he'd seen his father was a few months before he'd died and they'd had dinner and said very little. Once in the ambulance he got his first real look at her. One of the paramedics talking about head trauma and the lack of oxygen to the brain and how every second counted. *My wrist hurts. I think it's broke,* he wanted to tell them, but how could he say such a thing at such a time? A wrist hardly mattered. Clumps of blood clung to Anabelle's hair. Her eyes were closed. She was strapped in and the ambulance snaked and wailed. He couldn't really make out her face, recognize her as the girl he'd left home with. Everything was swollen and mangled and red. They had put one of those neck braces on her and now that was bloody, too. Another paramedic cradled her head, as if his hands were all that was holding her skull together. And maybe they were. Up front the driver yelled: "Fucking cars! Fucking traffic! What do people not understand about the concept of flashing red lights?" A group was waiting for them in the hospital parking lot: activity, a lot of words he didn't understand. They wheeled her away and he followed along and one of the doctors asked if he was OK and he said, "Yes, fine I think," and the doctor said, "We'd better check you out just the same, to be sure," and that's when he told them about his wrist, which was throbbing worse by then. He tracked down a pay phone. He had to call first, before anything else. He almost forgot his own number. Maybe it was shock. He slammed the phone in the cradle because he couldn't remember the number and people stared and he leaned there against the phone until the sequence of digits came to him, finally. He waited for Karen to pick up. What was he going to say? Where to begin? Shit. What had he done? Later he would wonder: What had Anabelle been saying before the crash? What were her final words? He couldn't even remember. It was probably nothing out of the ordinary: *I'm hungry. When are we going to get there? Can we go to KB Toys? Why was Mom mad at you this morning? When are you going to like each other again?* But even that would have been something. His daughter was quiet, mysterious, given to staring out windows and sitting on the sidewalk and mumbling to herself in that weird made-up language of hers. The last words she might ever speak and he couldn't remember them. His failure was complete.

* * *

She had been at home, paging through one of the women's magazines that she sometimes fell prey to in checkout lines, or maybe not even that: just sitting there doing nothing at all, perhaps contemplating housework and dishes and the *Buns of Steel IV* tape that someone had given her two Christmases ago (a hint?) and was still shrink-wrapped, or wondering which bills could be put off and which couldn't, or vaguely deciding whether she was going to shower that night or wait until morning. Did she know something was wrong when it happened, the accident? Did she feel something deflate and die inside her at the moment of impact when her daughter crossed over from one existence into another? No: she was too immersed in her stupid reveries, too glad to have the house to herself for a while, enjoying the silence and peace and space and still wearing her slippers and absently scraping off the last of her Burnt Sienna nail polish. How she'd like to change that part of it. How she'd like to have intuited that her daughter was in danger right when the crushing of metal and flesh and skull occurred; that their lives were about to turn inside out. But she didn't. Her motherly radar wasn't motherly enough, apparently. She'd tried her best to be the kind of mother worthy of those sappy Mother's Day greeting cards—the raised lettering, the elaborate cursive font, the couplets chronicling love and patience, understanding and sacrifice—but she knew that whatever she did or didn't do, it would never be good enough; that it was her fate to fall short; that people have kids for all the wrong reasons or no reason at all, because that's just what you do, and she was no different. They were no different. You bring a child into this world and you had better be prepared for the consequences. When he called, she almost didn't even pick up the phone. *Just let the machine get it.* But she got up. His voice did not sound like his voice. It had a fear in it she'd never heard before, not once in eleven-plus up-and-down years of dating and breakups and makeups and marriage. *John?* she said.

* * *

At first he thought she wasn't going to answer. *Fuck.* Then she did, right after the machine clicked on, the default computerized "Please leave a message" because he kept unplugging the damn thing by mistake. She uttered a sleepy-sounding "Hello." (Had she been napping in front of a movie she'd already seen six times on cable?) He started rambling. He didn't know what to say exactly, so he just dove in headfirst, rattling off details, hoping that if enough syllables spilled out of him, he'd be able to impart the necessary information. There'd been no time, no time at all to react. It all happened so fast. *The fuck just pulled out right in front of us like we weren't even there, like we were invisible. There was nothing I could do, I swear. Then he hit another car. The guy was obviously on something. How else could you explain? She's in surgery right now. Surgery. They're not saying much. They're saying it's too soon to make any kind of . . . what? . . . Prognosis. And we'll know more after the surgery. We'll know more later. My wrist . . .* But Karen wasn't saying anything back. She was quiet, absorbing, because that's what she did: listen calmly, make the other person mistakenly think all is serene and swell and fine, and then explode once all the evidence had been gathered. He kept going because he was afraid of the silence on the other end. If he continued talking then everything would be all right. His seatbelt had been on. Anabelle's, too. Secure in her booster seat. The car was too old to have airbags. But he ran out of words, sputtered to a stop. There was nothing left. He had said all he could say. He had done his best. He was ready for her response. Why wasn't she saying anything? What kind of reaction was this? Then it sounded like something happened with the phone. The static got worse. Everything got very far away. He said her name: *Karen?*

* * *

There was that empty, cavernous phone echo when no one is speaking but they're still there and you swear you can hear the lines and grids and all the technology you don't know anything about swirling together, as if everything that makes telephones and telephone conversations possible were suddenly audible. He had been talking nonstop. Like a crackhead crazy man. Like she'd never heard him speak before. She pieced it together as best she could: they were not at the mall, there had been an accident on the way, some guy had pulled right out in front of them and there had been no time to react. John was fine except for something with his wrist, but Anabelle was not. She was not fine.

She was the opposite of fine. She was in surgery and the doctors were saying things like *massive head trauma* and *major blood loss* and they'd had to use the Jaws of Life to pry her out of the car and a man had been on his knees praying. OK. Processing. This was the situation. How does a mother respond? How does anyone respond? This was one of those phone calls, the kind all parents dread, the kind that strip away your vague belief in a safe world, which is quickly replaced by the view that the universe is indifferent, especially when it comes to what happens to you and those you love and those you are supposed to love. Only, such phone calls usually come in the middle of the night, tearing you from womb-sleep and open-mouthed dreams. It was daylight, not night, so maybe it wasn't one of those calls. Maybe it was going to be all right. She had all the curtains and blinds pulled, but she knew it was daytime—the sun asserting itself, a simmering yellow, that desert planet sci-fi glow common to Los Angeles—and it was Saturday and there'd been an accident and her hand that held the phone began to shake like her great aunt who had what's-it-called—Parkinson's—and then her entire body began to quake and quiver and turn fuzzy, and soon she was no longer vertical but horizontal, and the coolness of the kitchen tiles pressed hard against her face felt nice like a damp cloth on your forehead when you were a kid and sick and home from school, sipping 7Up with a straw and watching daytime TV shows you didn't normally get to see. She decided it might have to be a while before she moved. Soon though. Her body was adjusting to something: a new weight, a brewing truth.

* * *

He waited in the waiting room. Doctors were paged; nurses slalomed by the door. *Buzz, buzz.* It was hard to keep up with

it all. But he had to because one of them might know something about Anabelle. Every doctor or nurse or orderly potentially carried information that would change his life, their life.
Somebody said, "Saturdays are the worst. Fuck me if I gotta
work two Saturdays in a row. Fuck me right here, right now."
A man with dreadlocks assaulted a vending machine, which had
consumed his dollar bill without dispensing the desired snack.
Families held hands, congregated, hoping to defeat death with
numbers: the more people assembled in the waiting room and
hallway, the less of a chance of . . . He couldn't even pace. Just
stood there. Time? What was time? He was alone and he was
the only one who was alone (even the dreadlocked man was
there with somebody) and obviously this was hurting Anabelle's
chances. More people were needed. Bodies. Safety in numbers.
Who else could he call? Karen's sister, but she'd always hated
him. Then Karen arrived and they waited together, two instead
of one. Still not enough, he worried. Karen said she had fainted
in the kitchen, but thank God she hadn't been out for more than
a few minutes and she'd called a cab because his car, of course,
was in the shop. Any news yet? *No,* he said. *No news. It could
be hours still, they said. Just wait and try to relax.* Yeah, right.
And he touched her face, traced her cheek slowly, softly with
his thumb, using his good hand, the one that wasn't bandaged.
He noticed the first inroads of lines around her eyes. He saw the
sadness permanently etched there—and everywhere in her face,
every centimeter of skin. He'd seen it before, but it had never
seemed so poignant and real, this sadness, and he knew that he
was responsible for it in ways he couldn't even begin to fathom,
because she hadn't always been that way; that his desperation
had become her desperation, and he wanted to rub it away like
smudged lipstick, make it disappear so she would no longer be

who she had become. And they were getting older, they had aged each other, he realized. It was true. Funny because they'd been thinking of possibly having another child, because that might be the salve they needed, the missing piece that could perhaps fill the ache that had afflicted them both. Because things weren't right, hadn't been since—well, who knows? They were only getting worse, and after a while you reach that point: *Let's have another kid.* Sometimes he thought, *Yes, that would do it,* but other times he thought, *No, what the fuck are we thinking here? It would only make things worse.* Another kid would double everything. Karen nuzzled closer, so close he could smell her tears. They wrapped themselves around each other tighter and tighter, rediscovering the fit of their bodies. What was happening? The fluorescent lights buzzed and the dreadlocked man launched a new series of improvised karate kicks at the uncooperative vending machine. And just like that they were a couple again. A real couple. How could they have ever doubted that? How could they have let themselves get to such a sorry-ass state, so distant and unknown to each other? One day you intimately know the curve of your wife's back and the next you don't. He stumbled through these snowy thoughts, groping. Anabelle would pull through. She would pull through because of what was happening here, their unspoken reunion, and they would become a family, a real family, not the cheap imitation they'd been before. And yes: they would have another child and they'd fix up the house and the yard and buy some new furniture and plates and sheets and then start to live the life where you lie down at night and reach out to touch the other person and they're already reaching out to touch you. He held his wife even tighter and mapped out their newly bright future and told himself to remember this feeling and not give it up, not to let things go back to the way they'd been (only minutes ago, true, but how much had changed since then!). He would try. He would really try. If Anabelle came through this then they would begin again. Whispering in her ear, he said, "Everything's going to be all right. Everything's going to be all right. She's going to be fine and we're going to be fine. *Shhhh.* There now. *Shhhh.*" It felt good to say the words, to make the sounds. This was what a husband, what a father did.

* * *

How long did they hold each other in the waiting room? She couldn't say for sure. A long time. Long enough for her to want to hold on for good, to be afraid of separating, of their bodies parting. Letting go would disrupt whatever was passing between them. Letting go would mean that soon a doctor would emerge from surgery and deliver the news. No, letting go was not an option. She remembered closing her eyes and telling herself to clutch him closer, if that was possible. She remembered burying herself in that silly Hawaiian shirt that he'd started wearing lately. He thought it was so uncool that it was cool. One hundred percent Rayon. Machine wash, tumble dry. But she couldn't remember if they'd still been holding each other when yes finally a doctor did emerge from surgery and yes he did have news and it was the famous good-news-bad-news speech (although he did not offer a choice of which they would like to hear first), the good news being that Anabelle has pulled through so far. She was a fighter all right and they had managed to keep her alive throughout the surgery, which was a victory in and of itself. But there had been massive—again that word, *massive,* which had never seemed so harsh to her ear—*massive* head injury and *massive* blood loss,

which meant that there was brain damage and they wouldn't
know how much or how little until later but for now she was in a
coma, or not really a coma but more like a state that was similar
to a coma, and he'd go into that more later, but there was one
other fact that he'd be remiss if he didn't tell them about and that
was that, besides the accident, which had caused such significant
trauma to the head (*You mean "massive,"* she'd wanted to cor-
rect him), there had been an initial discrepancy of sorts when
Anabelle had first arrived at the hospital and she had been given
too much of a particular drug, which had added a whole other
layer to the mix, and they wouldn't know the true repercussions
of this until later, but he's saying it right now, up front, so that
they'd know he's being totally and completely up front about everything because he'd be remiss if he wasn't. Again she faced the
question of how to react. Her daughter was alive, and for that
there was relief. Alive. But then: brain damage, unlikely to ever
speak or move again. And given too much of a drug. John was
asking more about this, about what was the deal with the drug
she'd been given too much of, the so-called discrepancy. "Are
you saying that could make it worse?" The doctor said, "I'm
not saying anything. I'm telling you the facts. I'm telling you the
facts of what happened and what we know so far and what we
don't know so far." The doctor wearing scrubs and glasses. A
tight, compact barrel of a man. And for sure by this point she
and John had peeled away from each other and the distance was
returning. Of course she wasn't thinking of that at the time. It
was all Anabelle. It was all her daughter, who was in intensive
care and would be for some time. And in the weeks and months
ahead she would be tested as a mother like never before. She
would discover a deeper level of motherhood, one of profound

vigilance and exhausting purpose, caring for a child, another soul, in such a consuming manner: cleaning, feeding, wiping, monitoring, ministering around the clock. It was an altered state of being that exiled you from the rest of the world. John having trouble with this, John resisting the gravity pull that would become a permanent part of their lives. She would also blame herself for the accident and everything it wrought—after all, she was the one who'd suggested Anabelle go with John. Ordinarily Anabelle would have stayed home. *Why don't you go with your father? Mommy's tired. Mommy needs a little downtime.* That's what she said. And of course Anabelle said all right even though she would rather have remained home and continued her coloring, and what do seven-year-olds understand about "downtime" anyway? What it came down to, though, was something else. What it came down to was that two people could love each other and this could happen. What it came down to was that two people could stop loving each other and this could still happen. She wanted to warn all mothers and fathers: *Do not take a moment for granted. Even when they are too much, when you wish your children away, either temporarily or permanently. Hold them and then hold them a little longer. Smell their hair, breathe their essence, marvel at the beating of their tiny, beautiful hearts, because a second is all it takes for everything to change.* The doctor then telling them they could see Anabelle and they followed him down corridor after corridor, left then right then left, the doctor walking his brisk doctor walk so that they had to move faster to keep up. When they arrived at her bed in the ICU, Anabelle was surrounded by people in masks and gowns, and the doctor said, *The parents,* and the people in masks and gowns parted so they could get closer. The machines and wires, the release and push of suction, of manufactured air. She touched Anabelle's face, stared at her closed doll's eyes and open, twisted mouth. This was her daughter now. She turned to John and tried to say something, but her voice was not there; it was gone, and she waited for John to say something, but he didn't, he, too, was silent and slowly backing away from Anabelle's bed, like he couldn't believe what he was seeing, this girl, this still, foreign creature so elaborately bandaged and manacled, this new beginning that was upon them, and they had to figure out what could and couldn't be fixed.

BELIEVERS

THERE'S THE TEN-YEAR-OLD with AIDS. There's the thirty-nine-year-old with cancer and advanced arthritis and glaucoma. There's the sixty-seven-year-old who's as physically healthy as a thirty-nine-year-old but cannot recognize his children or remember his wife's name. There's the rape victim. There's the sufferer of chronic allergies. There's the drunk driver who killed a boy around the same age and who thinks of the fucked-up, unjust nature of the world (he should have died, not the boy) on a more or less hourly basis. There's the homeless man who felt he had to come but didn't know why. There's the local politician who needs votes and a good photo opportunity to revitalize his flagging campaign. There's the aide who works for said politician and had suggested the visit, and who himself is terribly lonely and can't get this quote from Mother Teresa out of his head, which he'd read or heard somewhere, or maybe even dreamed (it's hard to tell these days, everything cloudy and part of the same general transmission), the quote that goes something like this: *The world is dying of loneliness.* There's the unemployed single mom who saw it on TV and was just curious. There's the woman who loves too little. There's the woman who loves too much. There's the woman who loves just the right amount but is not loved back in return. There's the man who cannot be true to his wife. There's the man who can be true to his wife but has big-time intimacy issues, and who, after decades of marriage and children, remains a mystery to his family. There's the mother whose daughter had slit her wrists and survived. There's the daughter whose mother had taken pills and succeeded. There's the young man who wants to die. There's the old man who wants to live. There's the old man's wife who doesn't want him to die before she does.

They arrive and arrive and arrive, all with their reasons, all with their doubts and certainties and everything in between. *Thank you,* they tell the mother. *Thank you for sharing this gift. Thank you for opening your door to the world. We need this. We need you.*

PART TWO

COUNTING DOWN

10

| Father Jim |

Nobody walks in L.A. This is a well-known fact. Everything spread too distantly, too arrogantly—the city, the county, the Southland, however you want to categorize it all. The only connection the great roaring freeways, like clogged ancient rivers, carrying commerce and travelers, people making their way in the world, industrious and air-conditioned and unaware, but not walking, no, never.

Nonetheless, Father Jim Hinshaw isn't going to let the limitations of his adopted hometown—still genuinely flummoxed to be among what he used to think of as the chosen of Southern California—ruin his lifelong love of a good, brisk walk. Growing up and living in a small liberal-arts college town in Ohio (as exotically foreign as France around here, he'd quickly discovered) for most of his life, he could walk anywhere, and did so, habitually, spending many a morning or afternoon or early evening on a leisurely stroll or therapeutic jaunt with no specific destination in mind, just a desire to cover ground and clear the head, and he'd never lost his attachment to the saintly idea of taking the more difficult yet ultimately more rewarding path/ route/road/whatever (he had become a priest, after all) and to the practice of traversing streets and neighborhoods by foot and thus seeing and noticing things you couldn't see and notice from a car. Life's different when viewed from the sidewalk as opposed to the insularity of metal and glass, and given his vocation Father Jim believes it's important to have as many vantage points as possible from which to contemplate, to understand, the human parade.

You can't, for example, ignore the stench, the urban affliction of this smeared section of downtown Los Angeles that he treks through twice a week, Sherpalike, as he makes the three-mile commute in his scuffed and city-stained Air Jordans, from his apartment to the Archdiocese's building on Wilshire, not only for the exercise and subsequent endorphin rush but also to re-mind himself of the reality of where he lives and works and breathes. Here he passes the forgotten, the banished, the surg-ing homeless, with their layers of clothing despite the unyield-ing wattage from above. Here he witnesses the man—always the same block, the same spot, the same anorexic dog curled dutifully at his side—with the sign that says HUNGRY BUT NOT HELPLESS on one side, the other less popular B-side bearing the proclamation WILL WORK FOR SPIRITUAL SUSTENANCE. Here he's subject to a steady stream of impressionistic yelling and rant-ing, usually religious and/or antigovernment in nature ("Father, Son and Holy Spirit—you are being watched by an unknown source!" and "God's real name is Denise. And she's Mongolian!" being two fairly recent examples that have stuck in his mind like commercial jingles). Here he can inspect, close-up, perhaps too close-up at times, the graffiti liberally splashed on dumpsters and bus benches and both abandoned and occupied businesses, the messages behind the boxy letters escaping him, so difficult to decipher in a nonsuspicious, nonjudgmental three- to five-second glance, which is all he allows himself. Here—where it's all too easy to rely on such adjectives as postnuclear, postapocalyptic, postsomething, yet there is an element of truth to this kind of overly dramatic classification, definitely a trace of the end times in the ravaged scenery and contaminated air and the inhabitants' purposeless shuffles and coded murmurings; something had happened, or is about to happen, some vast severing or shaking, a before and after, and now they're not sure how to proceed. Something almost medieval about their squalor. All of which brings to mind that quote from Revelation that had scared him as a child and scared him still: "And whosoever was not found written in the book of life was cast into the lake of fire." Then a little later, this whammy: "But the fearful, and unbelieving, and abominable, and murderers, and whoremongers, and sorcerers, and idolaters, and all liars, shall have their part in the lake which burneth with fire and brimstone: which is the second death."

Walking these streets, encountering these souls, one death seems enough. Where, he often wonders, are the swimming pools, the ocean views, the affluent suntans, the epic blue of magazines and movies that can make a man, a woman, ache all over and cause them to migrate hundreds, thousands, of miles in search of the promised—or at least more promising—land? Where are the chosen? Not here. Not in this stretch of depreciating real estate. But he walks it, he gets to know its edges and smells and eccentrics. And when he doesn't hoof it to work, he either takes the bus or rides the mountain bike that was donated by some parishioners last year, although none of the other priests had ventured to ride it yet, meaning that he has exclusive use. The robes can be a little cumbersome, that is, for those who still wear them regularly.

This particular Tuesday morning, his foot odyssey now well underway, only a few more blocks to go, the sun berating and beating down, Father Jim halts at a crosswalk, presses the Walk button, waits for the greenly lit frame meant to represent an anonymous pedestrian in motion (male, presumably). In Ohio the crosswalks all said WALK. But here you have this combo plate of cultures, a different language every block. He now knows how to say "Hello. How are you today?" in nine different tongues: Spanish, Russian, Mandarin, Japanese, and so on. So naturally you had to go with pictures, the visual. Otherwise imagine the consequences, the potential for accidents.

After crossing the street (noting a new influx of graffiti on a movie billboard for another would-be holiday blockbuster and a weather-wasted man wearing a USC sweatshirt and delivering a speech on Ronald Reagan and voodoo economics to a mute crowd waiting for the bus), he stops in a corner store where he buys some orange juice, doesn't even mind the inflated price, says thank you to the proprietor in his native Korean, which triggers a smile from the chap-lipped middle-aged man, who, like everyone else Father Jim comes across (himself included), sweats like Shaquille O'Neal deep in the fourth quarter and is reduced to the same old similes about the heat.

"Hot like sauna," says the owner.

"Hot as the devil's armpit," offers a more inspired fellow customer, a broken, toothless man meticulously extracting crumpled dollar bills and blackened coins from his pocket, handling the currency with the care of a jeweler, while simultaneously eyeing the big tub of beef jerky sticks on the counter by the cash register.

"Try wearing black all the time," jokes Father Jim, giving the toothless man his change, wondering if he'll just suck on the jerky or what.

Back outside, Father Jim tugs at his collar, then rolls the could-be-colder bottle of orange juice across his damp forehead and takes a pirate's swig of the name-brand beverage. He continues onward, northward, making progress and silently, hurriedly, blessing those he passes who seem in need of some kind of benediction (there are many, and a quickie is better than nothing) while also mapping out the morning ahead of him, multitasking, as he maintains his purposeful businessman's stride.

He figures Father Lewis will want to see him first thing and he's right—once he's in his office and finishes toweling (well, paper-toweling) himself off, Nancy knocks and informs him Father Lewis would indeed like to see him. Nancy already looking frantic and the day barely begun. Ever since the Miracle Girl story broke, the phone has been ringing nonstop and poor Nancy has been overwhelmed by the onslaught of inquiries, scribbling messages and assuaging relentless journalists on deadline and dispensing the standard unsatisfactory answer: *The Archdiocese is currently investigating the matter and has no comment at this time.*

And so, as part of that investigation, Father Jim and Father Lewis yesterday had driven to the house to find out all they could about Anabelle Vincent, doing what Father Jim jokingly liked to think of as their good priest/bad priest routine, arriving while the girl was getting physical therapy from a small, stout woman—and when the mother said, "The priests are here, Linda," the therapist kept working, replying, "Just a few more minutes, then we'll be done. This is important, too." Throughout the interview with the mother and the visit to the girl's room and the discussions with the faithful waiting in line and lingering in the front yard, he could tell Father Lewis did not want to be there, did not want to be there at all, did not want this kind of tricky situation so close to his impending retirement at the end of the year ("I like the . . . *poetic synchronicity* of bowing out at the millennium," he had explained after announcing his decision), like a lame-duck president who's hit with a major calamity in the final weeks of his administration. On the drive back he wasn't interested in debriefing or talking, choosing instead to console himself with the distraction of AM radio and Ed from El Segundo who expressed his concern about the lack of concern regarding the Y2K crisis.

"You're right," the show's host agreed. "You're absolutely right. Can I just say how right you are? Here we are on the cusp practically, and we're hearing about these thwarted terrorist plans, right, and who knows what else is going to happen really. You don't have to be a Nostradamus or Jeane Dixon to know that people aren't ready."

"When are we ever ready?" Ed added, his voice getting more excited the more he spoke. "And that's a rhetorical question, Marty, so don't answer. No, my real question for you, for you and your guest whose name I'm sorry—my real question is, is this:

What does it take to truly galvanize people these days? What is required to make an honest-to-goodness impact on the consciousness of this country? And I'll take my answer off the air."

Father Jim attempted to prod Father Lewis into commentary by mentioning how some religious communities—usually located in states like Montana or Idaho—had recently released statements saying that they believed we were in store for some kind of divine punishment come January 1.

"I don't think God works in round numbers," Father Lewis said.

That was typical Father Lewis: always to be counted on for a good silence-inducing one-liner. Many a debate (theological or otherwise) had abruptly ceased because of one of the old man's acerbic barbs. But his brusqueness, his outdated churlish manner and impatience with non-English speakers, and the abundance of SAT words that he regularly inserted into his speech and sermons (*perspicacity, magnanimous, mellifluousness*) didn't sit well with some of the younger priests, who certainly wouldn't miss the Hemingway-bearded Father Lewis, who also wore his hair long, too long for an old man, giving him the appearance of a crazed prophet, and Father Jim was not the only one to speculate that their elder foreswore haircuts in order to convey this very look. Still, he was a favorite of the Archbishop's, had been for decades, and even though Father Jim sometimes tired of Father Lewis's ways, he also appreciated the anachronism that the man represented. And no matter what you thought of him, you could not deny his oratory prowess, his ability to infuse an audience with wonderment and awe.

The only other verbalization that Father Lewis uttered during the rest of the drive was to note, out of the blue, the increase of "fusion" restaurants in Los Angeles and could someone please explain to him what that meant (Father Jim, being from the Midwest, could not). And for the rest of the day their paths did not cross, meaning that the two colleagues hadn't yet spoken about their visit to the Miracle Girl.

Now, apparently, Father Lewis was ready to talk. Or rather his version of talk.

"Tell him I'll be there in five," Father Jim tells Nancy, who's already halfway out the door to deliver the message.

"Nancy," he calls after her.

"Yes."

"You OK?"

"Oh you know, busy-busy-busy, buzz-buzz-buzz," sighs their most dedicated volunteer, a retired bookkeeper with a husband on disability and a son housebound with lupus. "What with all the phone calls, though, I don't think I'll be able to get the newsletter out on time. And then there's the annual holiday mailing which is coming up fast, with all these names that need to be added to the database, which I don't see happening because Phyllis had to go out of town unexpectedly for a funeral and Enid has some kind of viral thing and they're the only ones who know FileMaker besides me. And there's been this horrendous typo on the website that's been there for I don't know how long. 'Got' instead of 'God.' 'The word of Got.' It looks bad. Plus the links need updating. Don't get me started on the links."

"If there's anything I can do to lighten your load let me know. I'm sorry, Nancy. It's got to die down sooner or later, but for now we're in semicrisis mode. And don't let those media people get you down."

"Oh they're all right," says Nancy, remaining in the doorway, her posture as rigid as a ballet dancer's, her ink-black hair, dyed monthly, in the same reliable bob that she'd probably had all her adult life, Father Jim thought. Sixty-, seventy-odd years old, and where did she get the energy? "They're just doing their job, I suppose. But some of them are, well, a little pushy. I'm about to bust a cap at that Kellee Clifton person."

"Nancy!"

"Sorry, Father. I watched *NYPD Blue* last night."

Nancy gone, Father Jim sifts through his messages, fires up his computer. The internal network is down—again—so he can't check his e-mail. His screen flashes an "unable to connect" message, which sucks because he has to get a press release out today, just one of the many duties that fall upon his shoulders as Media Relations Coordinator and general all-around Spokesperson ("Spokespriest," they kid him) for the Archdiocese. So in addition to his normal priestly duties, Father Jim crafts policy statements, coordinates interviews, provides sound bites when necessary, and pesters various media outlets about issues they'd otherwise ignore. His minor in Modern Communication Theories, as well as his supposed uncanny resemblance to a primetime hunk, no doubt had helped him secure his current job and relocation to the West Coast. Not feeling very hunky now, however, just sweaty. Sweaty and stinky. He keeps some deodorant in the bottom right drawer of his desk, the way private detectives are known to stash bottles of whiskey, at least according to movie lore. He applies a few generous swabs under his arms before setting off down the hallway to Father Lewis's office.

The old man is writing, bunkered behind his mahogany desk, which is huge and of another era and inundated with paper and books and mail. Father Jim half expects him to be writing with a quill, laboring over a manuscript by candlelight. But instead, sunlight streams into the office and casts a Jesus-y glow over the elder priest's head, causing Father Jim to squint as he sits down and waits for Father Lewis to look up. But Father Lewis doesn't look up. Part of the dance. Part of the everyday power struggles and mind games that go on here. Like any other workplace.

"So the girl," Father Jim says finally, ceding defeat by speaking first and not waiting until Father Lewis has peered up from his important work. And when he does, having set down his pen (yes, it's a pen, a regular twentieth-century Bic), he smiles the smile of the cunning victor.

"Yes, *the girl*," repeats Father Lewis, as if referring to the stock movie character. "The Archbishop has made it be known to the necessary parties that this matter is to be of the utmost priority, of the, the . . . *exigent* precedence, when he gets back from Honduras. He's concerned. Very concerned. Which means, *concomitantly,* that we, too, are very concerned."

"I thought it was El Salvador."

"Maybe it was Guatemala, come to think of it," the older man replies, his speech uniformly slow and cadenced, emphasizing certain words, usually the big ones, in that grandiose manner of his (which works better with a congregation), each syllable carefully chosen as if he's distrustful of language, groping for a preciseness and clarity that's just not possible, eluding him yet compelling him forward to the next sentence. "At any rate, somewhere down there," he continues. "Some groundbreaking for a memorial for the disappeared. But when he returns, suffice it to say, he's expecting a, a, well . . . *meticulously exhaustive* report and presentation by the end of next week."

"I'll take care of it."

"Good."

"But what are your thoughts? What are your impressions? We should be talking about this. I need to start fleshing out some position statements. 'The Church believes this, the Church believes that.'"

"My thoughts, my impressions *in toto* are thus: this is the kind of hornet's nest that we all secretly dread."

"And?"

"And I'm dreading it. I'm in full ceremonial dread."

"With all due respect, Father Lewis, I'm going to need a little more than that. What about the girl? What about the mother? How do we feel about the claims that these people have been making? What is the Catholic Church's position on miracles circa 1999? This isn't something that's going to go away. We're beyond that now. We're on speed dial for just about every major network and newspaper in the country. Poor Nancy's talking like a rapper. What do we tell these people? I've got to tell them something."

Father Lewis resorts to an old tactic of his: the slow, there's-nothing-to-get-excited-about-here working of his tongue over his teeth, which are, incidentally, startlingly white, vigorous, like the rest of him. Despite his advanced age, despite the sea-captain limp that no one knows the origin of, he looks like he still throws the medicine ball around every morning, does his daily regimen of jumping jacks and other obsolete calisthenics. He'll probably outlive them all, many have predicted, up on his mountain or wherever he retreats to when he retires.

"We say we're continuing the investigation," he says, orchestrating calm in the wake of the younger man's growing panic.

"We reiterate. We make no commitments. We say a, a . . . *comprehensive* release of our findings—which include the conclusions, we emphasize, of not only theological but also medical professionals—is forthcoming in due time once the evidence has been properly . . . *accumulated* and . . . *analyzed* and . . . *scrutinized*. These things take time, we say. They cannot be rushed like so much else these days. We add that we generally do not approve of the veneration of weeping statues and the like, and we certainly do not like the, the . . . *egregious* equation of religion and the Church with superstition and miracles that cannot be quantified. We add as well that what is *inexplicable* might just remain that, inexplicable, but we acknowledge the hunger, the . . . *clamorous* need for guidance and comfort in these, these . . . let's say *ambiguous* times of ours, and if that brings people closer to God, well then, that's a good thing."

"All right. That I can use."

"But you see the dilemma we have here, Father Hinshaw. Say we say these aren't genuine miracles. Then we look like we're against the thousands of people, the . . . *hopeful* masses, who say they are. On the other hand, say we say they are—well, I don't know what. For one thing, in the secular mind, the Catholic Church has just jumped back two hundred years. So what's likely, what I'm assuming we'll do, unless of course the investigation is one hundred percent . . . *conclusive* one way or the other, which I doubt, what we'll do most likely then is articulate some middling response. Or rather you will. So think *middling. Middling* is your word."

"Middling."

"Yes. *Middling.*"

And at this point Father Jim knows that that's about all he's going to get from Father Lewis for now. Eye contact becoming less frequent, fingers straying to documents and religious-themed paperweights and beard hairs. He senses the old man shutting down; five minutes of one-on-one conversation is about his limit. Not because of age, but because of patience, his lack of it, which has nothing to do with the accretion of years and everything to do with temperament. Resigned, Father Jim says he'll have a preliminary status update on Friday, and the old man picks up his pen, returns to the hermetic universe of his desk.

When Father Jim gets back to his office, there's Nancy again, fluttering like a bird in distress, a mother unable to properly feed and shelter her young. But before she can speak—her prefatory forefinger raised, leaning forward to hasten her query—Father Jim sneaks in his own question as he sits down at his desk.

"Any news about what's up with the network?"

"Something with the server," Nancy says. "It's always the server. When in doubt, blame it on the server. They said we'd be back up by early afternoon."

"I've got to get this press release out this morning. Maybe I can run to Kinko's and send it out using my Hotmail account. And at some point I need to get online to do some more research on our little Miracle Girl. I came across this website the other day that has a lot of articles and stories, looks like it might be a good repository. I wanted to print some of them out. The Happy Skeptic.com or something. The girl's got her own website, too, of course. Who doesn't these days?"

"A man called while you were talking to Father Lewis. Not a reporter. I wrote his name and number on the message. He was distraught about his wife. Was kind of rambling. His name was Donald. He couldn't say exactly why he was calling or who he wanted to talk to. From down in Orange County. Laguna Beach. Ever been down there, Father? They say it's like the Mediterranean, which I've never been to, so I can't really compare. I think he just wanted to talk to someone."

"I'll call him back."

"What was she like, Father?"

"The girl? I don't know. I still don't know what to make of it all. She's paralyzed. It's sad. That was the shocking thing. Even though I knew this, I'd seen her on TV and knew what to expect, a paralyzed little girl who can't communicate either. But there she was. It was a shock. She just lies there in her room. That's her whole world, that room. While all this whirls around her. You can't tell what she's thinking or how much she knows. That's what the doctors say anyway. The people see it differently, though, and the people are there, Nancy. They keep coming. Lined up in front of the house and down the block. Part of this collective yearning that maybe before was general, not defined, and now it has a purpose, a focus. And they adore the girl. You talk to them and there's no doubt about what they believe is going on. Miracles. No matter what the Church or the TV or anybody else says. Miracles. Like they've read about but thought they'd never experience firsthand. Or secondhand. In 1999. In Los Angeles. Miracles. Miraculum, to quote the Latin."

"Because I guess I've been thinking that with Darrel—well, with both Darrel and Kenny, Darrel's ruptured disc and Kenny with the lupus—I was just thinking that why not, it couldn't hurt. You never know."

"Nancy, I think that if you feel the need to go, then you should go. If that's what you're asking."

"Thanks, Father. Maybe I will. I'm just mulling it over. What else did I come in here to tell you? Oh. There's someone who's been holding for about ten minutes. Says she's an agent or something. A woman."

"All right, I'll take it. Thanks, Nancy."

Father Jim presses the blinking button on his phone. Tugs at his collar. Still some residual sweat that won't seem to go away.

"Good morning, this is Father Jim Hinshaw."

"Yes, Father, Father Jim, hello, hello. Just switching off speaker. Hello. This is Christine Benfer here. Of Benfer and Sloan Artists Management. Saw you on the news the other night, Father. Nicely done, I must say. Although you might want to do something about that wardrobe. Ha ha. Joking, Father, joking. Has anyone ever mentioned that you resemble a certain actor who I'll have you know I once represented at one point in his career early on?"

"You're not the first. What can I do for you today, Ms. Benfer?"

"Well, Father, it involves, as you might imagine, the Vincent girl. Incredible story, that. And I'm involved in the development of a script based on these events. And I was wondering if you'd consider coming onboard and becoming a kind of advisor slash consultant for the movie."

"A movie? They're making a movie?"

"In development, Father. It's a complicated business. But things are moving faster than they normally do, which tells me something. A cable movie, it's looking like. One of the newer networks."

The requests keep getting stranger and stranger, thinks Father Jim as he shifts the phone to his other ear. Christine Benfer's voice is smooth, melodic, a well-honed instrument.

"And what would being this advisor slash consultant entail?" he asks.

"Not much really. Reading the script, making notes, suggestions, offering feedback. Religion-wise, we just want to make sure everything is up to snuff, that there are no major fu—foul-ups. Of course—and full disclosure here, Father, because I believe in being as honest as possible with people—that doesn't necessarily mean that what you say or recommend will find its way into the final product. No guarantee of that. Dramatic license and whatnot. Some of the rules and conventions of filmmaking do not always cohere with the rules and conventions of the world. That whole art-versus-reality thing."

"I'll have to think about it, Ms. Benfer. We're pretty swamped here right now with the investigation. But I'll think about it and look at my schedule and get back to you. If it's just a matter of reading the script."

"And how is the investigation going?"

Father Jim pauses before answering.

"We're . . . making progress," he says, trying to be as *noncommittal* as possible. "It's coming along. It's coming along fine. These things can't be rushed like so much else these days."

"That's all I'm going to get?"

"I'm afraid so, yes."

"I understand. Completely. Completely understand. Information is our most precious commodity, and this is after all the information age. Just think about it. Think about it and let me know. By Friday would be good. If you are interested, I'll have Daniel FedEx a contract and the script once this latest draft is finished. All right then. *Ciao.*"

Dial tone. That universal assaultive drone.

Had he ever spoken to anyone who ended a conversation with the Italian word for good-bye? Doubtful. Also doubtful: that while growing up in Ohio he ever imagined that he'd be reading scripts and talking to agents and showing up on the six o'clock news in the country's second largest television market. He stands and goes to his tiny office window, gazes down on Wilshire and the buildings of downtown Los Angeles, everything bathed in a hazy, sickly light. You are being watched by an unknown source.

And what about the Miracle Girl? He hasn't yet fully sorted out what he thinks about it all, this cresting commotion that has taken over his life, at least not much more than what he told Nancy. There's a resistance, sure, a skepticism that's probably healthy, the legacy of Thomas, the famous Doubting Thomas, who questioned the Resurrection until he touched Christ's wounds, and who said, "Blessed are those who have not seen and yet believe"; but there's also an elation, an expectant curiosity and delight reminiscent of childhood, when things hadn't been decided and there wasn't a name or word for everything you felt. In a way, he welcomed mystery back into his life. It was mystery, in fact, that had drawn him to the priesthood in the first place. As a shy little boy, then as an even more bashful teenager, he had been fascinated by the priests whom his parents had over regularly for dinner, these solemn, mythic men (Father Sullivan, Father Díaz) with their wise foreheads and forgiving eyes, like they knew secrets, had knowledge that was painful but beautiful to bear. His family strict Catholics, scornful of the cafeteria variety; however, regardless of their devotion, his parents, particularly his mother, had always discouraged him from becoming a priest: you're so talented, there's so much you can do, as if such a life would be a disappointment, settling for less than what he was capable of.

So yes: mystery. Which he found himself now savoring, not wanting to articulate his thoughts too much, to investigate too deeply—despite the fact that technically, yes, that was his job, his charge here at the Archdiocese—and therefore break the spell. And yet: even though the phenomenon of Anabelle Vincent had its questions and perhaps unanswerable Sphinx-like riddles, on the other hand it also seemed like something tangible, and maybe that's what has become so appealing for people. Here was this girl, this physical embodiment of pain and suffering and goodness and light and all the faith that has been diverted or distracted throughout the years. Karen Vincent, the mother, had told them a story about a woman who came all the way from Michigan. She was a widow, retired, no children, very little money, her health relatively good considering her age, her titanium hip implants, and her dubious family history of various life-threatening ailments. Had never been to California in her life. She took a Greyhound to Los Angeles and then a long, expensive cab ride to the house. She had nothing specific to pray for or ask for. Her life had been lived and now she was waiting, she said. She simply wanted to see Anabelle. She didn't know why, she just had to. The girl, her story, spoke to her as she sat watching TV in the day room of her assisted-living facility. She left without telling anyone. "I'm on the lam," she confided girl-ishly. After she met with Anabelle, a fellow visitor offered to drop her off at the bus station, and she returned home. "To wait some more, only now the waiting will be easier," she told the mother, who confessed to Father Jim and Father Lewis that she didn't know what to make of the story, it was one of many, and there were more and more every day, compiling like evidence, proof of something.

Father Jim returns to his computer, tries to log on again. Still the "unable to connect" message. He taps the keyboard, the screen an empty ocean of desktop green. Could it be that the Miracle Girl was a test for him? Some of the older priests talked about those who hit the Wall—referring to the younger priests who make a go of it for a few years but eventually leave the Church, who get married or succumb to doubt and selfishness and who knows what else, the thousands of reasons to live an uncollared life. Father Jim is near that vulnerable age when the Wall usually presents itself, either in the mind or in the flesh, confronting you, a reckoning to be had—what's your true com-mitment, your true belief? It all came down to this.

And because he'd thought of Thomas, he also thinks now of the Caravaggio painting, with the inspecting apostle sticking a finger into Christ's damaged body, probing the wound until it became real. Father Jim had wanted to touch Anabelle the same way, get the same kind of consuming verification. But he hadn't. Like countless others, he merely cupped his hand to her head, held it there, looked into her bottomless eyes, and waited, Father Lewis having already left the room, the mother standing quietly behind him, letting the moment breathe and be what it wanted to be. Later, after, it had been on the drive back to the office, while staring at his hand lazed on the steering wheel, he tried to determine if the slight tingling in his fingers had been his imagination, or from the strain of driving, or was it the girl speaking to him in a language he didn't yet know.

11

| Karen |

MORE EARTHQUAKES ENSUED — A series of subsequent bumps and aftershocks, fairly mild rumblings by L.A. standards—but nothing like the one that hit while she was on her "break" at Costco. People on the radio and TV and everywhere saying it was a warning, a sign of some kind. Just look at the number of quakes. Look at the weather, too. Look at the flooding in Indonesia and famine in Africa. Look at AIDS. Look at Ebola. Look at the Lakers' losing streak. Look at the whole Y2K thing—all the computers that were going to go haywire and blow up, causing power outages and gas and food shortages and riots and lootings, people stockpiling canned goods and bullets and water purification systems, the stroke of midnight on December 31, 1999, setting off a chain reaction of malfunctioning ATM machines, nuclear power plant meltdowns, a global economic, social and political collapse, and, eventually, if you went that far, the end of the world as we know it. And then there was what Anabelle's physical therapist, Linda, said: "I like my KABC radio and my Dr. Toni Grant, but I'm getting tired of all these folks calling up and saying apocalypse this and apocalypse that. The earthquakes, the weather, the price of tea in China. You seen that bumper sticker they have? 'Y2K Is Judgment Day.' The only signs I believe in are the signs at the gas station. You seen the price for a gallon of unleaded lately?" Karen liked Linda, a lot.

As for Anabelle, she was fine. After the earthquake and power outage, and after the doctor and paramedics and ambulance had left, they continued to monitor her closely—and nothing, she was fine. Stable. Unchanged. Normal—meaning the same as before the earthquake. But later that night, while sitting on the sofa in the living room and sipping chamomile tea, Karen had lost it, the hot beverage almost spilling as her hands shook uncontrollably, Bryce consoling her in his sweet Bryce way, making her feel, as he always managed to do, less alone in the world. She had cried harder than she had in months, harder, even, than she had cried when John left. It was getting to be too much. It had taken on a life of its own and it was now beyond her control, anyone's control. The people, the phone calls, the interviews, the letters, the e-mails, the requests, the devouring need of everyone who knocked on her door. Everything. The story of the Miracle Girl had officially grown "legs," to quote one of the many reporters she spoke to on a pretty much daily basis.

The crying lessened to a light whimpering and then subsided all together, and she was able to speak again. She pulled away from Bryce, noticing that his shirt was damp from her tears and that he quite possibly had an erection. She took a deep breath.

"I don't know if I want this to be happening anymore," Karen told him. "I don't know if I can do it."

Bryce crossed his legs; he drank the last of his now-cold tea. It was a rare moment when the house was dark and quiet, when she could almost imagine simply doing the dishes and going to bed without worrying about Anabelle making it through the night, and then the next morning waking up to her daughter gently nudging her and climbing next to her in bed, snuggling their way into the start of a new day.

"I don't know if it's a choice anymore," said Bryce.

"There has to be a choice," she said, leaning forward on the couch. "I mean, I'm her mother. This is my life. This is our life. I don't know if I want this to be happening anymore, Bryce. It's too much. Mostly, though, the main thing that's making me feel sick to my stomach, like I'm going to throw up, is I don't know what to tell these people anymore. They keep coming and I smile and I don't know what to say anymore. What if—what if I want this all to stop?"

The question went unanswered, and they both sat there for a very long time until Karen got up to check on Anabelle: she looked both peaceful and restless, alive and dead, the moonlight casting a celestial-looking white glow across her entire body—something, she knew right away, that she would keep to herself. It would not become yet another story about her daughter.

BUT THE WEEKS wore on. She did not know how to stop. Could it be stopped? More visitors, more fatigue, more indecision. She felt herself spinning, paper caught up in wind and tumult, controlled by a force beyond her.

PERHAPS THE FIRST miracle was that she did not die, and here it was, approaching a year after the accident. The doctors said not to expect much, maybe she'd have six months, maybe more if they were lucky, it's best not to get one's hopes up too much in these kinds of situations, take it day to day, be thankful for the time you have with your daughter. They also said Anabelle would be better off in an institution—an "extended care facility" was how they put it. Providing for her basic needs would be a full-time job—more than a full-time job, actually. But Karen wouldn't have it: "I can handle it, I can do it myself," she told them, without thinking of all that this entailed, the details, the day-to-day, hour-to-hour, life-consuming toil. "I'll learn what I need to learn. What I don't know, we'll get people to come to the house. Do whatever we need to do. I don't want her wasting away in some institution or whatever you call it. I can't accept that. A parent can't accept that. I can't . . ."

And they came back with: "That's our recommendation, Mrs. Vincent. There's a very fine facility in Brea and we'd be more than happy to make the necessary arrangements and they have a wonderful program there. Of course we can't make the decision for you. But understand that if you take this on yourself, your life will no longer be your own. Are you prepared for that? Because ask yourself. This is the kind of case where the patient, your daughter, Anabelle, will require constant care and supervision. Keep in mind there are financial considerations as well. It gets tricky with the insurance if you go it alone like this. We just want to make sure you're making an informed decision."

And she said: "I understand, thank you, you've made it perfectly clear, your asses are officially covered, but no, there are some things you know you're supposed to do. You just know. In your bones. In your chest, here."

And so, against the advice of several doctors and bearded specialists and pretty much everyone else she spoke with, from her husband and her sister Tammy to the mailman, they brought Anabelle home. Emptied her room. Redecorated with the machinery and equipment that would help prolong her life. John disassembled the special bed because it wouldn't fit through the door to her room, and then reassembled it once the parts were inside, and they had to hire someone to add a few more electrical sockets and redo some of the wiring (more bills, more credit cards surpassing their laughably high maximums, which meant it was time to apply for more cards), while she consulted technicians and spoke to pharmaceutical companies and asshole sales reps and figured out the intricacies of the tube that went into her daughter's stomach and through which she would get her nourishment. The great experiment began.

Even though she'd always known that Anabelle would come home, Karen, in her weaker moments, used to wonder what if—what if she had gone along with the doctors and everyone else? What would her life have been like then? Would Anabelle's supposed gift have remained hidden in such an environment? Had it taken her motherly love and devotion and unwavering belief in her daughter for it to flourish? When the reporters and media people ask her what's her role in this amazing story, she usually says nothing, brushes off the question like a celebrity being probed about a recent love affair gone wrong. Because she doesn't know. She doesn't know what to believe. Still.

Friends, family—they all thought she'd blown a fuse for bringing her daughter home. John freaking out. Or well on his way toward freaking out. Not sleeping. Not working. He stayed up late and zoned out in front of the TV. She tried to convince him that it was the right thing to do, the only thing to do, despite the fact that she knew that he would ultimately yield because this

involved their daughter, and up until then all decisions concerning Anabelle had been made by her and he wasn't going to start
getting all *Father Knows Best* now—nor was he entitled to, was
Karen's take. But he argued. Relentlessly. With a passion that
surprised and sometimes silenced her.

He said: "I don't think we can do this, I mean, I don't think *I*
can do this. Because think about it. We're still young. I know it
doesn't feel that way, that it hasn't felt that way in a long, long
time. But I can't. I can't give my life over like this. It's killing
me. Selfish, I know. I guess this is the kind of thing you always
wonder about, how if something like this were to happen—some
disaster or something—and you wonder how would you react.
Would you do the right thing or not. And I can't do this. I admit
it. I'm a selfish fucker. There. Is that what you wanted? Is that
what you wanted me to admit? OK, I'm admitting. Full fucking
confessional. Forgive me father for I have sinned. But Sweetie,
think long term here. What if the doctors are wrong about six
months or a year or whatever? Think ahead five, ten years. What
then? How can we possibly take care of her? What can we really
do for her? The doctors said. Wouldn't she be better off? I understand what's behind it, really I do. Totally. But look. Maybe
it's time to let go. Maybe it's time. Things have been so crazy,
even before all this. And I don't think we're in the right state of
mind to be like making these kinds of decisions, these huge, this-
is-going-to-affect-the-rest-of-our-lives decisions. We can always
have her go to that place and then later change our minds, too.
And shit. It hasn't been that long, not really, since the accident.
There's still the after effects of that, like that one doctor said
about how there's these different periods of like shock and sadness and then disbelief and then what was it—something else I

can't remember but you get the point I'm making here. I don't think either of us are in the kind of the condition to be caring for her like we're going to need to be caring for her."

Her mother, too, calling from Colorado (collect, like they could afford it), where she'd moved for a job that fell through and now was living with a man practically half her age and who worked part-time in a comic book store. Her mother: who once declared that she wouldn't wish motherhood upon her worst enemy (true story) and who lately has become more bold about displaying her selective amnesia, now an official unapologetic revisionist of the past, arguing that's not what happened, I never said that, did that, you were just kids, how could you possibly remember. Whenever they talked on the phone, Karen could hear in the background the forgotten TV, the restless tapping of her Lee Press-Ons, the metallic flick of the cigarette lighter signaling another smoke and a savored silence, inhaling. Her voice throaty and used up and resigned to the world's disappointments. Yet always full of advice. Always transporting her back to her ten-year-old self.

She said: "This is crazy. This is just plain straitjacket-me crazy. Hold on, dear. One second while—*Brian. Brian. No not that one. The other one. To the left.* There. OK, I'm back. *And don't use too much like last time. You remember what happened then, don't you.* Now where was I? John. And with things between John and you being what they are? Believe me, dear. I know. I've been down that neck of the woods and it's no day at the races. I know about relationships, there's something to be said for experience and old age and being around the track a little, and I know we've had our . . . *things*. And Baby Doll I know sometimes we don't see eye to eye on much besides the weather, and granted

. . . I'm not exactly the role-model type of mother which I'm perfectly willing to plead guilty here to . . . but there's one thing I do know about and that's relationships and in particular men and even more in particular men like John because I've known my fair share, your father included, these men of excuses of ours, and it's always something, because they've got that stupid idea stuck in their male brains that the world owes them something, and from the get-go you'll have to at least admit that you and John . . . you and John have been, I don't know, cursed. *Brian! By the sink, underneath.* Really think about what you're getting yourselves into, commitment-wise. Really think about it. And the money. That's a whole other bag of salami. I can come out and help for a little while, but I can't be gone too long. I've got a few job leads and I signed up for this computer training course next month. Who's your long-distance service by the way? I've got one of these referral deals where if I get people to sign up I get a discount and a tote bag."

Others offered their unsolicited counsel as well. She pretended to listen and consider. But she didn't give in, even though, yes, you bet, there were times when she wanted to, when she thought the lure of letting go would be too much. The sacrifice, sacrifices, that would be required. Her parenting skills probably never having been all that stellar anyway, and now this. Yes, she did pray. It had been years, since the summer when she suddenly had boobs and "Rhiannon" was her favorite song and she wanted to be Stevie Nicks. She got on her knees and prayed. No specific prayer or anything, just: *Please help me, God. Please help me.* Over and over, until the words dissolved in her mouth and it seemed like they no longer needed to be said.

And not only did her baby not die. She kept her at home, is keeping her at home. And perhaps that was another miracle, too.

SLEEP IS A luxury. Karen no longer believes in it. It comes in small, inadequate spurts, an hour here, an hour there, waking, checking on Anabelle, nodding off again, dreams that start and stop and never rightly conclude, always awake before dawn, and she's gotten used to it, sort of, though sometimes that lurchy haze of being on a different tape speed is hard to shake.

Last night had passed similarly, and now this morning, more than a month after the Costco Quake (as Karen has internally labeled it), she's up bright and early before the first pleas of daylight have begun to paw their way into Anabelle's window. Slowly, geriatrically, she extracts herself from the chair she's once again slept in and parts the lace curtains (made by a well-wisher, a homebound invalid who lives in Reno and also does award-winning needlepoint, according to the note enclosed with the package) and then she returns to Anabelle, caressing her daughter's long, dark fairytale locks, which drape over the side of the bed—like a princess waiting for a magical kiss from her prince, more than one visitor has remarked. The walls are painted a creamy, feminine pink. Next she removes the red bow from her daughter's hair, replaces it with a fresh one, also red, and begins combing—the morning ritual in motion, her brain and thoughts fighting against the lack of sleep and gradually narrowing into focus. When Linda arrives later they will change Anabelle into a new nightgown, bathe her body with the care of priests presiding over mass. Yes, it's holy work, this. But for now she combs, listens to the beautiful, gentle sound of hair gliding through the brush's teeth, the rhythm and the faintest hint of static, she's always appreciated this sound, as a daughter and now as a mother, how it consoled somehow, and layered behind that is the churn of the machinery, unvarying, monitoring her daughter's heart rate, allowing her to breathe and live. Everything looks all right this morning. Everything stable, normal.

Moments like this, her panic subsides. Temporarily, at least, she can deal. Things will move forward in a way that she can understand and perhaps control. But she knows once the day is underway, once the people file in and release their prayers and weeping and burdens, it will return and her heart will race and she will feel like locking the door and shuttering the windows and turning off all the lights. See? Nobody home. It's too much for her, too much for anyone.

Except wait—what's this? Had Anabelle moved during the night? Looks like it, yes. There. The slightest shifting of her midsection to the left. Her arms, too: last night they were at her side (weren't they?) and now they are more outstretched. And her lips: are they parted more than usual? With her open mouth, Anabelle appears always to be on the verge of speech, a cruel image that never fails to devastate Karen. (And sometimes, if she stares long enough, she swears she sees her daughter's lips come to life, struggling to say something, to utter one simple word: *Mom.*) But maybe not. Maybe it's all just a hallucination, a manifestation of her still-burning hopefulness, her motherly belief in her daughter's eventual recovery. This happens periodically. And she has to remind herself to not get carried away. Take it day to day. Accept the present. Accept everything.

She finishes brushing, the same number of strokes on each side: twenty-five. Then she applies ChapStick, kisses the waxy, cherry-smelling lips, and squeezes her daughter's hand—the last bit the final part of this particular morning ritual, a gesture telling Anabelle that the day is about to begin and that the people will soon be coming, that she should prepare herself for the flow of need about to enter her room.

It's past six and it's like the day has already slipped away. So much to do. She promised Bryce she'd spend some time getting more familiar with the computer and respond to a few posts on Anabelle's website. Then later in the afternoon a phone interview with a newspaper in Mexico City. There's probably more but she can't think of anything else right now. And of course: the visitors. Of course. She leaves Anabelle's room and commences turning on the lights, putting on the coffee, clearing space so people can sit, bringing the house to life. The temperature rising already, into December and no signs of the weather letting up. In the living room she opens the blinds only to quickly close them, releasing a frenzied clattering of plastic. Outside the people who have spent the night are stirring, waking up. They have noticed the lights. They are starting to emerge, sleepy and hopeful, from their tents and cars, a collective awakening, and again she feels bad for her neighbors: Debby next door, the black couple across the street (Morris was maybe the last name?), the mailman who lives on the corner, everyone who lives nearby, how they have to deal with this intrusion and inconvenience.

But she's not ready. She needs a little more time. Five more minutes. She can't help herself, though: she gets on her knees and takes a more covert peek through the blinds. She sees men and women and children. Scans the faces—and thinks there's a guy, half-facing the street, hands on his hips, leaning forward as if inspecting something on the ground, who could be John. This also happens fairly regularly. Yes, she thinks it's John, believes it's John, the build is the same, the walk and slouch is the same, and then the face comes into better focus and she realizes no, it's not him, this is a different face. John is still far, far away.

The question: What would she say if it ever was him, if he came back? What would he say? How long would they stare at each other before the words came? It's a scene she's played out in her mind many times, hundreds of times (and it's the scene in the movie that you expect all along, you know it's coming, the big moment of reconciliation, and yet you don't mind it, the cliché of it, even though it's obvious, because it feels right, it feels true, it feels earned), but it's always different, sometimes warm and forgiving, sometimes angry and bitter, sometimes awkward and frosty, sometimes all of the above. There's a soundtrack, too: soft piano music, accompanied by a swell of violins and other stringed instruments she's forgotten the names of.

The answer: She doesn't know. She doesn't know what she'd say, what she'd do, how she'd react. It was going to be something that would happen in the moment, discovering your way as you go.

The guy she's been watching, the one who isn't John, catches her staring, stares back, starts walking toward the house, and Karen jumps backward and almost falls on her ass, the blinds rattling once again. It was like the accident took away Anabelle for the first time, and now it was happening a second time, in a much different way. She just wants her daughter back.

Karen withdraws to the kitchen, tries to convince herself to eat. But there's nothing. The lack of food is daunting, a reflection on her character. She has fallen behind on condiments, salt, butter, the basics. So she sits at the table and cries. Again. The tears sudden and substantial. Why? Why is she crying? Because of nothing. Because she hasn't managed to run out to the market. Because her nails are chipped and gnawed. Because she doesn't know the answer. Because she doesn't know where John is right now, right this second. Because of everything. She must be strong. She knows this. Five more minutes (and why is it always five more minutes, that magical span of time that makes a difference?) and then I'll be better. There isn't time for this kind of thing anymore. I should eat something, anything, before it gets too late, like it always does.

After she dries her eyes and semi-composes herself and does a final check in the bathroom mirror (the bags, the bags; what can you do?), she's ready, or as ready as she has to be, for she's learning, too, about appearances and performance and the actor's credo about how the show must go on. They're waiting. Always waiting. So she opens the front door and once again welcomes the world into her house, smiling.

12

| John |

THEY GIVE HIM his own cubicle, as well as a computer that's ready to kick his ass and reduce him to a state of Cro-Magnon cluelessness. He really doesn't know much about it . . . them . . . computers, other than indulging in an occasional round of Solitaire or Minesweeper, the Internet still something of an otherworldly mystery to him. But he figures he'll be able to Lucy Ricardo his way around it all, at least for a week or two, or however long he'll be here, his latest TempPeople gig, after finishing a forgettable month-long warehouse job, another Monday-morning first day, which are always the worst, having to memorize all the people's names and system passwords and also learn the ins and outs and quirks of the copy machine, every time taking a deep breath as he begins the assignment and hoping this time will be better than the last.

After showing him where he'll be sitting, Ron, the supervisor, in his bland forties, a prolific perspirer who reminds John of a suburbanized David Bowie (the same snaggletooth, the same junkie skinniness, the same intense, accusatory cheekbones, all countered with a white shirt and patterned tie and tan Dockers, very un-Bowie), ushers him into his office and before John even has a chance to sit down asks how up-to-speed his database and 10-key skills are, and John pauses mightily, deer-in-the-headlights dumb, and finally says, way too late, *Uh pretty good, pretty up to speed,* wondering what the fuck is 10-key (database not exactly his area of expertise either). John remains standing while Ron rushes through his duties, what's expected of him, the company's policies on sexual harassment, affirmative action, personal hygiene, etc., John retaining nothing much except the overpowering brand-new smell of the office and Ron's frequent use of the word *copasetic.*

According to Ron ("Please call me Ron. That's just the kind of company this is."), things are kind of on the quiet side right now, but he'd better enjoy it because relatively soon, once the new promos hit the major TV markets, which would strategically coincide with a rebranded print campaign and a slew of banner ads set to inundate websites large and small, both horizontal and vertical markets (John nodding, still standing, contorting his jaw into a position of what he hoped would be interpreted as understanding and approval), the phones would be ringing off the hook.

John receives the official welcome-aboard handshake from Ron, who then plays tour guide and introduces him to the wonders of his new workplace, pointing out the essentials (bathroom, kitchen, supply area, copy machine), emphasizing the user-friendly nature of the floor's layout and design, finally circling back to John's minimalist cube. During the time he'd been away in Ron's office and taking the tour, someone had hung a plastic placard with his name in glaring caps, JOHN VINCENT, like an accusation, a wanted poster without the picture and fine-print details of his crimes. Attached by Velcro. Meaning that it can be easily removed, one effortless rip, nothing permanent like glue or screws.

"Any questions so far?" asks Ron.

John has about a hundred (horizontal markets? vertical markets? did he have to pay for parking?), but he answers the way he knows he's supposed to: "No, not yet. So far so good."

Ron, who does not have an English accent but John still can't get the Bowie thing out of his head, launches into an overview of the state-of-the-art and newly installed phone system. "The TeleTech 500," boasts an awed Ron. "Here's how you route, here's how you transfer, here's how you get an outside line." Ron fires up John's computer, clicking, double-clicking, configuring, typing with all fingers blazing (vs. John's single-finger chimpanzee approach), working the mouse and keyboard with shortcuts and a flurry of effortless moves, all the while continuing to narrate. *Here's how you take orders, here's how you submit orders. Click. And drag. Save. Then Save As. Import. Toggle over to other program. Alt-Tab. Alt-Tab, I'd highly recommend. Saves time versus the mouse and plus it cuts back on the chances of RSI and CTS, which has destroyed some of the best wrists of my generation, sadly. File, open. Copy, paste, again. Save. Submit. Easy, see?* John blinking, staring. Ron wears a high-school class ring about the size of a small crustacean. This, John finds, is highly distracting, making it even more difficult to follow along. *It's all pretty simple. I'm not too worried, John. You seem like a bright guy. You'll be good to go in no time.*

Next, Ron escorts John to an empty, echoing conference room. The large oval glass table where he sits is black and shiny and frosty to the touch. He can see himself, vaguely, in the surface's reflection. Ron cues up the video, which is an infomercial. It opens with a man and woman—husband and wife, presumably— who are ho-hum and beaten down, with a very male voice-over, which sounds like your pissed-off Dad, asking "Is this you?" and rattling off a bunch of symptoms posed as questions: "Tired? Burnt out? Lethargic? Listless? Unfocused? Disengaged? Forgetful? Moody?" The man and woman turn to the camera and simultaneously nod yes, that's us, guilty as charged; after this admission, there's a cut to two suited men seated talk-show style, lounging in white leather recliners, a square glass table between them, with a vase of imposter flowers, a pitcher of water, and two cups.

"You know," begins the man on the left, "they talk about the miracle of birth, and that's one thing, and then of course you have the miracles in the Bible and whatnot, and that's another, and I don't like to use the word lightly, but hey, that's really what we're going to be talking about here today with our special guest: We're going to be talking about a miracle."

The special guest is identified as a doctor. And as the conversation with the host ensues, the doctor gets increasingly worked up about neurotransmitters and people sleepwalking through their lives and the national crisis we're currently facing—a brain starvation crisis, is what he calls it. Which is why we're always so tired, so unsatisfied all the time, he explains. The product in question is some kind of pill, and when John asks a question and refers to it as such, as *pills,* Ron stops him right there, stops the tape, crosses his arms in football-coach disgust, and says don't ever refer to the product as pills, as drugs, but only as "the product" or by its proper name, Mira-Cure, or as "a revolutionary new dietary supplement and/or life enhancer," but never, ever *pills*. John adequately shamed, Ron continues on and un-pauses the video, which lasts almost an hour, and then it's practically lunchtime.

But before that, Ron introduces him to his coworkers, the members of his "team." There's Deidre and Mary and Mary Anne and Alexa and Lupe and Randall. Handshakes, waves, nods, gestures of neutral welcome. They all wear headsets and wrist braces. Security badges dangle from their necks. These are the people geographically near him and with the same job, more or less: Customer Service Representatives Class II.

"Where's the bathroom again?" John asks, and everyone points toward the elevators.

For lunch he goes to the food park across the street and shells out $9.50 for a "gourmet" grilled cheese sandwich, no drink. Someone in line behind him saying how he's finally vesting and the future is monetization and the future was like yesterday.

STILL FIFTEEN MINUTES left of his designated lunch break, and so John locates some shade in front of the building to wait it out. People are returning from lunch, grouped in clusters, chatting and laughing. Many carry colorful Styrofoam cups from Jamba Juice. He roots through his backpack, trying to look purposeful. And there. There it is: The postcard he keeps in the front zippered pocket. A reminder. It's a postcard he's never sent, a picture of the Nevada desert at sunset, the lights of Vegas gleaming in the distance. On the blank side he'd written, weeks ago, in his capital-lettered, nearly illegible elementary school scrawl: I WANT TO COME BACK IF YOU'LL HAVE ME. PLEASE.

"Don't leave," Karen had said many times over the years, whenever things got wobbly and complicated and cold. "Promise me that, if nothing else. Promise you won't leave. That's what my father did. Once is enough. Once is enough for any person."

"I won't," John had replied. "I promise. I won't leave."

But, of course, he did.

AFTER THE ACCIDENT, they had to give lengthy depositions, required by the insurance companies (there were either three or four involved, he was never sure exactly how many). The lawyers interviewed them separately. Lawyers with briefcases and ties and eye-watering aftershave. All dudes, the same age as John. Or younger, even. They were asked a series of questions, deep, personal probings into their lives and marriage and daughter. Trying to trip them up, uncover inconsistencies, as if they'd engineered this whole fucking disaster for profit and a bullshit lawsuit. *What kind of husband/wife was he/she? What kind of father/mother? Does he/she drink? Does he/she yell? Does he/she ever disappear for days?* It had left Karen in tears. They debriefed in the parking lot of a Home Depot, the car still running so they could have the AC on. Karen's deposition lasted three and a half hours; almost three hours for him. At one point, they were each asked: If you could describe your marriage in a single word, what would that word be? He had answered, "Regular." She had said, "Evolving." There in the car, after, he had kept his hands on the steering wheel, as if he were still driving, as if they were still going somewhere.

FOR THE REST of the afternoon, he's told by Deidre, Ron's robotic assistant who reeks of cat and perfume, to "get familiar" with his computer and the order-taking software, and to also continue going over the collated stacks of training materials.

He reads about Mira-Cure, about the company that makes it, which was actually a division of a larger company, which itself was owned by an even larger company, a multinational corporation located in Dearborn, Michigan, one of those companies that scarily does everything (energy, fast food, diapers), which was in fact this particular company's slogan: "Altco: We Do Everything." He examines the sample bottle of Mira-Cure that Ron had given him. It's about the size of a large Tylenol bottle, and features a sticker with a background hallelujah splash of bright light. He puts a handful of I GOT THE CURE!® refrigerator magnets in the top drawer of his portable file cabinet.

By 3:30 he's done all he can do. Neither Ron nor Deidre are around, and he doesn't want to bother his fellow hard-working, fast-typing CSRC IIs (the place is big on acronyms), so he detours onto the Internet. Stumbling along. Trying to remember what Phil taught him when he first started at TempPeople. Launching something called Netscape. Typing in searches—that's what you do, right? Hunting for the right keys, one finger at a time, pecking at the keyboard like a caveman. He tries his daughter's name. *A-n-a-b-e-l-l-e V-i-n-c-e-n-t.* Stares at the incomprehensible letters. Another language, it seems. He's almost afraid to click on the Search button, afraid of everything that has previously been hidden and now will be fully revealed.

Search.

The results are numerous, scary. He can't believe it. So much written about Anabelle. He scrolls and scans and reads, quickly, glancing over his shoulder every now and then. There are stories by news organizations and also stories on people's websites. Pictures, testimonials, quotes from those who'd been to the house. *Anabelle cured my arthritis. Anabelle took away the hurt in my heart. Anabelle gave me what no one else could: hope.* One link turns out to be a video. It starts automatically. He doesn't know how to stop it. There's nothing he can do but watch and hope that no one in the office hears or comes by.

The video jumps and flickers. Then footage of his neighborhood, the graffitied stop signs, the vibrant weeds, the high ratio of cars parked and forgotten on lawns—the kind of neighborhood you want to get away from if you can, if it's possible, which in their case it was not. The traffic, his street congested with a long line of idling vehicles, neighbors interviewed (he doesn't recognize them) and complaining about the disruption this is causing. Then it's Karen lowering the guardrails of Anabelle's bed, leaning closer, touching their daughter's face, Anabelle's empty eyes aimed away from the camera, as if seeking to avoid capture. Karen appearing even more tired than she looked in the TV report he'd seen, her hair more frizzed and frazzled. And that earlier glow seems to be receding as well. She's talking now about the people who are sleeping in tents and sleeping bags on the lawn and in their cars, wanting to be the first to see Anabelle that day. Karen adding that some people have been stealing stuff from the house—candles, strands of hair from Anabelle's comb, clumps of dirt from the yard, anything. "It's getting out of hand," Karen says. "We've tried waiting lists and scheduling appointments, but that hasn't worked. People keep coming. I don't know how long this can last anymore. But everyone's been so generous, donating money, wanting to help. It's truly amazing. Donations and any money from interviews and media and such first goes toward the cost of Anabelle's care, which is very expensive. Everything else goes into a special account we've set up for Anabelle. We're doing our best." There's a young guy in the kitchen. He's saying he's worried about the toll this is taking on Karen. Bryce. His name is Bryce, identified as one of Anabelle's Angels, a network of helpers and believers. One more shot of Anabelle, still as ever, hair framing her face, and the video abruptly stops.

Search and ye shall find.

After all that, he needs to clear his head, step away from his cube. He stands, looks around the open office space, and it appears that his fellow coworkers are still busy, buzzing right along with their computers and phone calls and 10-key Zen mastery. He's got to do something (people are turning, noticing him standing, wondering about the new guy and what he's up to), so he defaults to the bathroom even though he doesn't have to go, poses at the glistening urinal, unzips his fly, and pretends. Not that it matters, but there's an automatic flush. Everything in the bathroom is shiny, factory fresh. There's a red light blinking on his phone when he returns to his cubicle. He's never seen such a head-scratching phone. Buttons and codes and voice prompts. It's the size of a briefcase. The red light blinks and blinks and he doesn't know how to stop it from blinking. Oh well. He closes out the day with a few minutes of pen and paperclip organizing.

Back home at Desert Piss, he pulls out the bottle of Mira-Cure from his backpack. Takes one. Then two. Why not? Has a sweet taste, kind of like Advil. The color of cotton candy. Couldn't hurt, the pills. He definitely isn't eating right. His brain probably way starved. His neuros, neurons, whatever, all fucked up, too. He thinks of the part in the video where they showed Karen and Anabelle, Karen placing a hand on their daughter's forehead, a gesture that's simple, profound, beautiful; that sends a surging ripple in his blood—part warmth, part regret, part guilt. Was it too late to go back? This is always the question. And now there's a new question: Who the fuck is Bryce?

He swallows a third pill. It's a Monday night and it's too early for bed. The options are minimal. Dinner will likely consist of frozen crinkle fries and a peanut butter sandwich. Next door his neighbor's stereo thumps its familiar rap-inspired thump. John walks over and puts the palm of his hand against the wall separating them, and he can feel the wall vibrating. There's a person very close, his neighbor, another soul, only inches away, who he knows nothing about. They've never spoken or even seen each other. John closes his eyes and waits there. The music. The closeness. The distance. He needs something. Most definitely. He needs, he now realizes, the cure.

THAT NIGHT HE doesn't sleep, not a wink, not a lick, nothing.

TUESDAY, HE FLASHES his security badge at the pierced receptionist and rolls into the office raccoon-eyed and carrying a very large cup of coffee. He'd been up the whole night, unable to shut his brain off. Maybe the Mira-Cure had given him too much brain food, too many nutrients. From one extreme to the other, starvation to plentitude. Deidre already there in the cube next to his, her headset on, a flurry of fingers, bracelets, and polished nails that clicked and clacked as she typed.

"Morning," she says as John sits down.

"Morning," he replies.

His other coworkers haven't arrived yet, the office quiet and undisturbed.

"So," Deidre says, "you survived the dreaded first day and you're back for more?"

He notices the red light still blinking on his phone.

"I survived," he answers, trying to sound upbeat and light but it comes off sighed and weighted, like he'd been through cancer or something, and unexpectedly had beat the odds.

"Let me know if you need anything," Deidre says. "Ron's away at a corporate training thing all day. You should be all set with e-mail and access. I'll start routing calls your way once you get settled in. Good luck."

He settles in, turns on his computer, feels like he might be getting the hang of surfing the Internet. And why not: He takes another Mira-Cure. His body feels both massively tired and pulsingly pumped, both easy listening and heavy metal. He does a quick search for his daughter, reads first-hand accounts of Anabelle's healing power.

"Are you ready? For calls?" Deidre eventually asks.

He's supposed to say yes, he knows.

As THE WEEK millimeters along, he manages, after some trial and error and plenty of how-do-you questions and Gilligan floundering, to make a few sales, mostly to disoriented elderly women who'd recently lost their husbands. He learns about his coworkers: they're divorced or in the process of getting divorced, bitter and more than happy to recite the faults and fallibilities of their former spouses. He learns that Ron isn't around all that much, is a bit of a mystery man, one of those managers whose presence is defined by his absence. He also learns why he hasn't been sleeping.

Wednesday afternoon, while in the break room with Randall,

Mary, and Mary Anne, he asks what he's been wondering about ever since he saw the infomercial his first day: "What's in it?"

"You mean Mira-Cure?" says Randall, whose reddish neck and jowls suggest regular use of a low-end electric razor.

"Yeah, you know, the product."

"Well," Randall explains, "there are these things called neuro-transmitters."

"I saw the video," John says. "What is it really?"

Randall continues preparing the holy pot of afternoon coffee. Along with acronyms, they take their coffee very seriously here. Posted next to the refrigerator there's an elaborate chart, outlining who's responsible for buying and making coffee for each week of the month. Randall glances over at Mary and Mary Anne, who both nod, as if agreeing to reveal a sinister family secret. John has had a tough time figuring out which one is just "Mary" and which one has the extra "Anne."

"Speed, basically," Randall says.

"Speed?"

"Caffeine. Crazy-ass amounts of caffeine. It's what gets you all hopped up, makes you feel like you're Superman, makes your brain think it's smarter than it really is. Wait a minute—you haven't been taking it, have you?"

"Too late."

"Dude, stop taking that shit, pronto."

WHENEVER HE HAS a chance, he's back online, covertly looking for more information about Anabelle. He watches the video multiple times, scrutinizing each frame like it's the Zapruder film, pausing, replaying, pausing again. Was there something, a secret message perhaps, on Karen's face, in her expression? Was she trying to tell him something? Was Anabelle trying to tell him something?

Clearly, someone *was* trying to tell him something, because later that afternoon an e-mail went out to all his coworkers:

From: maryanne@altco.com
To: custservteam6@altco.com
Cc:
Subject: FW: FW: FW: Do you believe in miracles??????

hi all, you probbaly heard about the "miracle girl" on the news -- the little girl that got paralized & put in a coma then this strange stuff started happening like weird clouds in the sky & people with cancer suddenly getting better etc etc etc. i dont know if you believe in this kind of thing (not sure what to make of it myself to be honest w/ you!), and i know we all our very *respectful* of our religous diferences among tohers. But a friend sent me the link to this wonderful website which is the miracle girls website. its pretty inspirtational, i think (just imho), & it doesnt really matter so much how you define/dont define your own Personal Higher Power cause bottom line we could use more of this (hope, love etc) & not all the horible things you see and here about most the time. ok thats all promise. </rant> if you want you can read about the girl & check out some pictures there to. you can even post your ownn prayer. sorry this is so darn long. super sorry if this offends anyone but i thought why not we could all use a little pick me up in the. morning;-)

btw i brought bagels. there in the kitchen. yes miracles really do happen!!!!!

xoxxoxo,

mary anne

>> Have u seen this website? Very inspiring!

>> http://www.miraclegirlanabelle.com

He'd checked out the site before, but he'd mostly been reading news stories. So, as instructed, he clicks on the link in the e-mail and then, for the rest of the day, amid a spattering of phone calls, spends every sparc moment checking out the Official Anabelle Vincent Web Site, over 2 million visits and counting.

He makes it through Thursday, a new month, December, but on Friday morning, he crashes out big time, the lack of sleep caused by the Mira-Cure finally catching up with him, and he oversleeps, doesn't wake up until well after noon. It's too late to go to work. But he already knows he's not going back anyway—not to Altco, not to TempPeople. He leaves a voicemail for Phil, letting him know, then notifies the rental company that manages Desert Piss—which is more than what most of his neighbors do, people routinely disappearing without a trace. Friday night and Saturday morning is spent packing and preparing. It doesn't take long, and that has always been the idea: to be able to move on and vanish quickly, in a blink-and-you'll-miss-it flash, like he'd never even been here. By Saturday afternoon, he's on the road again, the red light of his phone at work still blinking, the mighty Corolla chugging toward the 15, which will take him west, which will take him home. Yes, it's time to go home.

13

| Anabelle |

SCHOOL WAS WORSE. Sometimes worse. Sometimes not. She pretended to be a robot. Or she pretended the other kids and teachers were robots and she was the only real one, the only real person left in the entire school, the whole universe. Alone she went. Aware of her place. The line she must follow.

The girls and their secrets. The boys and their spaziness. The things you had to remember. Names and numbers. Dates and places. People who did stuff in history and you were supposed to know. How it was all there and also not there. She didn't raise her hand. She drew and counted and double-dutched. If she blinked her eyes, it would all go away. Walking to school was an adventure through a jungle. Walking back home a journey through a magical forest. She blinked and blinked and blinked.

Mrs. Stinson called on her and she didn't know what to say. She had been thinking about something else. Mrs. Stinson's face was round and puffy like a pumpkin.

"You're not daydreaming again are you? Why don't you join us here on Planet Earth?"

Giggles, laughs. Mrs. Stinson also had huge boobs that shook and jiggled when she ran after kids. One time her husband came to the classroom and he gave her flowers. Roses that smelled up the room for days.

She wanted to answer with one of her made-up words. But she'd tried that before. More giggles and laughs. So she said, "I wasn't. I won't."

At recess, sides were chosen. It happened quickly. She had been blinking, trying, and then it was over and she was there by herself. She drank from the drinking fountain for as long as possible. Water. Water was water. You need to drink it or you die. Had she learned that at school, or from her mom and dad? Her mom helped her with her homework and when her mom was too tired she asked her dad to do it.

Lunch lasted forever and ever.

Then you had to wait in line before you went back in the classroom. The boys sweaty and smelly from running and playing. The girls whispering. Not to her. She was last in line. Staring at the ground, hoping that one day a crack in the concrete might grow, get bigger, open up, and take her away. Something small could become something big.

The best part of the day was when they read stories. All those words. All those things happening, seeming so real. It was all made up, she knew, but that was better, that somehow made it even more true to her.

During afternoon recess, an older boy, Oscar, told her, "I have hair down there if you want to see it."

She decided on the first day of class that she did not like Mrs. Stinson. She would have to wait a whole other year for a new teacher.

When she got home no one was there. The TV was on. But no one was there.

14

Nathaniel | Linda | Mavis & Marcus | Donald

THE PRODUCER PERSON asks Nathaniel if he'd like something for all the sweat waterfalling off his forehead, which is long and sloped and unfortunate, the subject of lifelong scrutiny. At the last minute, he'd switched from what he wore to work—his usual high-school teacher ensemble of a button-down shirt and pleated khakis—to a jacket and tie, more formal, more professorial, but he now regrets the decision. The sweating is only going to get worse.

"And maybe without the glasses?" she suggests, as she hands him a roll of paper towels.

It's all been a blur and so he didn't catch the producer person's name. She's rushed and jittery, engaged in numerous tasks at once—talking to him, talking on the phone, writing on a clipboard, ordering underlings around, sipping Lipton tea from a Styrofoam cup. Probably too old for him, a little Mrs. Robinson, but who is he to be picky? And, at thirty-seven, he's not so young anymore either.

Nathaniel dabs his forehead and face, does what he can to

temporarily stem the flow of sweat, then doesn't know what to do with the damp paper towel. The producer person brings over a trash can.

"Thanks," he says. "I think I'll keep the glasses. Can't see without them."

Yesterday he was contacted by MSNBC and asked to come in to a local TV station to be interviewed about Anabelle Vincent. Without really giving it much thought, he said yes—meaning that this will be his official coming out as the Smiling Skeptic. No one at work knows; his parents don't know; basically, nobody knows about his other life. And sure, plenty of people, including his mother, have wondered about the other kind of coming out. But he's not gay. He's definitely hetero. Hopelessly hetero.

"You'll hear Ben in your earpiece," says the producer person while she also opens a FedEx package. "You'll want to look straight in the camera when you're talking. Just pretend you're talking to a friend. We're almost ready. I'll count you down."

They've got Nathaniel seated in a chair, with a picture of the San Francisco skyline and Golden Gate Bridge behind him. For the past minute and a half, possibly longer, he's been debating whether or not to cross his legs. He tells himself not to blink too much, not to imagine how much larger his jowls will seem on TV. Ben is Ben Jenkins, host of *The Big Ben Hour,* a nightly cable news show focusing on the day's events, today being December 4. The segment before his is about another poison-gas attack, another shadowy doomsday-type cult trying to get their message out in time, before the end of the year. The sweat has already returned, though, all that dabbing for naught. But they're probably just filming his head and shoulders, so it really doesn't matter if he crosses his legs, right?

"And counting down. Three. Two. One. Go."

Nathaniel hears the growly, whiskey voice of Big Ben introduce him, and it's almost like the Smiling Skeptic is suddenly transformed into someone else. Big Ben mentions the website and the articles, says there's been a lot of media attention devoted to this Miracle Girl in Los Angeles, and they'd like a skeptic's point of view on the whole situation. And then Nathaniel—the Smiling Skeptic—is talking.

"These things can be explained," he says, quoting himself. "They can be rationally, scientifically explained."

He stares into the camera and perspires and talks about the girl. He talks about the increase in such occurrences as we near the end of the millennium, but also points out the historical precedents. This is nothing new. He talks about hoaxes, citing once again the Miracle of Saint-Marthe case in Montreal. He talks about other examples—apparitions appearing in the sky, like the supposed "sun miracles" reported in Fatima, Portugal, and the village of Medjugorje in the former Yugoslavia. (The latter was the subject of a Woodward-and-Bernstein-worthy take-down in the most recent issue of *The Smiling Skeptic*.) It's often just meteorological phenomena, such as a sun dog, which creates the effect of there being another sun. Or it's optical effects, such as the retinal distortion that happens when you stare at an intense light—like, duh, the sun—causing the sun to move or "dance." And when it comes to healing the sick—well, the body recovers on its own, doctors misdiagnose, psychosomatic illnesses are never real to begin with, and the power of suggestion is a powerful fucking thing indeed. (Except he doesn't say *fucking*.) No matter that religious leaders themselves are skeptical, do not authenticate or condone such events, and even warn against parishioners basing their faith on them.

Hopefully he's sounding coherent. He's a better writer than speaker. Off the cuff isn't his thing. Which is why he's memorized a speech if he's asked how he came to skepticism, how it can be traced back to the death of his beloved grandfather when he was twelve, when he was told that prayer could save the old man, that God listened if you knew how to speak to Him.

"Once people start believing something," Nathaniel says, "it's hard to get them to stop."

But Big Ben cuts him off before he can finish his thought.

"What would you say then, sir, to all these people, all these folks from all around the country, who are coming to Anabelle's house, lining up outside, waiting to get their turn, praying for her help and intervention?"

Nathaniel pauses. He doesn't mention that he'll be there soon, that his plane ticket to Los Angeles has been purchased, that in a few weeks he'll be up close and personal with the Miracle Girl and the questing pilgrims.

"That there's another way," he answers. "There's another way."

* * *

Then the pains started.

As Linda Santiago prepares for the half-hour physical therapy session with her celebrity client, the girl's mother, Karen, tells her how a visitor had been kneeling, praying, seeking intervention for a parent cursed with an incurable ailment and who had been given the usual six months, and then something happened. When she, the visitor, who was herself fighting multiple addictions and

currently involved in a WWF custody battle with her ex, finished
and opened her eyes and stood to leave the room, she paused to
take one last look at Anabelle and noted how she seemed, well,
different—agitated, uncomfortable. It was all in the eyes: pulsing
larger, intensifying, an alarming accumulation, screaming a silent
scream, like her blood was fire.

"The woman ran and got me," Karen explains. "She was frantic, saying she didn't touch her, didn't do anything, it wasn't her
fault. By the time I made it to the room Anabelle was crying."

"Crying?"

Linda massages and exercises Anabelle's white, wasted legs,
while Karen strokes her daughter's cheek, her hair. The bedroom
seems more cramped (chairs, boxes, balloons, flowers) than on
her last visit, the air conditioner and various machines working hard to keep the room cool, the girl alive. Today Linda had
to park three blocks away from the house, navigating the traffic and visitors and looky-loo neighbors. The guy who's usually
here, Bryce, isn't here.

"Yes, crying," says Karen. "And it went on for ten, fifteen
minutes. It was like she was in great pain. And she was trying to
tell us this. Then it just stopped. Then she was just like before.
And it happened again this morning. The tears gushing. And
when it happens her forehead feels like it's burning up, like she's
got a fever. There's this cluster of little red dots, too, really slight,
but right there above her brow, in the middle of her forehead.
Her eyes all bloodshot. Her face looking like she's been holding
her breath. I put a cold compress on her. Anytime I touched her,
though, it seemed to make it worse. I called her doctor and he
came over and couldn't find anything wrong and said to keep
an eye on it. The visitor from yesterday was saying how she's

Catholic and how there's something called a victim soul. How Anabelle's pain wasn't just her pain but the pain of others. She was taking on that pain. The pain of the world. Do you believe in that kind of thing?"

Linda repositions herself at the foot of the bed. Sometimes when she's working she stops and thinks how other people work with computers, build things, manage things; she, however, works with the body, with skin, with touch. Her hands regularly run over moles and freckles, wrinkles and cellulite, dry skin, oily skin, blemished skin. The girl's legs are like bird legs. Linda has to be careful. This is her fourth visit, and she's still trying to find a way to talk to the girl with her hands. Some of her clients take longer than others. But she'll get there. And today could be the day. This could be the breakthrough, when they connect, when they learn to speak the same unspoken language.

"I'm not sure what to believe in anymore."

"Are you religious, Linda?"

"Well, you'd think with a name like Santiago, right? But no, not anymore. I grew up as Catholic as they come, and like any good Catholic girl I wanted to be a nun. I read *57 Stories of Saints for Boys and Girls*. I slept on the floor and put rocks in my shoes to get closer to God. That was the idea. We used to go to school with ash on our foreheads and the kids in our neighborhood, the public school kids, would try to rub them off, calling us Jesus freaks. But that was a long time ago. Religion is one of those things that you lose over the years if you don't keep up with it. I started working. I got married. I had a kid. I got unmarried. I had another kid—well, you know how it is. You get busy. Life sneaks up on you and then years have gone by, in a flash. The world don't stop for no one."

"And there's something else, too," Karen adds. "Something that happened last night. I mean, something that I think happened."

"What?" Linda asks, switching to the left leg now, her hands working the skin and atrophied muscle, imagining the flow of positive energy from herself to Anabelle, emanating from her heart to her hands and then to the girl, infusing her with what was needed, Linda's own miracle cure of touch and simple human contact.

At such moments Linda realizes: She's doing what she's supposed to be doing. Work soothes, has a burning purpose. And there's great comfort in that, no matter what happens—or doesn't happen—in your life.

Karen asks, "Is it possible for her to move because of some kind of muscle spasm or something?"

"What do you mean move?"

"Well last night, I'm pretty sure, last night when I fell asleep her arms were by her side like usual. But when I woke up they were more spread out, like this."

And Karen demonstrates, spreads her arms open.

"Ah, you mean like *Jesús*."

"*Jesús?*"

"*Jesús*. Jesus. J.C. The big man. You know, like the crucifixion. Arms outstretched like so."

Karen stares at her daughter.

"I hadn't even thought of that."

"Someone will. I did. Another part of the story. Every little thing can mean something to somebody."

"I don't know, Linda. I could be wrong. Maybe I moved her last night and that's how she fell asleep. I don't trust my brain anymore."

"It could have been a spasm. Involuntary or something. The muscles realigning. It happens."

This doesn't seem to satisfy Karen, who moves away from the bed. She gazes out the bedroom window toward the front yard. Sighs as she sees all the people waiting to have their turn with Anabelle. Once Linda finishes, Karen will let them inside, and it will all begin again.

"A woman who came yesterday," Karen says, "she came because of her son, who was in a motorcycle accident and hasn't been able to walk on his own since. She came to see Anabelle and then when she got home, there was her son, waiting for her at the door, without the crutches he'd been using since the accident. Said he just had a feeling that he could walk again. A miracle, she said. She called this morning to tell me. You hear these things, Linda, and it's hard not to believe."

Karen taps the window with a finger, continues: "Someone suggested we put a larger window in here, so visitors could file by and view her. More people could make prayers and there might not be such a big waiting line and there might be more privacy. We could have designated hours for when people could walk by and see her. And do you know what else? Someone from Hollywood called the other day. There might be a movie. It just doesn't stop. There's always something else."

Linda fully extends each leg, slowly bends it back toward Anabelle's chest, twenty times, gentle, rhythmic repetitions, counting to herself, then releasing the leg, moving on to the arms and shoulders and neck, the face, the temples, the scalp, pressure and release, pressure and release, the simple truth of skin touching skin, navigating, understanding muscle, tissue, tendon, soul, and when she's done she covers Anabelle back up with her Hello

Kitty sheets, tucking her in and patting the girl's hand, as if to say: *There, dear, all done.*

"She likes it when you're here," Karen says. "I can tell."

"Good. I'm glad. I like being here, too," says Linda, as she begins to pack up her things.

"There's also been the suggestion of some kind of event."

"An event?"

"An event where a lot of people could come and see Anabelle at once, all at the same time. Bring her to the people who want to see her instead of the other way around, is the idea. Maybe at the high school football stadium."

"You need sleep. You need rest. You need a break."

"That's what Bryce says. That's what everyone says. But I don't think that's going to happen anytime soon."

Karen returns to the side of the bed, holds her daughter's arm, then says: "I just don't want to be alone."

Ah, thinks Linda. That's what it always comes down to: being alone, the fear of being alone, that constant, murmuring panic of having no one there next to you when you turn out the light.

"I'm going to let you borrow some of my relaxation tapes," Linda tells her. "Might seem like bullshit but they really work. They're in my backpack."

Linda has two other client visits this afternoon, so there's no time to linger, and she has to take a rain check on the offer of coffee, even though she can tell Karen wants some company, isn't ready to deal with all those people waiting outside.

By the time she's back on the 605, she's sitting in traffic (part of the job when you're an in-home physical therapist who lives in Los Angeles), and she knows she'll be late for her next appointment, way over in Long Beach. It's that time of day when she's driving directly into the sun. Sunglasses help, but she still has to squint as she drives, the cars and trucks crawling along, eventually passing an accident, two cars, minor damage, the far left lane blocked, and so she has to merge, and because people are generally assholes no one lets her in until she practically hits another car. How much of her life has been spent like this, braking, stopping, starting, on Southern California concrete? All that time spent dream-thinking, life-reliving. Because what else can you do? If she had done X. Said Y. Ignored Z. Mostly she ticked through the list of men that had appeared in her life, starting with her father, and including both those with major roles and those with walk-on parts, and somehow they all equally haunted her. Brake. Stop. Start. Traffic is traffic. Men are men. Because what else can you do?

She doesn't want to be alone either. You have your kids, sure, but kids are different. You can have kids and still feel alone. You need more. And her "more" these days was Victor. She knew things had gone as far as they could go; there had been no progress or forward momentum for months. But he was a body. He was a man. He made her laugh, too, sometimes. People said he looked a little like Erik Estrada.

And by the time the day is done and she finally makes it home, five client visits in all, a different city each time, back and forth between L.A. and Orange Counties, eating a late lunch (El Pollo Loco) in her car while driving yet again, she's exhausted; it's already dark, the lights in the apartment not on, just the familiar TV glow visible behind the mini blinds as she climbs the stairs to the second floor; and inside she finds the dishes from the morning still stacked in the sink; the kid's homework not done; her sons, David and Danny, holed up in their room; no dinner made,

no laundry done; the apartment in the same state as when she'd
left at seven o'clock that morning; and Victor sprawled on the
couch, like a teenager, waiting, wearing sweatpants, taking up
space. He'd been home all day. Her "more."

Linda stands there in the living room until he's forced to notice her, acknowledge her. It wasn't going to get any better. His
body still did not listen. Maybe she should give in and talk to
the girl. Make her prayer to Anabelle. Ask for the necessary
strength. Nothing else had worked so far. And look where that
had gotten her.

"Hey," says Victor. "What time is it? I think I fell asleep."

First there was Steve, who she'd made the mistake of mar-
rying, father of her first son: welder, drummer, cheater, liar, car
tinkerer, addict, charmer, lover of Tommy's burgers, distant,
unwilling to give. Then there was Antonio, who she'd had the
wisdom not to marry, father of her second son: carpenter, poker
player, movie quoter, buyer of Lotto tickets and imported beer,
unremarkable, plain, constant maker of promises he could not
keep, two kids of his own living back East somewhere, also distant, but willing (sometimes) to give, though usually giving the
wrong thing. And now Victor.

"It's late," she says. "It's very late."

How many times could you be wrong about love?

* * *

Just ask her husband: Mavis Morris isn't one for patience. So
there's no way in Hades she's going to wait in that line. She's a
neighbor after all. Has paid her dues. Has lived here in El Portal
for most of her life. Can remember when the neighborhood was
mostly white, then mostly black, then mostly Mexican. Now it's

sort of a combination of all the above, along with a scattering of Asians, Middle Easterners, Ukrainians, you name it. "Multi-cultural," she guesses, at least that's what they'd call it if they were doing some study or an Eyewitness News Special Report on Channel 7. But that makes it sound like a grand experiment when it's not. It's just people—people living together but separate, the usual suspicions and boundaries remaining intact.

"I'm going," Mavis announces, finally, emphatically, huffing away from her husband. "I don't care if it's crazy or what, doesn't matter, I'm going right up, walking across the street, marching up the driveway and ringing the doorbell, and I'm not waiting in line, Mar, I'm going right up to the door and say hi there, I'm your neighbor from across the street, Mavis Morris, pleased to meet you, we never met proper before, which I apologize, but you know how it is, and but we used to wave and such sometimes, every once in a while, we'd see each other and wave, from a distance—you remember that? —and but here I am now, saying hello, introducing myself, one neighbor to another, official, and I know there's a line, there's all these people waiting, but I was wondering, talking to my husband, Marcus, wondering if it's different for neighbors, like some kind of exception where you can go to the start of the line. I just figured maybe there was. It's Karen, right? We shop at the same stores, probably. Have the same mailman. You know, the guy who never smiles and wears the funny straw hat? I used to wave at you in the mornings sometimes. You remember that? Just neighbors being neighbors. Waving at you and your little girl when you were driving her somewhere, school I guess. It was school, right? Neighbors are different, is what I figured."

Marcus puts down his newspaper for the third time. It's a

significant gesture. He goes about it slowly, folds it into the four quadrants, then places the result calmly on the kitchen table. Then the final flourish: he removes his reading glasses and sets them on the table, too. There. Now he's ready.

"And if you do this," he begins, "like you say, going there and cutting in line. Say you do these things. And the mother, she takes you to the girl's room. She closes the door. Says you got your five minutes. Then what? Then what are you going to do? What, exactly, are you going to ask her for?"

Mavis had been walking over to the refrigerator. But that last line stops her. She turns and stares deep into Marcus's eyes. He can only hold her gaze for so long. It's always been this way.

"You *know*, Marcus. You know what I'm going to ask. What else?"

Marcus has no need for this, indignant about it all. But she—she's willing to try. Why not? What could it hurt? All those years ago, not long after they were first married, still flush from the newness and surprising intensity of their bond, when they lost one—a child. The baby was born early, dead: a tiny, blueish creature, all veins and goo, no bigger than a Kleenex box, re-sembling nothing Mavis had ever seen before nor would ever see again. And after, the doctors said that was most likely probably it. No children for Mavis. Too much damage to the wiring and circuitry of her traumatized uterus. Leaving a dusty ache inside them both.

"This could be our last chance," she says. "I'm going to be forty soon, and once a woman hits forty all those birth defects and three-headed babies are way more likely."

"That little girl, across the street, in a coma, possessed by the Holy Spirit or whatever, she—she's our last chance?" he asks, searching his wife's face to see if she really means it. She does.

"It's something, Marcus. We got nothing else."

Neither speaks for a while. Mavis continues on to the refrigerator, retrieving from the top a plate of cookies she'd baked yesterday (now he understands why he hadn't been able to have any). Marcus then puts his glasses back on and returns to his paper, resuming an article about the rape and murder of a fourteen-year-old girl down in Fullerton.

"Wish me luck at least," says Mavis.

Marcus almost goes through the whole newspaper-and-glasses routine again. But he doesn't. He just says, "Good luck, Mav. I hope you don't have to wait. Let me know if you see Geraldo or somebody over there."

"It might help if you came, too. Better odds. Two's always better than one."

His wife's voice is hopeful, urgent. It's the same voice that said "yes" when he asked her to marry him. It's the voice that said, "It's OK, we'll figure it out" when he fell and fucked up his back and couldn't work anymore. And it's the voice he wants to hear when he closes his eyes for the last time: *Dear? Dear? I'm not going anywhere. I'm still here. Dear?*

Marcus stops his reading again. He's older than her, by almost six years, maybe not a huge difference, but still. The years accumulating harder on him. He complained about being an old man even when he was a young man.

"All right," he says, standing up. "Give me those god-damned cookies. Let's go."

* * *

Ever since Donald Westerfield took his place in the long, theme-park-worthy line, the woman standing in front of him has not stopped talking. That was approximately over an hour ago, maybe longer; checking his watch only makes it worse. And why is he here? He's here because of his wife, because he doesn't know what else to do at this point, the days accelerating away from him. He can't let Patricia down. He wants this to be like anything else: if you do something the right way, if you follow the rules and precedents and prepare yourself properly, then you'll succeed. That's always been his credo, what he taught his children, what gave him grounding, meaning. But after the Diagnosis (he internally capitalizes the *D* whenever he thinks of the word) that foundation has seismically shifted. And he now knows more about Cassie Solinski's life and its circular script of woe and disappointment than he knows about most of his friends and former coworkers and some family members even.

To begin: she has two academically challenged ADD kids and two worthless ex-husbands (one kid with each) and works in sales (her supervisor a total perv) as a Transaction Processing Specialist (he didn't ask) and lives in Brea near the freeway, a rented house that's about to collapse and there's probably toxic stuff everywhere and that lead paint thing they're always talking about, too. It's not so bad, she guesses, she tells him, there's worse, it's life, it's how it is, you just get used to it, you know? (No, he did not.) Plus there are more important, more pressing matters. Like: she thinks she might have one of those syndrome deals, the one where you don't feel like doing anything, you're like total blah, and her cousin who's a nutritionist's assistant said it sounded like maybe it was some sort of chemical imbalance, which is probably hereditary, which means you're screwed, genes and biology and whatnot, that's your destiny and what can you do about that, you know?

He nods a nod of noncommittal acknowledgment, doing his

small part to maintain the social contract. But Donald doesn't want to hear about someone else's troubles, he's got enough of his own, he has no space for people like Cassie Solinski who so readily share themselves with the world, who believe it's their constitutional right to publicly chronicle the days of their lives. He's always been the opposite: privacy, withholding certain information, the covert mentality of a Cold War spy. If nothing is secret anymore, then can anything be of value? He wonders. Maybe it's his age. That's the way he'd been brought up. Holding it in instead of letting it out. That was the norm back then. (His father never talked about "feelings"; his mother, he found out only after her death, had been married once before, to a man who died of tuberculosis when she still lived in Minnesota—an episode she had chosen to keep private from her children.) Now it's all about sharing and confessing and broadcasting your own personal narrative. You want an audience to know about your pain, as if that somehow makes it more real, more true. And who's to say, Donald concedes. Maybe it does.

And Cassie Solinski has a lot she wants to share. So she monologues her way through a variety of other topics, from Irritable Bowel Syndrome to the latest blockbuster movies to the inadequacies of our public school system. The line advances at a staggeringly slow DMV pace: he estimates it will be at least another hour or two of shuffling and waiting and periodically interjecting a "Really" or "I didn't know that" to appease Cassie, which is short for Cassidy. Donald notes there are no visible tattoos, but he's thinking she has them, somewhere, hidden—on her back, her ankle, shoulder, somewhere. If one of his kids had come home with a tattoo, what would he have done? Anything he sees or experiences in life, his thoughts eventually boomerang back to how it relates or could relate to his family. Once a parent, always a parent. He can't help himself. Early December now, and the sun microwaving above him and the crowd—it has never before looked like such a powerful, intimidating force, anchored up there in the sky.

Yes, he's here for his wife, he reminds himself. It's why he drove all the way from Laguna Beach on this most foolish of fool's errands that he's embarrassed and still not too sure about. Because of his wife. His loving-wonderful-suffering-yet-flawed-like-all-of-us wife, who, as he waits his turn, is in the hospital, in Intensive Care after last week's sudden fall in the backyard, the frantic surgery to remove one of her lungs, the subsequent complications, now breathing with the assistance of machines, no longer really alive. Take that back: her eyes are still alive. That's it, though. And that's the hardest part, too, witnessing the watery whispers of memory pooling futilely between blinks, because he can see her in there, in her eyes; in fact he can see their entire history, their entire lives contained within those two muted orbs.

What is left for her? Time has stopped. There is no time. Or rather it is all time. Her days are nothing but stabbing pinpricks of the clock ticking away, carrying her farther away from who she was, is. There is nothing he can do. So he sits in a chair next to her bed, getting up whenever a nurse or doctor hurries in and out, and he talks to her (and to himself, a recent development he's uneasy about, fretting that the first wave of Alzheimer's troops has been deployed against him). He reads to her, gives her updates on family members (weddings they'll have to miss, births that only remind him of the nearing completion of their own deathward arcs) and tells her about the world. The news is usually not good, despite his filtering out the more violent and macabre tales: the babies left in dumpsters, the school shootings, the incarcerated rappers. The doctors said they couldn't say for sure whether she is cognizant and aware or completely vacuous, her brain nothing but a TV channel tuned to snow. Like the little girl, Donald thinks. Same worthless diagnosis from the magicians of modern medicine. Fifty-fifty chance either way, they said.

"I hear that sometimes there's a light that shines right out of her eyes, right at you," says Cassie Solinski.

"Really," he responds.

He tries not to make too harsh a judgment about his fellow pilgrims (he is, after all, one of them, standing here, doing things like calling up the offices of the Archdiocese of Los Angeles, talking to priests, investigating alternative cancer treatments in Germany and Mexico), but what he finds himself coming back to is this: they are mostly poor, or at least poor-looking, or poor-seeming, in his admittedly privileged estimation. He doesn't know if it's just the neighborhood or the nature of the event. Regardless, this is not a part of the greater metropolitan Los Angeles area he's been to before. So he turned to his trusty Thomas Guide map. Taking a while before he zeroed in on the exact location, thumbing through corresponding numbers and letters and multicolored grids. But even then he had some difficulty. Some of the streets here did not have signs. Either they'd been taken down by roving vandals or no one even bothered to put them up in the first place. It struck him as that kind of place. He got lost.

After circling for an hour he stopped at a gas station, Super Gas N More, not a brand name he's familiar with, no Shells or Chevrons in sight, and asked the slack-eyed young man behind the counter (was he an employee or had he tied up the real clerk and disposed of him in back?) if he knew where Shaker Street was, very aware of his Lexus of recent vintage idling outside. *Oh, the girl,* said the clerk. *You want to see the little girl, the little Miracle Girl, sí?* Sí. Then the clerk (no uniform or name tag, fostering further suspicion) imparted a flurry of difficult-to-decipher directions: right here, left there, second stop sign, past the railroad tracks and the closed-down MacFrugals, and Donald got lost again, but still he drove, noting the high concentration of liquor stores and cigarette outlets, the billboards for movies from two, three years back. He pulled over and queried a woman walking on the sidewalk. She did not seem to speak English. Then he drove some more, giving himself over to random turns and going on instinct, triple-checking to make sure the windows were fully up and the door locks locked, then coming upon a block with a heavy concentration of parked cars and seeing the people congregating outside, just like on television, lined up in front of a small one-story house like a matinee movie crowd. Budding entrepreneurs were selling water, soda, oranges cut into fourths, Popsicles. All at highly inflated prices. Everything went fast.

When he turns his attention back to Cassie Solinski, she's lamenting the heat, but then she pauses to watch a man and woman walk past them, bypassing the line and heading right to the front door of the house, the woman carrying a tray of some kind, the man walking with a slight limp, nervously scanning the crowd, hands in pockets, coughing into his fist.

"Who's she, gets to go right in like that?" says Cassie, who doesn't wait for an answer and moves on to a discussion of her sister's chronic skin problems.

Donald again tunes her out—as much as he can tune her out without manifestly appearing to do so, meaning that he continues to make the appropriately timed nods and attendant facial gestures. He hasn't been out of the hospital in days, desperately needs a haircut, has given up on shaving regularly for the first time in his life. Behind him a woman chats away on a cell phone, informing the person on the other end where she was and what she was doing and how her mother has incurable blood cancer and how she'd never heard of that kind of cancer before—*blood? blood cancer? what the hell?*—but now she's pretty much a de facto expert and no it did not look good, multiple myeloma, what happens is that the cancer erodes the bones—*can you believe it? the bones?*—and half of those who get it are dead within five years, *I'll call you after, I'm on my cell, waiting in line, this is costing me a fortune, bye.*

It wasn't all that long ago that he'd retired. So many years spent on his career, away from his wife and children, the trips for work, the conventions and working vacations, the strategic cocktail parties and hellish commute to Century City, Patricia always making sure he had his Saturday golf, his Tuesday night tennis. Retirement would make up for all that. That would be her time, Patricia's time, when he was finally fully available. There's a picture he can't get out of his mind from the Laguna Beach fires of 1993: Patricia grabbing a hose, defiant, watering down their roof, refusing to leave their house until the very last minute, firefighters with bullhorns practically threatening to drag her away if that's what it took. That time they got lucky. Their house was spared. Life went on as before. If you do something the right way, then you'll succeed. The day before she'd fallen, Patricia had told him, "It's stupid. I still don't think I'm going to die. I still don't think it's possible. How can I not exist? How can I not be? How can there be one of us and not the other?"

Two elderly women exit the house. The crowd instinctively quiets. A wave of questions ensues. Are the women transformed? Did they get what they'd hoped for? Which one is in need of help—the taller one or the shorter one with the stern brow and glittering earrings, or both? Or are they here for someone else, a grandson with leukemia, a childhood friend almost completely blind, in the final stages of macular degeneration? What was the girl like? Could you tell just by looking at her? But these two ladies, dressed similarly, in stretch slacks and floral print blouses, are not saying: they stare at the ground before them as they solemnly make their way past the hushed onlookers, arm in arm, European style, each doing her best to ease the burden of the other. There is, however, this: they look like something has transpired, spent and worn out, like a great deal of energy has been exerted since they entered the house. Or was it just the heat, the long drive from Fresno or Bakersfield or wherever? Who could say really? No one asks them anything, though. The reverence lasts a while, longer than seems necessary. The crowd soaks up every last drop, it is their primary sustenance at this point, the day lurching onward, and the conversations do not fully resume until the women are far down the sidewalk, trying to remember where they'd parked their car. The line moves forward. A little. A young woman in a wheelchair is next. They have to lift her out of the chair to get her through the front door.

Why didn't he bring a hat? He wipes his forehead with his sleeve and gazes up at the sun, the sky: clogged with eyesore haze, congested with apocalyptic gunk. That's what you get inland. No saving ocean breezes here. Mountains veiled behind, vague shapes that have been there for millions of years. They've been saying L.A. is no longer the worst, that Houston is the worst, and that the air quality has been improving. That is until this past summer, when there was a triumphant return of the smog. Only they don't call it smog anymore, because they're not sure if it's technically smog or something else. So they're calling it Abnormal Atmospheric Disruption, or AAD. Might be related to global warming, might be related to El Niño or La Niña, might be an entirely new pattern. They just don't know. But ever since the summer and well into the fall and now the approaching winter (if you believed there were seasons in L.A.), there have been more frequent reports of people having trouble breathing, passing out on the sidewalk, claiming disorientation and delirium. Donald reminds himself not to inhale too deeply. Take it slow. Who knows what's out there.

Past midday now, the thick of it, and it's certifiably sweltering. It's going to take much longer than he thought. His son and daughter-in-law, currently staying with Patricia, will be wondering where he is. Cassie Solinski is off on another tangent—unprovoked, of course. Vaginal polyps, radiation, date rape drugs. So much that's wrong with the world, how truly fragile everything is if you only take the time to fully realize. Closing his eyes helps: her voice seems farther away, like a distant radio. After all, he can't save Cassie, he can't save her kids or any other hapless participant in her messy life. Heck, he can't even save his Patricia. He can't save anyone. Which—and finally he's getting back to this—is why he's here. And he's come this far. It's about time to take the leap. He can't leave and turn back now.

Then up at the front of the line, there—someone collapses. Standing, then down in a broken heap. Everyone sees but it takes a while for the sight to register; there's a delayed reaction, a spell of time when those waiting in line mentally check off the possibilities (the heat? the smog? the girl? millennium madness?), before a woman snaps them out of their collective trance and yells, "Call 9-1-1. Somebody. Call 9-1-1. We got ourselves a situation here."

15

| Karen |

THEY BRING THE woman inside, put her on the couch in the living room, where her recently arrived across-the-street neighbors (their first names already having slipped her mind) have been sitting, waiting their turn. The woman is unconscious, strands of damp, dark hair pasted to her face, her body limp and uncooperative, carried by a younger man and an older man.

"What happened?" Karen asks.

"We don't know," the younger man answers. "She was standing in line, like the rest of us, just standing there, and then all of the sudden she collapsed, she's on the ground, down for the count. Me and—"

"Donald," exhales the older man, almost out of breath.

"Me and Donald helped pick her up and brought her in. Figured it would be a good idea to get out of the sun. Ambulance is on its way."

Karen rushes to the bathroom and wets a towel, places it on the woman's forehead, which is beaded with trails of perspiration. The woman doesn't move. She is ghost-white pale. You can see her bra straps. Her shirt untucked and askew, revealing a series of startling stomach folds. Her bra is beige. Karen wants to pull down the woman's shirt for her, cover her up, something, with all these people looking, but she refrains.

"Probably the heat," says the older man, Donald, his face and bald head patched with red and sweat. "It's brutal out there."

The woman's mouth remains open. Karen isn't sure if she's breathing or not. There's nothing they can do now except wait for the ambulance. She stares at all the people in her house.

What's next? Karen wonders. What could possibly happen next?

THAT MORNING, NOT long after getting off the phone with her mother (she'd been calling more frequently, asking about all the media coverage and hinting at the possibility of a visit), Bryce had tried to kiss her. It was an awkward grope of the mouth that drew part cheek, part lip, part nose—and she'd turned away just as she saw it coming, a belated reaction, Bryce's face hovering close and smelling of aftershave and guy, but it was too late, it was happening, a two-second incident that no doubt would change everything between them. They'd been sitting on the backyard porch, which overlooked a large patch of dirt that was supposed to be a lawn—and that, for the most part, was the extent of the backyard. She was wearing shorts and flip-flops, the cool, early morning air like a balm on her toes, a welcome respite from the heat that would soon dominate the day. Her legs almost touching Bryce's legs (the porch was narrow, not much of a porch really). He'd been growing his hair out and not shaving regularly. From there in the backyard, the San Gabriels loomed in the distance. You could also see other yards, other houses leading toward the mountains. The patio concrete had tiny tributaries of cracks all over, a lousy job done long before they'd moved in, which they'd never fixed. She'd been staring at the cracks and thinking about John, wondering how often he thought about her, if he was awake yet, wherever he was. And then Bryce leaned in.

"Oh god. I'm sorry. Shit, I'm sorry."

Why, she thought later, after breakfast, and after a BBC reporter interviewed her and also informed her that some of the neighbors were considering legal action because of all the disruption her daughter was causing—why did the kiss initially take her by surprise? It shouldn't have. The constant helping, the taking care of things, the scheduling, the organizing; the shoulder massages. How could she not notice? But really, Bryce could have walked into her bedroom naked and she'd probably say, "Hey Bryce. What time is that guy from the *Chicago Sun-Times* coming tomorrow?" She felt so removed from her body that such possibilities didn't even enter her head. Or heart. Or tingly lady parts. Another place, another time: would she have said yes? Would she have turned to him instead of away?

"It's OK," she said.

"That was dumb. Man. That was messed up. What was I thinking? I'm so sorry."

"Really, Bryce. It's OK."

"Do you want me to leave? Do you want me out?"

Bryce's neediness: she was not used to seeing this in a man. Sometimes it was endearing, sometimes she wanted to tell him to buck up, to act like, well, a man. And plus he was so big, so burly, yet so reserved and breakable, which makes it all the more odd to her. John had longer hair, John didn't shave regularly.

"No I don't want you out. Of course I don't want you out. And it's not like if things were different or . . . But my life right now is so . . . You of all people know that . . . there's just no place even if I wanted, even if I had the, you know, energy. Which I don't, I so don't . . . and, I'm married . . . Bryce, I'm sorry, too. But I can't. I just can't."

Bryce started moving toward her, then stopped himself.

"I understand," he said. "I completely understand. It's just that I get caught up sometimes. I start thinking things in my head, start convincing myself that things are one way when they're actually another way. I convince myself. I'm sorry."

"Please stop saying you're sorry."

"OK. I do that, I know. Apologize too much."

Sounds of the couple next door fighting, something about coupons having expired. The sky above was lightening, turning bluish-gray, the clouds looking flawlessly white and sculpted. The other day someone said an angel had appeared in the cloud formations above the house. That night Bryce had showed her an article about it on the Internet. People believed and believed. It wasn't going to stop.

"Let's go back inside," Karen said.

"I fucked up, didn't I?"

"You didn't fuck up."

AND THIS, TOO: Yesterday they arrested someone in Port Angeles, Washington, trying to cross the border from Canada. Customs officials found explosives and timing devices in his car. Said it all could have caused an explosion forty times greater than your average car bomb. The guy's plan—a guy from Algeria—was to detonate everything at LAX on New Year's Eve. And

there was, of course, the weather, the earthquakes, the computers that would self-destruct. Every day another story, more evidence of some kind of reckoning ahead. Things were happening,
it seemed, an intricate converging had been set in motion, and
Karen was having a hard time telling if Anabelle was part of that
or outside of it all. Or maybe both.

THE PARAMEDIC'S CONCLUSION: heat exhaustion. Just as
they all suspected. The smelling salts do the trick and the woman
snaps awake and sits up on the couch. She immediately wants
to know if they would save her place in line. She'll be back as
soon as possible. This was no big deal. It wouldn't take long.
She didn't even have health insurance. She'd be in and out in no
time. I need to see the girl. Please. It's about my son. He has this
condition. This thing the doctors can't figure out. They've seen
specialist after specialist and the bills have been staggering. He's
always tired, distracted. He has no energy. So would you mind
terribly while I'm gone to just hold my . . .

"Relax, ma'am," the paramedic instructs. "We need to get
you hydrated. I'm going to start this IV and you'll feel much
better. It's best if you don't talk."

Another paramedic, whom Karen recognizes from the earthquake visit, helps lift the woman into the gurney, and they
roughly wheel her outside. Karen follows them out the front
door and then watches them push her down the driveway and
deposit her in the double-parked ambulance, the now-silent
crowd outside watching, too, some doing that sign of the cross
thing. There must be forty, fifty people out there, waiting still.
With foldable beach chairs. Umbrellas. Blankets. Coolers. In it
for the long haul. But Karen decides they need to leave. Now.

"Everyone," she begins. "Everyone, hello. Can I please have your attention please?"

Heads turn. The crowd collectively surges toward her, gathering around her in a haphazard semicircle, causing Karen to take a step back. She tells herself to speak up. She's never given a speech before, nothing like this. She doesn't like crowds or speeches or having to deny people what they want.

"I think that's going to be it for today. There's been a lot of excitement and Anabelle needs her rest. I know you've been waiting and some of you have come a long way, and I'm sorry about that, but we need some—I think we need a little break here. These past few months have been amazing but it's been exhausting. Our lives are so different now. Everything is so different now. I'm very sorry. I hope you understand. You can come back tomorrow, if you'd like. Tomorrow is fine. But today we need some rest. Thank you."

Back inside the house, her neighbor from across the street (Mavis, she now remembers) extends an arm and walks her over to the same couch where the heat-exhausted woman had been. "Sit, dear," Mavis says. "You look like you're about ready to collapse yourself. You look like you could use a cookie."

Someone else brings her water. She drinks. She eats the cookie. Chocolate chip. Fresh. Delicious.

"Thank you," says Karen.

"Do you want us to go, too?" the older man, Donald, asks.

"No. Please don't. Why don't you each have a visit with Anabelle. You've all been waiting and so helpful and you're here. So that's fine. I hated to do that, to tell everyone to go. But I had to."

Mavis nods, and she and her husband go first, Karen insisting on showing them to the room, and when she comes back, the other visitors—the older man, the younger man, and a woman with a ponytail and hippieish tie-dye dress—are sitting and eating cookies. Karen apologizes for the state of the house, tells them she wishes she had more food to offer them. They shush her, say don't even think about it considering all that you do, who has the time when there is . . . And here they gesture with hands, with tilts of the head, in the direction of Anabelle's room.

The younger man—Ted from Tacoma, wearing a button with Anabelle's picture on it—explains that he's on vacation with his family and when he heard about Anabelle before their trip he told his wife that they'd be in Southern California anyway and he would have to come, to see for himself, he had to, it was one of those things you just knew deep in your bones, and his wife and kids went to Disneyland and here he is and sure there was a little familial tension but looking back now he wouldn't have it any other way. Today has been the most amazing experience, he's met the most amazing people and heard the most amazing stories. This is the other Magic Kingdom, he concludes.

The older man, who's quieter than the rest and more formally attired, nervously avoiding eye contact, not as excited, presses the sunburn on his arm, it goes from red to white and back to red again, repeating this several times, and it's as if he's enamored by this simple transformation of the human body: red-white-red. The hippie ponytail woman comments on how someone could have used a little sunblock today. And he, the older man, looks caught, his face shading even redder, says yes, he wishes he'd had the wherewithal (a direct quote: "wherewithal") to remember a hat. He burns easily. Always has. Like his mother and brothers, a hereditary vulnerability; they'd all be lobsters in the summers.

This was Pasadena, growing up, before it was developed like today and you could see Mount Wilson all the time and there was one postman for the entire town and believe it or not Pasadena used to be a place where people moved because of the clean air. His skin would burn then peel then burn again. He had to be careful. His wife is always telling him—and then he pauses, and it's hard to tell if he's pausing because he realizes he's kind of rambling and folks are beginning to wonder where this is going, or if—but no, he continues, corrects himself, switches to the past tense, *was*. His wife *was* always telling him. So: that was the reason for stopping. Then he stops completely. Sucking breaths. Saying the words is too much. You can tell that this is a man who does not cry often, if ever, let alone in front of people he doesn't know, and who still adheres to the tears-equal-weakness philosophy, and who quickly wipes them away before they have a chance to trail down his proud, bank-president cheeks. Ted from Tacoma places a priestly hand on the man's shoulder, keeps it there. I'm all right, Donald assures. I just need a second here, sorry.

The living room is quiet, acknowledging the moment. Karen has witnessed so many similar moments: of people, complete strangers, sharing their grief, their hope. The tray of cookies gets passed around again.

The hippie ponytail woman asks if it's true that sometimes you can feel an immediate jolt when you touch her, the energy and power is that strong.

LATER THAT EVENING, after she has sponge-bathed and prepped Anabelle for the night ahead, Karen calls Bryce.

"Again, Karen, I'm really really sorry about today."

"It's OK, Bryce. And I'm not even calling about that. You said you knew someone who worked at the high school who might be able to help us get permission to use the football stadium. For the thing we were talking about, the event."

"I have a friend who's a teacher there and also an assistant coach on the football team. He could maybe help."

"Let's do it. I want to do it. December 30. It happens to be the one-year anniversary of the accident. We'll have a big gathering and people can come and make their prayers and do what they need to do and that will be it."

"What do you mean, that will be it?"

"It will be a big send-off. After that, I'm done. We're done. Anabelle and I are done."

"Done?"

"We're going back to being a mother and daughter again, a family. We're done."

NEXT SHE TURNS her attention to the six diehards in the front yard, former strangers who are now chatting away like old college roommates who haven't seen each other in years, who have either ignored her earlier request that everyone leave or they showed up after the incident. They pass around photos from their wallets and purses, explain genealogies and the diseases afflicting their loved ones. (The overnighters will come later, around midnight, carrying sleeping bags and Igloos and radios, establishing their space and trading stories of their respective journeys here, from near or far.) Then she does what she's taken to doing lately: inviting the last few visitors in for snacks and drinks. Surprised, delighted, they follow her into the holy house where it all began, past the daily overflow of flowers and balloons and stuffed animals (monkeys, Anabelle's well-publicized favorite, heavily represented), and past the gauntlet of hallway photographs (and are they wondering about the man with the mustache, is that perhaps the mysterious father we never hear anything about?), and into the kitchen. Tonight there's not much to choose from, only some Cool Ranch Doritos and the last remnants of a Whitman's Sampler. But the people are grateful. They feel blessed, she can tell, being shown such generosity in an age of ignoring. And then they turn, with rapt faces, in the direction of Anabelle's room.

16

| John |

THIS, APPARENTLY, IS as close as he's going to get; he can't make it any farther on Shaker Street because of the traffic. So instead he pulls over and parks blocks away, resorts to sunglasses and a baseball cap as a half-assed disguise, sticks to the other side of the street as he approaches the house, noting the buildup of trash in the gutters, the proliferation of weeds and wheel-less cars, the skeletal trees that seem to have given up. Crossing street corners (Slauson, Mills, Oak), zombie-lurching his way down the block, ignoring the growing gnawing in his stomach—the last time he'd eaten anything was back in Barstow, a 99-cent cheeseburger at McDonald's, inhaled while driving, not wanting to stop for longer than was necessary, fighting off sleep for the last fifty miles before finally popping the last two Mira-Cures. Christmas lights, cheap-looking Santas and Frostys and candy canes, 'tis the season, he'd almost forgotten. There's wind, the warm Santa Anas rendering everything dry and vulnerable. The sun daggering down. Now in front of a house across the street from his, skulking like a teenager, hands in pockets, slouching guiltily, it's just like he saw on TV: the people lined up, the tents and chairs, the crowded sidewalk, the blazing heat and buzzing activity. Some of them are holding signs (Bible quotes, his daughter's name, various diseases and medical conditions, Y2K predictions); others are taking pictures and holding video cameras, filming. Standing there, he witnesses at least three hugs and one high five. Like a football tailgate party, he thinks. A few cops patrol by on foot, scanning the crowd, talking into their shoulders. Passing them is a guy with a Styrofoam cooler strapped around his neck, selling tamales and oranges and bottled water. John doesn't see Karen anywhere.

OK then.

He's right across the street.

He's back.

He's home.

He's here.

The person who lives in the house he's loitering in front of comes out to check the mail. John recognizes the man. He has a limp and sometimes uses a cane to walk. But he's not super old. Middle-aged, kind of defeated. He'd always seemed a little angry, this guy, barrel-chested, collared short-sleeve shirts and slacks (always slacks), darting in and out of his house along with his wife, who was a little more friendly and would even wave now and then. John had never caught either of their names.

"You here for the circus?" his former neighbor asks, not looking at him, sifting through a stack of letters and junk mail with the skepticism of a judge dismissing evidence.

"Yeah, I guess so," says John.

"The other day they had to call an ambulance. A woman

passed out. Heat exhaustion. You hear the latest? The one about the heat causing people to forget their names, who they're married to, their Social Security numbers, who the president is. I was reading about it this morning. Solar Inflicted Temporary Retrograde Amnesia, they're calling it. SITRA for short. The heat makes you dumb, that's all. Now it's a thing. But of course people were saying she, this woman who passed out, she got so caught up with the holy spirit or whatever, and that's why she passed out. Every day it's something new. People walking all over my yard, leaving their crap all over the place. Takes my wife and me about a half hour to get out of here just to go to the store or bank. The mail doesn't come until the end of the day now. Mailman can't get through. I'm a subscriber of periodicals. Now I got to wait."

John doesn't know what to say. The neighbor shuts the mailbox.

"Didn't you use to live around here? You look familiar."

John yanks down the brim of his cap. And was he not wearing sunglasses, too?

"It was a long time ago," says John.

"How long's a long time?"

"Seven months, actually. It's only been seven months."

"Well," says the neighbor. "A lot can happen in seven months, friend. Just look at all this."

ALL THE WAY back, on the drive from Vegas to L.A., he played the "if only" game. *If only, if only:* those two stabbing words, how they collapse the chest and crowd the heart.

If only he'd been taller, smarter.

If only he'd applied himself in high school instead of dicking around.

If only he'd had the ability to recognize what was important, what mattered, and what, in the grand scheme of things, did not.

If only he'd stuck with learning to play the bass guitar.

If only he'd taken a different street, missed a light, sped up instead slowed down, slowed down instead of sped up, picked a different time or a different day to run the errand—an errand that didn't mean shit, that was shit, that was nothing and yet everything. If only he'd been paying more attention to the traffic and other cars, reading minds and anticipating what was about to happen.

If only he'd gotten up more at night to take care of Anabelle when she was a baby and crying, crying, crying, like she was broken and could not be fixed.

If only he'd been more patient, more understanding, with his daughter. Then maybe the dynamic that developed between them (argumentative, combative) wouldn't have grown and grown and grown until he was the type of parent he thought he'd never be: angry, exasperated, impatient, distant (he had morphed into his own father, which he'd sworn would never happen). You never know what kind of parent you'll be until you become one.

If only he was a different man, a better man.

That whole time in Vegas (well, Henderson), not once had he gone to the Strip, not once had he visited a casino or seen a show or gone bat-shit crazy or done any of the things you're supposed to do in Vegas, not once had he put a coin in a slot machine and pulled a lever and stood back and waited for a miracle. It seemed like yet another failure.

If only he'd said certain things to Karen, made her feel better instead of shittier. The right words at the right time could save you. They could save your wife and daughter, too.

If only he'd had the strength to stay. Then he wouldn't be in this fucking mess. He wouldn't be doing what he's doing.

If only he believed in something. And wasn't always dangling like this, making it up as he went, merely winging it instead of actually living his life. You reach that point. Why did thirty-one feel so old and far gone?

If only, if only: it could go on like that for hours, Monday-morning quarterbacking his way through his past.

It was never pretty.

HE DOESN'T GO in that day. He doesn't go in the next day, either. Instead he becomes an inept stalker. Driving. Parking. Passing the house. Relying on the hat-and-sunglasses disguise. When he's not stalking, he drives around, spends afternoons at the Wash N Go, subsists on vending machine food, sleeps in his car in the T.J.Maxx parking lot. He doesn't call anyone. The people's faces, the people he sees coming outside after having been inside the house, praying or whatever to his daughter: they look transformed, like they are now something else entirely.

WAS IT ALL true? What did it mean? Would his daughter really be different? Would his wife be different? Will she say no? Did she still love him? How much time is too much time—too much time to ever forgive? These are the questions he asks himself over and over.

"I KNOW IT'S the holidays and getting to Christmas, I know the timing is bad. Horrible, actually. Fucking horrible. But when is it ever good for something like this? But I had to, had to. I had to break free while I could still break free."

John is sitting in one of Wash N Go's red plastic chairs,

awkwardly contoured for a species other than human, meaning he has to readjust his back or stand up every five minutes
or so to avoid sharp pains shooting through his neck and spine.
For the past fifteen minutes he's been contemplating a load of
clothes tumbling away in a dryer, imagining what if they were
his clothes, if he was the person they belonged to, if he was the
one who would eventually pick them up and then leave and then
resume his already-in-progress life. The woman talks on her cell
phone from the other side of the Laundromat, over by the tables
for folding clothes. She doesn't even try to lower her voice. All
of Wash N Go can hear. Except it's just John and her, no other
customers on this Tuesday (is it Tuesday?) afternoon. So why
bother with being discreet?

"He doesn't know yet," the woman continues in a calm,
matter-of-fact voice, holding up a pair of jeans for inspection
before commencing to fold them. "He doesn't know what's coming when he gets home."

The dryer stops. No one comes to retrieve the clothes. The
woman finishes her phone call and laundry, and leaves. Then it's
just John. He goes to his car to check if there's any change in the
ashtray. There isn't. The Corolla looks like it could disintegrate
into a heap of dust and metal at any second. It smells like sweat
and French fries and motor oil. Back inside Wash N Go he stands
in front of the vending machine. It should be a verb: "to vend."
He would have gone with C7: Ruffles, sour cream and onion
flavored.

Maybe she has a good reason to leave. Maybe it's totally and
completely valid.

• • •

THE NEXT TIME he doesn't put on the cap or the sunglasses. He has to park even farther away now. That's because it's been announced that after the high school football stadium event on December 30 they will no longer be letting people into the house to see Anabelle. So there's a mad rush, a final surge of visitors seeking help and salvation. They want to get in while they can. He read in the paper that the wait is now up to six hours. More and more people camping out and spending the night in his front yard.

There's a camera crew, again—today there are actually multiple camera crews and vans and reporters roaming around, wielding microphones. The tamale guy is doing a brisk business.

One of the reporters, male, with brown surfer hair and an abundantly tanned face, approaches him and inquires if he's willing to be interviewed. About the girl. About the last-minute hoopla. About why he's here and what he's come to ask for. He declines. The reporter moves on to the next person and the person says yes, sure, and launches into tales of a sister with diabetes, an abusive childhood, a friend whose two sons may or may not have autism.

Then John gets in line and waits his turn.

17

| Anabelle |

SHE DIDN'T WANT a birthday party. She would be seven, and then the next year she would be eight, and nine after that, and if she had a birthday party when she turned seven, which was soon, there would be people and presents and sounds and voices and eyes and adults and cake and candles and bodies and people. The time would be *drip-drip-drip*. The light from outside filling the house and making her sick. She would want to go outside and wait in the car. Lock herself in there. Once in the car, she would sit for a while and then open the glove compartment. She would look at maps. She would find things like melted crayons and paper clips and straws. The maps would be hard to fold and get back to the way they were before. Why did they call it a glove compartment? Her mother would come outside. Knock on the window. *Are you sure? Honey? Sweetie?* The glass between them, separating them. You didn't put gloves in there, after all. Her father would try, too. *We're about to do the cake. You don't want to miss the cake, do you?* The window would be cracked, just enough to allow in some air. She'd breathe. Sit. Stare. *Drip-drip-drip*. She didn't want a birthday party.

They'd talk about it, the birthday party. Over time, again and again. The day itself getting closer and closer. She'd say no every time.

"But isn't there anyone you'd like to invite?"

No.

"What about Danielle from school?"

No.

"What about Aunt Tammy and Dom? What if it was just them, and here, here at the house?"

Fine. But no singing. A cake but no singing.

"It's your birthday, Honey. Are you sure? Are you sure that's what you want? You only turn seven once."

I'm sure.

She was sure. The cake would be strawberry. An ice-cream cake from Baskin-Robbins. She'd lick the candles, the icing cold and sweet on her tongue. The night before her birthday, the night before she would turn seven, she had a plan. She'd stay awake until midnight when the change would actually happen, awake and aware of the exact moment when she went from six to seven, crossing over like that, becoming something else, something new, but also keeping the old, what she was before, the old her, plus the new her, she'd be both things at once, if that was possible, her face pressed against the glass, pressing harder and harder against the hot, hard glass, her skin burning like fire now, something or someone stepping on her head is what it felt like, running an errand at the time, she remembered being in the car and the radio on and a wild crashing and loud sound and her father's loud scream, she remembered being there and not being there, being elsewhere, watching it happen like a movie, except she was there, she was in the movie, and not in the movie, the way her mother leaned over her and smelled like flowers and said *shhhhhh shhhhhh*. Sometimes things came back to her and sometimes they did not; it was a dream within a dream, floating, waiting, reaching out, people coming to her and asking her things and telling her things, and sometimes she wanted them to stop and sometimes it was fine.

SHE LISTENED, ALWAYS. It was different from other kids. It was like a superhero power she had. She knew. She listened. She heard things others didn't hear.

The report card came in the mail that afternoon. They hadn't talked about it yet. She watched her mother and father read it after dinner, passing the piece of yellow paper back and forth, in front of the TV, people arguing and laughing and falling down.

"You need to sign it," she told them. "So I can bring it back tomorrow."

They were still reading, squinting at all the grids and columns and letters and numbers. She hadn't seen the report card yet, but she knew, she could tell by their faces, the squinting, the chins lowering, disapproving.

"Belle," her mother said. "This has some really good things. Some really good improvements from last time. You're making progress, and that's good."

Her father took the report card from her mother, pointed his finger at something, read to himself, shifted his stubbly jaw back and forth.

"Definitely," he said. "Definitely some improvements. But Belle, we've got some things to work on. I'm seeing a lot of 'needs improvement,' 'unsatisfactory,' things like that. You don't want to be unsatisfactory, do you? Don't you like Mrs. Durbin?"

She did not. She did not like Mrs. Durbin, who favored the girls with perfect ponytails and the boys who raised their hands and always answered her questions correctly, so sure, so certain, always. She liked Mrs. Durbin even less than Mrs. Stinson from first grade.

Later, at night, after the report card had been signed and discussed and stored in her backpack, she brushed her teeth and went to bed and pretended to be asleep. But she wasn't asleep. She lay there in the dark. The world would come to her. She didn't move. Her parents were still talking and she listened.

"This part here, for example," said her father. "'Anabelle hasn't developed habits of behavior that we would expect from a girl in the second grade. She does not accept the responsibility of a citizen who has to live with other people.' What the hell does that mean anyway?"

Quiet, TV sounds, someone standing up and walking. It was like she was there in the living room with them, invisible and powerful.

"Belle isn't your typical kid, John. We know this."

"I just wonder if we should get her tested."

"Tested for what?"

"I don't know. The attention thing. Autism. See if she's on the spectrum. Something might be going on with her brain."

"She doesn't need to be tested, John. We've been through this how many times?"

"I just feel like . . ."

"What?"

"Like we've done something wrong. That we've somehow created this situation ourselves."

"You mean *I've* done something wrong."

"No. I didn't say that."

"You don't have to."

"I didn't say that and you're jumping to conclusions. You're inferring. Look. Have you talked to the teacher? What does the teacher say? Have I met her?"

"No, John, you haven't."

No one else had her name. No one else knew what she knew. She listened. She heard things. As long as she didn't move, was as still as water in a lake: She heard things, knew things. She sometimes had the idea of writing these things down, like maybe in a book or something. But then they'd no longer be a secret. They'd be there, on the pages, for everyone to see. They'd no longer be hers.

18

Message Board of the Official Anabelle Vincent Web Site

Comments:

THE HOLY SPIRIT LED ME TO THIS SITE ... I FEEL THE PRESENCE OF GOD WHILE VIEWING THIS SITE ABOUT HIS MIGHTY WORK THROUGH HIS PRECIOUS VESSEL ... ANABELLE! I BEG HIS PRECIOUS ANOINTING AND BLESSINGS THROUGH THE MARVELOUS INTERCESSION OF THIS YOUNG SAINT! ANDERSON HOUSE MINISTRIES IS A COMMUNITY OF DISABLED MINISTERING TO THE DISABLED AND CARING FOR STRAY ANIMALS AND HOMELESS PEOPLE. THE EVIL ONE HAS CAUSED US SEVERE FINANCIAL HARDSHIP, HINDERING WHAT JESUS HAS CALLED US TO DO ... BY THE POWER OF THE HOLY GHOST THR UGH THE SANCTITY OF ANABELLE GOD SHALL SEND US FUNDING ENDING THIS CRISIS ... KEEPING ANDERSON HOUSE DOORS OPEN TO THOSE JESUS SENDS FOR HELP, HUMANS AND STRAY ANIMALS; AND ALL THE EVIL ATTACKS ON THIS MINISTRY AND MYSELF SHALL BE HALTED AT ONCE IN JESUS` MIGH Y NAME, THROUGH THE INTERCESSION OF THIS PURE HOLY ONE, ANABELLE.

Comments:

It is a great website. May our lord keep blessing everyone who sees this website.

Comments:

I am very interested in the "victim soul" designation. My son is autistic and disabled. He recently underwent surgery for kidney cancer, and the pathology report confirms the malignancy of the tumor. I am concerned that a child, my own or anyone else's must suffer so very, very much. Is that the philosophy of the "victim soul?" I admire the faith and love of those who surround Anabelle.

Comments:

This is a very beautiful site. Enjoyed the articles and pictures. What an amazing God we have! He is with us always and in a special way with souls like Anabelles'. Thank you Lord!

Comments:

needs more pictures and more info.

Comments:

I find that is very inspirational.

Comments:

Congratulations this website is really god. I feel really touched, I will continue to visit it and praying for Anabelle's and all ill people.

Comments:

God Bless You AnaBelle! I continue to pray that you will be healed.

Comments:

I believe that this is true. I do pray that she may be healed. My pain for her mom and her family is felt here. what Hardship they have felt I'm sure.

When I heard of her story broke my heart. my daughter is three and I lost my son who lived for 2 da .s in nov of 96. The comfort of knowing that the Lord os working threw her I has given me some comfort threw my own sadness. But I still pray for her healing God willing. Thank you, Donna

Comments:

I am thrilled to see so much information about Anabelle on her own website. I have already printed out most of the information so that I can share it with others who do not have access to a computer. Thank you for enabling me to find out answers to so man things through your site. I pray that I may someday be able to actually get to visit Anabelle and pray with her.

Comments:

Anabelle's vocation as a victim soul is a story that the world needs to hear. Your website is a good tool to help accomplish this. She has been a source of an increase in my faith. I'm sure many can say the same. Pray for us, Anabelle.

Comments:

I found it helpful in understanding what is happening. And have come to realize that life is to short and to live life to the fullest. Everyone should love there neighbors and respect each other. It is so touching to see this & what Little Anabelle has given.

Comments:

a friend sent me a video about little Anabelle,and it was wonderful.The facts were very infomative.I think that little Anabelle and her family are a wo derful statement for life in this culture of death i

Comments:

Really nice site. I heard about Anabelle from some friends of mine in Los Angeles. We plan to visit soon. Our son David has CP and relates to her also.

Comments:

I thoroughly enjoyed the site. Hopefully no one is taking advantage of this little girl's misfortune.

Comments:

It's a magnificent website. I teach religious education to children in grades 1-6. I will share Anabelle's story with them this afternoon. I am glad I saw it on 20/20 this Monday, or I would not have known about her and wouldn't be able to share her story ith my classes. We will pray for her.

Comments:

I am a 13 yr old girl from PA. I first learned about anabelle's extraordinary case on 20/20. Her story moved me so much I decided to look it up on yhe internet. I told my mother about it and all we could think about was my grandma. She has been blind or 27 years. It's heartbreaking when your grandma can't see how her grandchildren and children have turned out. Therefor, I would give anything to see Anabelle. She's a saint. She's the hand of God. Thank You

Comments:

I saw Anabelle on 20/20 and I was deeply touched not only by the grace of God but by the love and devotion Karen has for her daughter.

Comments:

My Grandmother and I saw the 20/20 episode on Anabelle and were compelled to find you. The show did not list a mailing address or web address so we found you on our own. We were very moved by the story of Anabelle. We have had many problems in our lives bu our faith keeps us strong. We pray for you and Anabelle. Please keep us informed of updates on the web and personal. Stay strong God loves you! In our prayers, Marcella and Anita Rivera

Comments:

People feel the need to believe. I understand, it's part of human nature. But people please!!! If you'd like another view of miracles, weeping statues, etc. please check out my Website: www.smilingskeptic.com. Thanks!

Comments:

VERY INSPIRING. THANK YOU AND GOD BLESS.LOVE ELAINE

Comments:

The website is a beautiful site. I pray a small prayer for her and her mother that she be able to have the joyful strength to bear the burden of her daughters care. Also that maybe one day Anabelle will come back and tell us about her journey. I also submit to her my little niece Julia who suffers epilepsy. She is a brilliant little girl but is emotionally spent. Please Anabelle intercede on her behalf. My 2 boys are healthy thank God and Anabelle I pray you do come back.

Comments:

Good, you have put alot of effort into this, Please pray for me and boyfriend kenny estep and I to to stay together. Thank you, God is w/ you, Barbara Seligman.

Comments:

I think that the website is fine. I originally heard about anabelle's store on the news, I have a brother name Tommy who has been in a coma for almost 20 years, his was the result of a motorcycle accident which occurred on May 9,1981.Please pray for HIM!

Comments:

You're doing a super job, Bryce ... can't wait until more articles are up, as well as pictures. I wonder when the Church investigation will be done. Have you heard anything? I have been telling as many people as possible about your website. God Bless!!

Comments:

More people should know about this.

19

| John and Karen |

THEY MET AT a party. The house and the backyard overflowing with people, so many people, so many drunk people, from high school and also the recently graduated, a mix of those who were free and those who were not, not yet. A party that turned out to be one of those parties that was discussed and dissected for the rest of the summer and beyond and later became the measure for other parties, all of which forever failed to live up to Mike Rico's kick-ass summer of '87 party, you know, the one where Ginny Thompson and Adam Hupp supposedly did it in the bathroom and the music was so loud a stereo speaker blew and then Steve Silva saved the day by backing his truck up on the lawn and blaring heavy doses of the Stones and Led Zeppelin (a heroic feat that, according to legend, earned him a complimentary blowjob from Trish Vanderwende). A Saturday night, late June, that feeling of the summer never ending. Multiple pukings, hookups. A window was broken, a bathroom trashed. Of course the cops came. And later there was disagreement about who saw who first, but over the years Karen stuck to her version: she spotted him not long after arriving, camped out on the couch, plastic red beer cup in hand, his hair still wet from a shower, his body slim and dangerous and muscular underneath a white T-shirt and baggy chinos, looking like he was charmed, chosen for some princely adventure. Dark hair, dark eyes. She recognized him, knew that he went to the rival high school (sports, notoriety for his prowling black Mustang and dreamy smile), or rather had gone, because he was a year older, had graduated, worked somewhere, and that was about it, all she knew at that point in time. He, on the other hand, always contended he noticed her the moment she walked in the door. Played it cool. Acted, for a while, like he didn't notice her staring, too, but did. He'd worked all day at the dentist's office, making molds of people's teeth. It was a shit job but it paid pretty well and he could show up stoned and get away with it. Now it was the weekend, and he tasted the promise of that. It had been only a week or so since he broke up with Karla Bloomquist (Karla with a "K," she liked to say, Karla who worked at Winchell's Donuts and could tie a cherry stem into a knot with her tongue), so he looked forward to new beginnings, maybe a hookup, someone he didn't know perhaps. The girl who walked in jumped right to the top of his list. He made the mental note. He thought of possible lines. But she looked like a girl that required more than a line. Something in the eyes. An intelligence that both excited and frightened him. Mike Rico was two years older, John knew him from sports, and Mike had just moved into a new place. A little housewarming party, he told John on the phone. Word spread.

THEY TALKED ABOUT people they both knew, the lack of furniture in Mike's house, the ongoing renovations at the

Whittwood Mall, the merits of the Who without Keith Moon (unlike other girls, she had an opinion here), how they didn't want the summer to end. Yes, summers were magical. Warm and long and magical. And it was technically her last, the summer between her junior and senior year, when she wore shorts and tank tops and learned what it meant to have hips, actual hips, womanly shapes and contours and smells that bestowed a power, a place in the world that had been there waiting for her and now, finally, had arrived. She practiced a certain smile in the mirror. She smoked cloves and, when those weren't available, cigarettes. That, plus the right pair of sunglasses and enough cherry-flavored lip gloss, and you were somebody else, the movie version of yourself. Nights were the best. Each one an adventure, a promise. Somebody usually could borrow a car and then they were good. Tanya and Beth and sometimes Lisa Frosch when she wasn't being a bitch. And if no car was to be had, they made do. They stayed in the neighborhood and sat on someone's porch steps and made phone calls to boys they'd met the previous weekend. She did not, like most of her friends, drink wine coolers or Vodka Dews. She drank beer like the boys. This also gave her a power. This guy at the party, John, cute, also commented: *Wow, that's cool, you drink beer.* From the couch they moved to the backyard and then the kitchen, where the keg was, touring the house and its mostly empty bedrooms (Mike had several roommates). The music got louder. You had to raise your voice, practically yell, to be heard, their throats growing raspy from that and the alcohol. Right before they kissed for the first time, she said, "I'm kind of intense." He said, "I like intense." And she said, "Then you can't say you weren't warned." Hips locking together as their lips met, bodies falling in place, a gentle, inevitable fit. She stayed out all night with him. But she didn't have sex with him, that wouldn't happen until weeks later, but they slept in his car, in the backseat, like children, a Mexican blanket wrapped around them, it came from the trunk, smelling of sand and grease. Nothing had ever felt so warm or beautiful. She caught hell at home in the morning, her mother awake and fuming, what kind of girl does this, but it was worth it, worth it, and she knew something had changed, and he felt it, too: a beginning.

THEY WENT TO the county courthouse over two years later, a few ups and downs along the way, plenty of doubts never fully tamed, but they were ready, felt ready, for the most part, and it was time. Not the wedding she'd imagined, for sure. Sharing a flask filled with Southern Comfort. Digging through her purse to scrounge up change for the parking meter. No family came: John's father was dead, his mother in Michigan, while Karen wasn't on speaking terms with her mother at the time, her father and his second wife couldn't leave the cats alone, and Tammy was hardly guest-list material, since she'd rendered her verdict on John, nicknaming him BL, or "Beautiful Loser," after the Bob Seger song. The judge reminded her of Uncle Fester from *The Addams Family*. The witness—a bifocaled secretary who got roped in last minute—kept sneezing. He was hoping for at least Vegas until they checked their respective savings accounts. The room smelled strongly of Pine-Sol. Two other couples were waiting to go next. Outside they were back in the car and a little dazed and a parking ticket graced their windshield: the meter had run out. The wedding dinner consisted of Taco Bell, drive-thru, two Burrito Supremes and Cinnamon Crispas. But they were married, they had done it, they were together, till death do us part and all that, rings, documents, signatures, consummating to *Van Halen II.* They honeymooned by looking for an apartment to rent, finding a one-bedroom place in La Habra, making frequent trips to KMart to buy things like dish-washing brushes or toilet bowl cleaner, listening to their favorite radio stations, KMET and KLOS, wondering what DJ Jim Ladd looked like, if he was high while he did his midnight show *Headsets,* getting high themselves, gaining weight, shopping for a new car, sending in sweepstakes forms, and for a while he was working and then she was working, too, and then he wasn't working. When he came home or she came home, the other person was there, waiting.

THEY TRIED TO have a baby. Similar to getting married, it felt like it was time. So Karen stopped taking the pill, and they had more sex than they'd ever had. They got strategic with their fucking. Morning, night, then morning again. During the day when Karen was ovulating they rendezvoused at home whenever possible, soldiering on like this for months, the bursts of tactical intercourse followed by periods of celibate recovery time. And much to their dismay, the superhuman humping produced no results. They stuck with it, though. Did some research. Karen put pillows under her hips after John came and didn't move for half an hour, sometimes longer. They monitored Karen's cervical mucus. "Your cervical mucus doesn't lie," they'd read in one book, which also suggested that Karen take Robitussin (which she did, two teaspoons a day, starting four days prior to ovulation), because it not only thins mucus in the lungs but also does the same for cervical mucus, thus potentially assisting the passage of John's sad, searching sperm. Another book recommended that they refrain from oral sex (bacteria in saliva can "degrade" semen and decrease the chances of conception). Foreplay options were therefore significantly reduced. But again, they had nothing to show for their efforts. Nada. John switching from tighty-whities to boxers didn't help either. The holidays were approaching. They thought: wouldn't a special Christmas or New Year's announcement be nice? So they labored onward, their respective organs resigned to the entrances and exits, withdrawals and deposits. If they hadn't known the difference between making love and fucking they did now. Another month, another ovulation cycle wasted. They grew to hate the sound of their bodies slapping futilely together, the sheer defeat of their genitals. "It's like porn," said John one night, or morning, or afternoon. By then it had become a coitus blur. And when the unfertile holidays came and went, and it was a new year, and they were unable to make that special announcement, John and Karen visited their doctors. Karen was fine, her blood pressure a tad higher than normal, as well as some slight vaginal tissue scarring (due to the frequency of the Mr. Roboto sex), but otherwise very healthy and certainly capable of reproduction. John's news, on the other hand, wasn't so good: low sperm count. *Oligospermia* is what it's called, the technical name. A common enough male affliction, to be sure, but understandably John took the news poorly, staying up late, alone, eating pistachios and playing Nintendo and watching movies. But just when they'd almost given up, when they'd started talking about things like adoption and in vitro, a miracle: a baby was on the way.

THEY WANTED TO be surprised, so they didn't find out the gender. During the ultrasounds and checkups, he held her hand and she squeezed back as the doctor said the baby looks fine, the baby is healthy, you can see the baby's fingers, you can see the baby's heart, things are moving right along, Mommy, Daddy. The down payment on the house was made and they moved in and brought what little they had and dreamed of more and it seemed like the day would never come.

THEY DIDN'T KNOW what to do. Anabelle, named for a beloved aunt (Karen's side, a relative who had died early and mysteriously), would not stop crying. It was like she was broken and they'd lost the instructions and the hotline number; they were on their own. She cried when she was held and when she was not held and every variation in between. Rocking didn't help. Swaddling didn't help. Begging didn't help. If you *looked* at her, she'd cry. They felt like they were doing something wrong, some key piece of parenting information had eluded them completely, and they were horrible, horrible parents. You heard about crying babies, sure, and you heard about sleep deprivation, yes, but this seemed extreme; she wouldn't stop. Colic, the pediatrician said, prescribing a pacifier and Raffi. Anabelle also had trouble latching. She wouldn't stay on Karen's breast, Karen now crying as well because not only was she exhausted but also because her nipples were crusted and tender and this supposedly natural, beautiful, essential, life-affirming experience was fucking hard and it wasn't fucking working. No one was sleeping. They took turns getting up during the night, though more often than not it was her, Karen was the one. This was not the beauty of parenthood. This was not what you saw on TV or heard from your friends. People came by to see the baby, to ask how the lucky new parents were doing. The lucky new parents wanted to bite their fucking heads off. *See? Can't you see the watery, washed-out eyes? The nails that have been chewed raw? Can't you see this constantly crying creature we've created? Why don't you try?* The grandmothers were the worst, coming to visit and *tsk-tsk-tsk*-ing. Obviously John and Karen were at fault. They (the grandmothers) had never experienced anything like this, *oh my, no, you were a little angel, have you tried a little rum in her bottle yet?* They (John and Karen) often barked at each other, too, coming apart instead of coming together, arguing about everything from whether they should pick up Anabelle when she cried ("Is it OK to pick her up every time she cries?" "Crying babies need to be held.") to how were they going to afford diapers and college and braces. Karen turned away, then John turned away, and after a while it was hard to tell where it had begun, the turning away. "Here," she said one particularly unbearable night, around 3:00 a.m.—and she practically tossed the swaddled Anabelle at him. "You try. See what you can do." And he paced the house, bouncing her, his wailing, inconsolable daughter, on his shoulder, in his arms, shushing, humming, singing songs, the only ones he could remember all the words to, inappropriate songs like "Stairway to Heaven" and "Cocaine." ("If you want to hang out, you've got to take her out . . . cocaine," he whispered/sang, wondering what the hell he'd gotten himself into.) He had assumed since he was a mellow person he would have a mellow child, this being the first of many mistakes and misperceptions that would come to define his spotty career as a father. Karen was in the bedroom, head under her pillow, tallying the number of days it had been since she'd showered (four). They'd expected it to be hard but not this hard. This wasn't normal, was it?

THEY ALSO EXPERIENCED moments of great joy, random wonder, ferocious love they never thought possible. The times when baby Anabelle yawned and time stopped, when she clasped her fingers around one of theirs, gripped with such primordial need, and seemed, finally, to be content, not wanting to let go. Or when she burped unexpectedly, surprised herself, and then laughed, they all laughed. The sound, once she was walking, of her pajama'd feet, pattering on the hardwood floor in the hallway while they lingered in bed, listening. When she demanded hugs, saying, "Hug, Mommy. Hug, Daddy." Those times when they knew they'd walk through fire for her, their child, they'd do this or anything else without hesitation. A fierce, complicated love. A love like no other. And they somehow got through those early years, bags around their eyes, wrinkle lines deploying on their faces, even though the crying never completely stopped. At two, three, four, five—Anabelle cried. She cried when she woke up. She cried when she went to bed. She cried when she was put into the car seat and when she was taken out. She cried because she didn't like it when her Cheerios got soggy, or when it was mashed potatoes instead of French fries. She cried because she didn't want her hair combed. She cried at the doctor's, the dentist's, the babysitter's. And so on. And she had nightmares, too, woke in the middle of the night, every night practically, climbing into their bed and settling between them (they'd allowed this once and then it became a regular occurrence, something that John stewed about, regretting that they'd said yes the first time and set a precedent). Anabelle was also a light sleeper, so they didn't dare go into her room and watch her sleep. That was something that parents did, right? Stand in their child's room

and watch them sleep and be amazed? One of the few times John
tried it Anabelle woke up and started crying. "John," Karen
snapped when she came into the room (this was also probably around 3:00 a.m.). "What did you do?" He shrugged like:
What? He was trying. He was trying to be a parent. Earlier that
day Anabelle had said something that haunted him then and continued to haunt him. She was six now. She said, "I wish we didn't
live in a house with mirrors." What the hell did that mean? He
asked her why. "Because I don't like to look at myself." And he
found himself thinking what he often thought when his daughter said something like this: How to respond? He wanted to ask
more, get at the root of what made his daughter uncomfortable
when seeing her own reflection, but, as Karen reminded him, it
could make things worse to interrogate, to bring more attention
to the issue at hand. But that was just it: with Anabelle he was
never sure of the issue at hand in the first place. The psychologist
they saw once or twice referred to her intense emotionality, her
inability to regulate her emotions, telling them that it was just
the way their daughter was wired. Karen agreed, reading books
and articles on the subject; John did not read books and articles
(well, a few articles), instead clinging to the belief that they could
fix the problem, that if they just cracked down and molded and
guided her the right way they'd be able to control her personal-
ity. Karen was of a different mind completely. Weren't kids supposed to bring you closer together? But with them it had been
the opposite. Throughout the years, among all the good and bad
and everything in between, all the discussions, filibusters, and
long silences, all the measuring themselves against other seemingly happier, more competent parents (which made them feel

even shittier), their abiding fear remained: that their unhappiness had infected Anabelle and caused her unhappiness.

THEY WERE, ONCE again, at odds—this time over what to do after the accident, that time of doubt and stabbing panic, the world collapsing around them, Karen adamant about keeping Anabelle at home, John wishy-washing his way through a series of half-assed counter-arguments, afraid, genuinely fucking can't-sleep-at-night afraid about the effect this kind of 24/7 burden would have on their already fragile lives. He knew he wasn't that strong a person, didn't have the heroic gene necessary to carry him, carry them, through this. They were dealing with the hospital, lawyers, bills, doctors, social workers, insurance companies, their mechanic who was holding John's car hostage (Karen's had been totaled in the accident) until they paid for the new transmission he put in. At some point they were doing what Karen wanted; he was going along, yet not going along; he was saying the words, yet he was not believing them; he was there in the house doing his share, yet he was not there in the house, not doing his share, already leaving, already gone, already living his life of regret and remorse, a marked man. "I want to do this with you," Karen said, sensing him slipping away, day by day, the frequency of actual eye contact between them now about as rare as a two-dollar bill, adding, "I can't do this without you, John." One of the fluorescent ceiling lights in the kitchen started to flicker. They didn't say anything about it. Waited for the other to give in and make the first move. The standoff lasted for days until she said, "Are we going to do anything about it?" She meant the flickering light, and he of course knew this, and it was as if the flickering light and their lack of mutual acknowledgment signaled something deeper, was symbolic of some larger failure that neither of them was ready to admit. That time in the waiting room, right after the accident, holding each other until they did not. On the other hand, though, it was just a light. All they had to do was replace it and that would be that. Simple. When he did leave, she watched him go like it was a bad TV movie where you knew what was going to happen before it happened; the sound of his car, the vast silence after, a long time standing there at the window in the living room, noting the dedicated layers of dust on the mini blinds, windows needing to be washed (inside and out), repeating to herself *he's gone, I'm alone, he's gone, I'm alone;* and when she finally roused herself to go check on Anabelle, surprise—Anabelle's catheter bag had broken and the sheets and her nightgown needed to be changed, the piss a dark, disturbing, seeping yellow, a color that did not seem possible.

HE'S STILL IN line, waiting his turn, all this time, three people ahead of him, roughly four hours having elapsed so far. When asked by others why he's here, he keeps it simple, keeps it vague. After a while people stopped talking to him. Fine. He can now make out the inside of the living room. Bodies moving through. He can't tell who. The first words will be the hardest. And when he does see her, in that initial blooming instant, he'll know right away whether he can ever be forgiven and if there's a future for them. Her eyes will tell him everything he needs to know. Someone behind him says the Lord works in mysterious ways indeed but there's no place she'd rather be than here. Someone else mentions the weather, says Fritz said it would be like this—quoting the famous L.A. TV weatherman, known for his large glasses and ability to remain on the air for decades despite turning gray and looking like a used car salesman. John hears a helicopter circling above, peers up; he watches it cross the sky, tilting into the low clouds and then disappearing. A person (female, in tears, consoled by Karen's niece Dom) exits the house and everyone moves up a little, including him.

SHE HASN'T SAT down all day, answering the phone, returning calls, reading mail and e-mails, writing a response to yet another delay in the lawsuit against the hospital and doctors, reviewing the itinerary for December 30, talking to visitors, fielding questions, listening to stories, taking pictures, trying to clean the bathrooms, organizing all the Christmas presents she and Anabelle had received, skimming through the movie script FedExed from a Hollywood agent named Christine Benfer. Bryce was around earlier (though he didn't stay long) and now Dom is helping out, earlier apologizing for not having been around much lately, currently cutting lemons and making iced tea for everyone. She's also giving Karen updates on the line outside, which is dwindling as nighttime nears. Dom passes out the iced tea and then checks the window again as she takes a sip of her drink. Karen puts a stack of magazines next to the sofa, creating another toddler-sized column of reading material. Then, from the window, she hears Dom say: "Oh shit. It's him. It's John. John's out there in line. That's him. Look." Karen looks, confirms. Of course. Of course John's there. Dom asks, "Should I go get him?" "No," answers Karen. "No, let him wait. It's been this long. Let's just wait a little longer. I need a minute."

AND WHEN HE sees her for the first time he doesn't automatically know if they have a future together, her eyes don't tell him that story. It's not like he thought it would be, but they, her eyes, which are just as richly, intensely brown as he remembered, do tell him another story: yes, it's still possible, there is hope despite everything, you still have a chance.

AND WHEN SHE sees him for the first time it's not like she imagined it would be, there isn't this roller-coaster rush of emotions, it isn't anger, it isn't relief, it isn't gratitude, it isn't certain, and it isn't final—it's more like: *this is the way it should be, this is what I expected, this is what everything has been moving toward, and now we're here, it's right in front of us, the moment, this moment, and I can't wait to find out what happens next.*

THEY ARE ALMOST touching, only inches apart, aware of a shared electrical current between them, sparking to life now that they were so physically close again, the years, the history undeniable, like a large, invisible shawl wrapped around them both. He's in the house; she's in the house; their daughter is in her room, where he'd just been, the first time, and he's still crying, hunched and buckled and disbelieving. The house otherwise empty. Just the three of them. Like it was before. She'd asked everyone to leave. Instinctively, they find their way to the kitchen, the most neutral room in the house. A plate of enchiladas—brought by a visitor—remains untouched on the kitchen table. They sit there and stare at the enchiladas. Like really contemplating them in a deep way. But food does not seem like an option yet.

"It's going to take time."

Somebody had to start, and it was her.

"I know. I've got a lot of work to do. I've got a lot to prove. But I will. And I know how it might look, me coming back like this. You know how everyone's saying what's happening is a sign? Well maybe it's a sign for me, too. When I saw it on TV, I thought . . . I thought that I still had a chance. That I could come back and do good. I'm not asking to stay or anything. Or for anything permanent or for anything to be decided. I'm just asking for a chance. To be here sometimes. To be a family. As best we can."

"And even then . . . I don't know."

"Day by day, week by week, month by month. You'll see. It'll take time. But you'll see."

Much does not seem like an option yet. But they are getting there. Along the way there will be long pauses, there will be overlapping words, repeated stops and starts, a general awkwardness and distance that will gradually decrease. They will have to get through it, now, later. And the more words now, the more back and forth there is, the more likely they will eat the food, edge their way to this communal consumption, sitting, eating together, talking.

"John?"

"Yes."

"Even then, I don't know."

Christmas presents are stacked on top of the refrigerator, on top of the stove, underneath the table. He notices this. And she notices his noticing. They are getting there. Arriving at something. They will have to get through it. And this is progress. This is words and proximity, mutual sitting and trying, contemplating enchiladas and Christmas presents and the future.

"We'll start slow. Day by day. It won't happen again. That's the same question I'd be asking myself right now. I don't want to be in the place where I was ever again."

"Tell me something."

"What?"

"What were you thinking when you first saw me?"

"The very first thing? At the party?"

"Yes."

"That . . . she's drinking beer. That she's different. That she stands out. Not just the drinking beer part, I mean. It was more than that. That if I don't talk to her it's going to be something I regret for the rest of my life. But you know all this. I've told you all of this before."

"I know. I just wanted to hear it again. It's been a while."

THE ROOM

PEOPLE SAY: *The room breathes. The room is life.* They pass on this whispered wisdom as they leave the house and as others inquire how was it, what was she like, how do you feel now, after.

The line moves slowly, but that's OK, that's part of it, too—the waiting, the anticipation, the interpreting of the facial expressions and words and body language of those who have just seen her and those who are about to see her. And next up: a young couple, holding hands, nervous, the husband significantly taller than the wife, every now and then leaning down to kiss the top of her head, her hair, as she presses farther into him—that is, as close as she can get given the fact that she is very, very pregnant—and when they enter the room, see the girl there in her enchanted state, they immediately know it's true. *The room breathes. The room is life.* Despite the pale skin, despite the absence of movement and the faraway gaze in her eyes, the girl glows, actually glows, as if lit from within. She is holy. She is touched. This is so eff-ing obvious.

The couple stands at the foot of little Anabelle Vincent's bed and pauses. Do they continue standing or do they kneel? Because neither the husband nor the wife is particularly religious. The husband speaks up first, says softly, "Let's kneel just in case, to make sure we do it right," and then he helps his wife down to the floor, guiding her, one arm wrapped around her lower back and stomach (gentle, gentle), the other supporting her legs. She is eight months along, slow and pained, and moving around is difficult, as is sleeping, as is waiting out these last few weeks, knowing what they know. They kneel. They hold hands. They close their eyes. The machines sigh, hum. They begin. They tell their story in the room where so many other stories have now been told.

Their doctor had news. Something was found, the way the spinal fluid looked in the ultrasound. Then the AFP test, which confirmed further. "News that isn't good, I'm afraid," the doctor continuing, a man who habitually wore his eyeglasses perched atop his forehead. "In all likelihood, from what the numbers and statistics tell us, knowing what we know, our best approximation, the baby will likely, very likely, be born with Down syndrome." The doctor told them this and didn't know what else to say. His glasses perched there, like they were sunglasses but they were not sunglasses. The baby was a boy. They hadn't settled on a name yet, though they were thinking of naming him after the husband's grandfather, who'd died not long after the couple found out they were pregnant, a family name, an old, solid, nineteenth-century-style name, not one of the newfangled flashy ones. Finally the doctor said, "Well, there are options, even at this point, though we'd need to make a decision very soon." But they said no, it wasn't their way, no, we can't. This, then, was several months ago, in the doctor's office, a much different room. And now, they are here, in the girl's room. This is it. This is the final thing. Nothing else left for them to do.

So they ask for her assistance, for Anabelle's intervention in this matter. They pray. They cry. They hope they are saying the right words. They don't want to leave. How long they'd been trying. Years.

The room breathes. The room is life.

This is what the husband and wife repeat, repeat to themselves now, and then later, in the days and weeks that follow, like a chant that imparts more meaning, further clarity, with each utterance.

And a month after their visit, in the middle of the night, the wife gives birth to their son, Joseph Matthew. He is fine. He is beautiful. He is perfectly, wonderfully fine. The doctors and nurses marvel. The husband says how they knew. From when they first saw the girl: *they knew.* How the room existed elsewhere, another realm entirely. He'd never been in such a physical space, never felt such golden warmth and electricity within a confined area, be it another room, house, church, football stadium, whatever. Driving home that day, after asking the girl for her help, he remembers reaching out to touch his wife's stomach, to reassure her, as well as himself and his son, too, and thinking: *There is no doubt, there is no way it cannot be true.*

PART THREE

December 30, 1999

20

THE POLICE ESTIMATE is six thousand, but Captain Dave McGinnis, aka KTZ-AM radio's venerable Eagle Eye in the Sky traffic reporter, who's just now circling El Dorado High School in his trusty white-and-yellow Cessna 177B, predicts it will be more like ten thousand, possibly even higher, based on what he's surveying below: the event is supposed to start at noon and here it is only ten thirty and the surrounding side streets are already jammed with cars and people on foot, the backup now reaching all the way to the 605, while the freeway itself resembles not the sleepy (relatively speaking) mid-day intermittent stop-and-go but the full-on morning/evening rush-hour, hand-wringing, shoulder-tensed crawl. Yep, it's going to be a doozy, Captain Dave further predicts, as he swoops over the parking lot (full) and notices at least a dozen news vans as well as several large passenger buses chartered for the occasion (*doozy* being one of the Captain's frequent euphemisms for a huge fucking vehicular mess that you want to avoid at all costs). At the last minute it was announced

that the event would be broadcast live on Channel 11. Rumors
are that CNN might cut in, too.

Having flown the smoggy skies of Los Angeles for over twenty
years, Captain Dave has pretty much seen it all: O.J.'s freeway
odyssey, the riots after the verdict, earthquakes, floods, fires, car
chases and crashes, grisly pile-ups on the Grapevine, an elephant
named Misty escaping from Lion Country Safari down in Orange County and causing an epic traffic jam on the 405. He's an
L.A. institution, like Lasorda, like Vin Scully, like Chick Hearn,
like Dr. Toni Grant. Known for his good-natured on-air barbs,
clever quips, and throaty baritone. Reliable as a goddamn dic-
tionary. Never out sick except for the time he had a colonoscopy
back in 1982, missing only a day. If he's not in the cockpit, patrolling the comings and goings of the Southland, reporting on
this daily mass migration of souls, something seems off with the
universe; it's where he belongs. His wife is worried what he'll do
when he retires. He is, too.

Perspective. That's what you get from up here. The chaos below,
the serenity above. He savors the space, the quiet his mind can
achieve from the cruising altitude of two thousand feet. There's
nothing like it on the ground. You're sort of God. Or God-like.
Watching it all from a distance. Which is, he guesses, apropos to
the day's festivities and what all these people are here for: little
Anabelle Vincent, the Miracle Girl, eight years old, bed-ridden,
incapable of speech, instant celebrity, possible instrument of
God, the talk of his talk radio station, a well-timed phenomenon,
to be sure, what with all the Y2K and millennium craziness. He
just hopes that the Almighty calls in a favor and does something
about all these damn cars or there's going to be a lot of disap-
pointed civilians. Counting down to his next live report in five

minutes, how he'll open with his trademark "From high above, from the surf to the mountains and the desert and everywhere in between, this is Captain Dave McGinnis, your KTZ Eagle Eye in the Sky, with the latest traffic, and boy, have we ever got a doozy over in El Portal, folks."

First, though, he banks toward the football stadium for a closer look, seeing the bleachers filled to capacity, the activity in one of the end zones, a stage there, chairs, a podium, speakers, some kind of plastic tent, people rushing around like insects, making the final preparations, setting up large white pop-up canopies like they use for outdoor weddings. As Captain Dave circles back over the school again, he spots two police cars, with sirens flashing, entering the school parking lot, and behind them an ambulance, sirens also flashing, breaking news he'll include in his update: She's here. The Miracle Girl has arrived. In this outlying area of L.A. The kind of neighborhood where there's always a devil dog barking, a kid doing something he shouldn't, a parent about to cross a line.

He lowers the Cessna a little more, gives thanks for the day's relatively clear skies. Visibility is decent. Slight northwesterly winds. Feisty heat. That Biblical sun, burning with an Old Testament vengeance. In all his years in the sky and on the air, he's never seen anything like it.

* * *

The Smiling Skeptic, flush with the excitement of a spy who's successfully ventured behind enemy lines, sharks his way through the bubbling crowd, passing faces and bodies that are demographically diverse, visibly needy, finally finding the end of the viewing line, which is already enormous and twisty, snaking all the way from the football field itself and under and through the stadium bleachers, past a chain-link fence and gate and empty ticket booth, before then spilling out onto the basketball courts (and yes, the rims have no nets, it's that kind of school, that kind of sketchy area, he quickly surmised once he pulled up in his rented red Taurus, one of those cars that might as well have RENTAL CAR spray-painted on its doors).

So he'll have some time to kill. He'll wait in line with the true believers. And that's fine with him. More opportunity for research. Maybe he'll even manage to convert some souls. He's filled with information and data he wants to share. If only they knew the evidence, if only they knew the facts. People were ultimately reasonable, weren't they? This was the progression of humankind, what we've been moving toward over the centuries, was it not?

Even though the flight from San Francisco to Los Angeles is short, he feels jet-lagged, a little soul-lagged, like he left behind some piece of himself on the plane. Or maybe it's the weather, or the whole Northern California versus Southern California thing. Whatever the reason, he shrugs his backpack off, unzips it, and digs out the article he'd been reading on the flight. He has to keep up. Now more than ever. Since his appearance on *The Big Ben Hour,* there have been more requests for interviews, more traffic to his website, more all-nighters spent online and writing and chugging Mountain Dew. He's called in sick to work twice. And his mother is asking questions that go beyond his bachelorhood.

The woman in front of him, he now realizes, is on the verge of crying. Head bent forward, hand covering her eyes, shoulders twitching. She has long dark hair, pale white arms, a husky build—the overall girth and sturdiness of a waitress, Nathaniel concludes. Someone who's spent too much of her life serving others. She's actually half facing him and half facing the person who's in front of her in line, a man, also on the husky side, who has his back turned and is wearing an Iron Maiden T-shirt.

"Sorry. I told myself I wouldn't cry. But I can't believe I'm here. I can't believe it."

She is, it turns out, talking to him.

"I can't believe it either," Nathaniel says, which is true.

"When I first heard about it," she tells him, fully facing him now, revealing heavy eyeliner, smoker's teeth, "I knew I had to come. It's the last time—the last time people can come and see her. I knew I had to be here, in California, when it happened."

The woman fortyish, perhaps a bit younger. The hair obviously dyed. Puffy in the face. There's some kind of accent, too, but since Nathaniel has never been outside of California, he can't make any kind of a geographical connection.

"Where did you come from?" he asks.

"Maryland. Baltimore area. I drove. Straight through mostly. Stopped in Albuquerque to see my sister but that was about it. I kept driving to make sure I'd make it in time. What're you reading?"

The article is about visitors to the girl's home trying to steal locks of her hair, grass from the front yard of the house, bits of straw from the welcome mat, anything that can be fit into a pocket or purse or closed fist. Anything to get closer to the girl, closer to God. Nothing new there, Nathaniel thinks. It's always been so, this veneration of holy objects purported—and he heavily emphasizes the *purported* part, italicizing the word in his mind—to belong to holy people. One of his recent late-night online excursions took him to a site devoted to religious relics. Some crazy voodoo there. Apparently, during the Middle Ages, and especially during the Crusades, relic hunting and collecting was a booming business. Among other sought-after collectibles, the bones, hair, teeth, and fingers of saints and martyrs were highly coveted, said to be capable of miraculous feats. (Poor Thomas Aquinas: when he died, in 1274, some monks who just couldn't wait to have at his valuable bones quickly got to boiling his flesh away before his body was even cold.) Predictably there's much, much more from the relic files. As for Jesus memorabilia, there's plenty to choose from: splinters from the cross used in the crucifixion (enough reputed specimens to build a ship with, or so goes the old joke); thorns from his impromptu crown; plus Jesus's swaddling clothes, baby teeth, umbilical cord, even his foreskin (the latter claimed by at least six different churches). Several heads of John the Baptist found their way onto the market. And Mary: her hair, clothing, vials of her breast milk as well as pieces of the rock upon which the milk had supposedly fallen, which turned the rock white and blessed it with curative powers. And really, it hasn't changed all that much today, is Nathaniel's take. The objects are a little different, sure, and now you can track down just about everything under the sun on eBay (you'd probably find a saintly relic or two listed for sale there, too, along with the occasional human kidney or soul), but it's still a matter of the possession possessing us. A celebrity's autograph. A famous home-run ball. A pen once used by John F. Kennedy. We are transformed.

"It's an article about the girl," he says. "How people are taking stuff from the house, anything to remind them of her."

"Well," sighs the woman, who is officially crying now, tears making steady, streaming progress down her cheeks. "I don't condone. But I do understand."

Still holding the article, printed out from the Internet, he wants to launch into an impassioned, spiritually devastating speech. He wants to tell her about the hoaxes, how they use oil for tears, how it can all be rationally explained, how people believe what they want to believe, and he wants to clinically deconstruct it all for her so she understands, so she knows the truth. He would be doing her a favor, actually. And eventually, if need be, he'll stump her with the ultimate stumper: If little Anabelle Vincent is capable of performing miracles, then why can't she heal herself?

"It is real, isn't it? Don't you think?"

There are families here, clusters of adults and children. Babies wail. Men and women talking on cell phones. Talking to each other. Sweat and suntan lotion. Beach chairs and Igloo coolers. The sun baking all below it, casting a burning yellow glow. Cops patrolling. Young, burly neckless men with yellow shirts that say SECURITY on the back. People wearing shorts who should not be wearing shorts. Excitement in the air. Like waiting for a concert. He doesn't know what to say.

"I'm going to die," the woman confesses.

And now he really doesn't know what to say.

"Wow, I've never said it out loud like that before. *I'm going to die.* Wasn't so hard, saying it. It's one of those six-month deals. 'You've got six months, Amy.' What the hell do you say after you've been told something like that? More importantly, what do you do?"

With his grandfather, they said there was nothing to do except pray. This from medical doctors, people with framed degrees and prolific beards. So you knew it was bad. And so he prayed. He prayed like no one had ever prayed before, blazed a trail in the history of prayer. Every waking thought a plea to God. *Pleasegod-lethimlive. Pleasegodmakewhat'shappeningtohisbodystop.* On his knees, standing, walking, waiting for the bread to pop out of the toaster. He never missed an opportunity to argue his case. The prayers came fast, a rush of words and syllables, a new language that had the power to transform. *PleasegodifhelivesIwon't evertakehimoranythingelse for granted. Iwonteverwishanything badonhimoranyoneelseinthisworld. Pleasegodplease.* He prayed at school, in the car, in his dreams, while watching cartoons. His mother told him good. It was helping. It was working. So he prayed more. The frequent visits to the hospital, on weekends, before and after school—he prayed there, too. Not only for his grandfather but for the doctors and nurses, the machines and medicine. Everything. He prayed. Still, his grandfather died. To his twelve-year-old mind, this was an act of the highest betrayal. He had done what was required, he had *prayed,* he had said the right words, many words. *PleasegodifIdidsomething wrongtocausethispleaseforgivemeitwasn'thisfaultsodon'ttakeit outonhimplease.* Still, his grandfather died. Many people told him it was part of God's plan. But if this was part of God's plan, then he didn't want any part of it. He wanted another plan.

Did people from Baltimore have accents?

"What did you do?"

"I don't know," says Amy. "I was alone. I was sitting in an exam room. Wearing one of those papery gown things. The doctor was real cold about it. They do that kind of stuff every day, I guess. Tell people they're going to die. Still, like 'here's a Kleenex' or something would have been nice. Every time I moved that white tissue paper you sit on made this super loud noise. I was fixated on that. The white tissue paper. It seemed so loud.

Later, after, when it finally sunk in, was when I first started hearing about the girl. I knew that was it, that I had to come."

He can't do it, no, not to this weeping, dying woman. He's thought of this moment so many times, of making a believer not believe, of undoing the years of slavish thought in a single, well-reasoned, secular humanist instant. But the Smiling Skeptic can't do it. He can't do what he's thought so long of doing. Bringing someone into the light of reason right before his eyes. Watching the belief and certainty drain from their face. Replaced by the doubt and uncertainty that is our true state. He can hear the sound of that white tissue paper.

"Look," the woman says.

And then they turn to see the ambulance, lights flashing, siren blaring, driving toward the football field, people starting to clap, to cheer, a collective euphoria rising, and he has to catch himself because he was about to join in, too.

* * *

The boys had hugged Linda like they hadn't hugged her in ages. Big, boyish, bear hugs. Trying-to-hold-you-as-close-as-humanly-possible hugs. I'm-so-happy-there-are-no-words hugs. Life-affirming hugs. Validation hugs. They were happy, the way boys should be happy, not how they usually were these days: moping, frowning, afraid. They felt fantastic, the hugs, giving her the courage she'd need in the coming days and weeks. Hugs that would have to last.

As of yesterday, he was officially gone, out of her life. Linda had expected more resistance, having put off this decision for so long partly because of the fear of what he'd do. She'd witnessed his temper firsthand before. One shit little thing that could transform him from David Banner to the Hulk, Jekyll to Hyde,

Regular Joe to Supreme Asshole. She was afraid. His track record of hearing bad/unwelcome news not exactly stellar. She did
not leave a note, it was face-to-face. He called her a cunt-bitch,
but left it at that, then stormed out, leaving behind all his things
(there wasn't much).

Just yesterday, thinks Linda. It's only been since yesterday and
yet it already seems like she's been free longer. This morning: that
first intoxicating breath of air, savoring it. Noting the empty space
in bed. Where he'd be, but was not. Amazing how much larger the
apartment seemed with just one less body in it, how much room
he took up both physically and emotionally. Reliving all this, those
revealing opening moments of the day, as she now rides in the
back of the ambulance with Karen and John, the newly arrived
husband, looking over at Anabelle, who's strapped in a gurney but
perpetually jiggling, as if her body is capable of movement, but it's
only the movement of the vehicle, driving to the high school where
she will be on display one last time and then it will be over.

Or will it?

People will still come. They will still show up at the house.
They will still believe. When Linda brought this up, Karen said
she hasn't gotten that far. She's dealing with today. She's dealing
with the return of her husband. Linda not sure what to make
of John yet. He's quiet. He seems stunned, a little like a shell-
shocked soldier who's returned home and is having trouble adjusting to taking out the trash when he's been used to shooting
at people. Pretty regularly he reaches out to touch Karen, as if
to confirm something with her, to bring her closer to him, and
sometimes you can see her jump, physically jump, the surprise
at his fingers being there.

Besides the three of them, there's also Anabelle's main doctor,

Dr. Patel, who's busy monitoring the machines and making sure Anabelle is comfortable and breathing without distress. Periodically, he readjusts her oxygen mask, which keeps slipping off. Others will be there to help, too—a small army of volunteers organized by Bryce. For the occasion, they had bought a special tent for her, as well as a portable generator and air conditioner, to keep Anabelle cool and shaded and regulated. Dr. Patel would be there at all times, the ambulance standing by if something went wrong and they needed to get Anabelle to a hospital. Karen had asked Linda to come, said "I'd really like you to be there," and so here she is, the ambulance moving slowly, navigating through the high school now, getting closer to the field, and at some point they hear cheering and clapping, and it's like they're rock stars.

Yes: Linda had finally broken down and prayed to Anabelle. A little quickie while Karen was out of the room. Prayed for the strength to do what she needed to do. And now she had done it. And it did not seem like a miracle. It seemed like a simple transaction. You asked for something and you got it. That's how the world worked sometimes, if you were lucky.

The boys had come home and hugged her and asked "Where's Victor?" and she told them. There they were in her arms, her beautiful sons, David and Danny, and she didn't want to let go.

The ambulance comes to a stop, and Karen says, "We're here."

* * *

Inmates at California's Avenal State Prison are allowed one hour of television during the day, from 11-12, right before lunch. This happens communally, in a large, gray concrete room with rows of folding chairs, and the TV gets rolled in every day, like it's some kind of daily blessing. It's also kind of cutthroat with regard to who chooses the station, the program. Usually it's the guard, Marty, who typically goes for ESPN. Marty hardly ever talks because he has a lisp. A prison guard with a lisp. Imagine that.

Today Matthew Ronald Kimbrough makes a point of being the first one in the room so that he can convince Marty to let them watch coverage of the girl at the football stadium. He pleads his case once Marty arrives, and the guard just shrugs, clicks the remote over to Channel 11.

Others begin to assemble and fill the seats. There is some grumbling when they see it isn't sports but the news. These men, too, say little, and Matthew Ronald Kimbrough is thankful for that. He has twelve years left in his sentence, will be up for parole in eight. He doesn't understand how that time will pass. He doesn't understand how you get over something like this. He will always be the drunk driver who caused an accident that paralyzed a little girl. This will be the single statement that defines his life, no matter what he does from here on out. It's all he'll think of. It's all his mother or sister or the person interviewing him for a job will think of. He has become someone else, familiar but no longer fully known, not fully his core self anymore, this whole other complicated layer that takes away from who and what he used to be. It was vodka gimlets that night, a woman next to him at the bar who laughed at his jokes and he thought maybe there was a chance.

On the TV, they cut from the anchors in the studio to the high school. Everyone waiting in line, the police cars, the ambulance, people getting out now. Then the mother. Then the father. He remembers them from the trial, their shattered faces, the few times when he could keep his eyes on them for more than two seconds. And then they carry out the girl. She's cocooned in one of those beds with wheels and straps, which they gently place on the ground, the legs extending to the proper position. They start pushing her. Photographers jockey around for the best angle, snapping away, cameramen filming, too. There are also machines on wheels, and other people are pushing the machines along in unison. The machines are connected to the girl and vice versa. They all move together, move as one scrum, move slowly, toward the end of the football field, where there seems to be some kind of shrine, only it's not really a shrine, it's a clear plastic dome-shaped tent, about seven feet high and eighteen feet long, which is up on a stage and which reminds him of the movie from when he was growing up, *The Boy in the Plastic Bubble,* where this little kid had this weird disease and couldn't go outside or touch anyone and he had to live in a bubble, which really wasn't a bubble but a completely antiseptic and germ-free plastic enclosure thing in his room, and he remembers it being one of the few times he cried as a child, watching this movie. He figures that's where they're going to put the girl, that's where the people will pass by and say what they'll say, pray what they'll pray, do what they'll do, and Matthew Ronald Kimbrough suddenly wants to be there, very badly, he knows what he'd ask for: forgiveness. And he'd not only ask the girl but also the mother and the father, and he's picturing it in his mind, these conversations, what he'd say, and how the parents would reply, when somebody, a fellow prisoner, snaps him out of it by saying, "What the fuck is this fuck-shit we're watching? Someone change it to CNN. I want to see the countdown for when everything goes up in smoke. Only one more day to go. Then all this, all this here, won't matter. We're all the same. We're all equal. Free at last, free at last."

* * *

He decided not to go. Because of the long drive from Laguna Beach, because of the crowds and the parking (he'd had enough of that at the girl's house). But as he sits in his living room, watching it on TV, sipping reheated coffee and debating whether or not he's going to ignore Patricia's wishes and have a memorial service anyway, he kind of wishes he had. The mother, Karen, has just walked up to the podium to address the crowd. She looks overwhelmed, tired, nervous. A man stands next to her, close, suspiciously scanning the audience and scenery the way Secret Service guys do, seeking out the one deadly anomaly amid a sea of ordinariness. The mother utters "Good morning" and the microphone responds with squealing, high-pitched feedback.

Donald can't explain exactly why he wants to be there. He visited the girl, he made his entreaty, he drove home, and Patricia died three days later. His desire, he figures, probably has something to do with being around people who understand what he's been going through. Who were also dealing with life and death— mostly death. If you weren't immersed in this intense, narrowed existence, this tunneling down to questions of what constitutes living and how long you'd want to prolong something that might not be living, you just didn't know. You just didn't know. He supposes he wants to be around people who know.

His son and daughter-in-law, who had taken care of Patricia while he made the journey to El Portal, didn't know about the visit. He'd lied, fabricated something about lunch with an old friend from work, from way back in the day, no, no one you'd remember. If they had known they would have wondered about him, just as he was wondering about himself. What was next? Psychics with 900 numbers? Poorly toupeed late-night TV preachers whose mere touch sends the faithful into mystic convulsions? Whatever it took, he'd decided. Whatever it took to have his wife for a little while longer. And whatever it took to make the decision that will either liberate him or destroy him. Which was what led him to Shaker Street, another seeker of miracles and wonders, one of many.

It had taken all day, what with the driving and getting lost. Then hours to get in. Hours with his new best friend Cassie Solinski. Hours to consider the mysteries of faith. Hours in the sun. Then that woman had collapsed. Heat stroke was the general consensus among the crowd. Or smog stroke, if there is such a thing. Or maybe she was overcome by the spirit of the girl, even from outside. He heard such stories from the people in line. And other tales, from the papers and TV: communion wafers that leaked blood; the teenager with chronic acne who visited Anabelle and the next day was clear-skinned for the first time in her life; the elderly neighbor who took a photograph of the girl and an angel appeared in the background.

The room was small and locker-room stuffy, smelling powerfully of flowers and bodies and incense. Barely enough room for the bed—one of those hospital beds that has retractable railings so the sleeper will not fall out, similar to his wife's bed in ICU, but smaller, girl-sized—plus the respirator and the other anonymous gadgetry keeping her alive, breathing. He didn't know what to do. Kneel? Stand? Pray? The Father/Son/Holy Spirit thing that the Latino baseball players do? Think of his wife? He should have been more prepared, done some research, paid more attention in that Intro to World Religions G.E. class he'd taken sophomore year at USC. He wanted to ask the mother: What do most people do? But she had already left, respectfully giving him his time alone. And then there was the earlier breakdown in the living room. An open wound that worsened the more he dwelled on it. But how could he not? How had he let that happen? Crying in front of strangers. Bawling. This was not like him. This was not like the man who'd paid for his children's college educations by mastering the stock market in his spare time. He was letting his wife down. Failing her.

It was hard to look at the girl for more than a few seconds. Seeing her so immobile and helpless, a miniature version of his wife. So removed. Reduced. All the motion and momentums of life gone. Is it worse to have a child like this or a spouse? Is it valid to even entertain such questions? He tried to avoid the girl's eyes: Hershey's brown, eerily open, blinking occasionally. Thinking what? Looking for what? And he told himself to banish the next thought, to blot it out before it fully formed, but it was too late, there it was, it had already mutated too far, he was fucking up: She didn't look holy or blessed or anything. She looked like a sad, crippled little girl. That's all. Then he became aware of the passing of time, the seconds slipping away. He had to make good use of his allotted minutes. He had to concentrate, focus. The mother said she'd knock before she came back in.

Out of panic, what he did was this: He explained what had happened to his wife. Quickly summarizing the details, the *Reader's Digest* version, making sure to point out the similarities between his wife's situation and her own, the girl's, a little sympathy couldn't hurt, might as well, working up to the pledge they'd agreed to years before—that if one of them wasn't really living that something should be done—and thus his current dilemma. He wasn't sure if he said all of this out loud or merely recited it internally (had he bowed his head? closed his eyes? would his ignorance of protocol lessen the chances of the girl helping?), but either way the information was out there, passing, he hoped, maybe, from him to the girl and then who knows.

The mother did indeed knock, gently said, "How are we doing here?" Her voice soft and floating. She touched his hand. He touched back. There were still three more people waiting for their turn, including the sort of loudmouth guy, Ned, Ted, who had placed his hand on his shoulder and called him brother.

Driving home that night, he thought how rare it was these days for him to brave the traffic and travel northward to L.A. People in Orange County were generally afraid of Los Angeles, and Donald Westerfield was no exception. He also didn't usually listen to the radio when he drove, but he was doing so now because today was a day of irregularity and impulse and why not follow it through all the way. Someone, a man with a regional accent of some kind, was talking manically and circularly, the general thesis involving the U.S.'s uncertain international role in this post–Cold War era.

The question, then, that kept snapping back at him as he steered the Lexus: Do you have to be a true believer for it to work? And what if you're not? Does that make him an impostor? Always, always his instinct to gravitate toward the here and now, the tangible muck of his day-to-day life, not what may or may not be above the clouds, elsewhere, unknown. He's probably agnostic, though he's never used the word to describe himself. (It means maybe there is, maybe there isn't, right? Hedging your bets, playing it safe, which makes perfect sense to him.

Actually, there was one thing he remembered from that religion class: something called Pascal's Wager, which basically said that we're incapable of really knowing whether God exists, yet we must wager whether he does. And it's the smarter wager to believe in God because if it turns out that God does exist you'll be rewarded in the afterlife. But if you wager against God, if you don't believe, and it turns out that he exists, well, then you're screwed and you'll be punished for your disbelief. On the other hand, if God doesn't exist, you don't lose anything either way. The gist, then, being: it's better to believe than not to believe.) If cornered on the subject at a cocktail party—not that they went to cocktail parties anymore—he'd just say he's not that religious and leave it at that. Patricia a little more certain, believing there is some kind of force out there, a truth and mystery beyond us, a higher power, but never taking it much further than that.

The radio garbled out chunks of static as he scanned the stations. A Costco lasagna awaited him at home, ready to be microwaved, bought by his son the previous day, along with army-sized rations of pancake mix, almonds, mouthwash. He hadn't eaten all day, his stomach reminding him with periodic gurgles and snarls. The faraway voices on the radio continued to fight through the poor reception. Wyatt from Dime Box, Texas, was concerned about the country's lack of purpose.

The Lexus almost drove itself. It should, considering how much it set him back (Patricia not complaining, allowing him the indulgence because he had so few), and it was a good thing, too: Donald's thoughts consumed him as he drove, ping-ponging from the girl to Patricia to his family and back to the girl again, large blocks of time disappearing without him realizing it, and suddenly he was on the 133 and weaving through Laguna Canyon and almost home. He thought how he would soon pull into the garage and turn off the engine. He'd sit there for a while, then go inside, shower, check the mail, water Patricia's plants. Next he'd head back to the hospital, greet his son and daughter-in-law, thank them, apologize for being late, the traffic, time flies, etc. He'd wait until after they had left. Then he'd confide to his wife that he went and saw the little girl, the one he told her about, the girl on TV. He'd say: *I prayed. I think I prayed. I hope I did it right. I should have checked. We'll see. Now there's nothing to do but wait. Wait and see. Wait and hope that it's all true. That miracles exist, are still possible in this day and age, so late in the century. What do you think of that? And how are you, my dear? How was your day? Tell me. How was your day?*

And that's pretty much what had happened that day. And it was OK that the little girl did not save Patricia; she had died, was gone; and that meant he no longer had to grapple with the decision of whether to take her off life support, so perhaps he didn't get what he asked for but he did get something else. And now he's here on the sofa and on TV the mother has finished speaking and he wishes he was one of the people surging forward to see the girl one last time. He just wants to tell her that Patricia is gone and that it's OK, and yes there will be a service, something small and intimate for friends and family, because they need to remember his wife, his beautiful dead wife, and the remembering was beginning now and would last as long as he kept waking up in the morning, as long as he breathed and ate and walked the earth and was capable of recalling her face, her smell, her essence, her love.

* * *

She knows, yes, she can feel it, she can tell: there is something growing inside her belly, life taking root, a baby, a boy, yes, another boy. Things are happening and cannot be stopped. This not long after her time with the Miracle Girl, her neighbor. She and Marcus waited with the others, chatting, after the woman had passed out, small talk among strangers, the mother's eyes scanning back and forth like radar as she spoke and listened and spoke, nice and cordial, but obviously there were like eight thousand things on her mind.

And then Mavis and Marcus were inside the room, just like it looked on TV, only smaller seeming; and there Mavis was, so close to her own her house and yet in this famous room, this newly designated holy place, that had been broadcast to the world.

"Belle honey, this is Mr. and Mrs. Morris, our neighbors," the mother introduced. "From across the street. They wanted to meet you. They're going to spend a little time with you."

The mother smiled at them, slipped away, closed the door, though not completely; a just-in-case-you-need-me crack remained.

Now what? Mavis thought. She tapped an uncharacteristically unpolished nail on the rail of the girl's bed: the metal, or whatever it's made of, cool, smooth, like something you'd want to press your cheek against on such a hot day (she did not, however). The voices and activity elsewhere in the house. The factorylike churning of her thoughts. The heart's inadequacy when confronted with the magnitude of its raw wants.

Mavis assumed the position, followed, reluctantly, by Marcus. It'd been a while. Her head swirled. She went back to the hospital and when they pulled it—him—from her womb and how when she saw Marcus crying she knew it was bad, bad. Nobody would tell her anything at first and she was so narcoticized that even when they explained what happened she was thinking, *fine, I can deal, I'm floating here, floating along like a dream and anything that comes along I can handle, I can incorporate it into the dream and make it right.* Other snapshots of her life flashbulbed in her mind, too: the time her brother brought Marcus over for Sunday supper, their first introduction when she was just fifteen years old; her father's easily provoked fury, his children forever disappointing him in some vague, unacknowledged way; her mother retreating to her baked goods and Billie Holiday records. But she told herself to focus, to pray. So she prayed. She prayed for her dead son with no name. She prayed for the fertility of a rabbit. She prayed that one day they might be able to have another child, that whatever had been corrupted inside her would heal and disappear like a paper cut. She prayed that Marcus wanted this as much as she did. She prayed that she and Marcus were not too old. She prayed that the statistics you hear about older women and birth defects would not apply to her. She prayed and she realized it had been years since she'd clasped her hands like this, palm to palm, dropped down to her knees and humbled herself, eyes shut, head bowed, and it felt good, it felt right, it was a goddamned (sorry) relief in fact, and it was as if there was this great unburdening of something, an internal relinquishing that shuddered through her pleasantly submissive body. Nice. She prayed for the mother, the neighborhood; for Marcus, if she hadn't already, specifically singled him out, that is. And while she was at it she prayed for her aunt, for her parents, for her nieces and nephews, for anybody whose life basically intersected with her own, amen. Opened her eyes and the girl hadn't moved, hadn't budged, because she couldn't move, couldn't budge; but that mouth, those eyes; the eyes of the living dead; the eyes of her son had they ever opened.

She knows, yes, she can feel it, and she could feel something was already changing right after they left the girl's house that day and came home and she said now and he said what? and she said upstairs, now, while the magic's still fresh, and he said fine. She's been telling Marcus this—the knowing—all throughout the morning, while watching TV, switching back and forth between the girl and the coverage at the high school and *The Price Is Right*, Marcus now shuffling to the bathroom, in need of a break—from the TV, from her.

"It might be a while," warns Marcus, who's known for camping out in the bathroom for long stretches of time, typically working his way through multiple magazines in one sitting. "My stomach again," he adds.

The baby boy's name, by the way, is Anthony. He is growing and will continue to grow until he's ready to come out, the eight and a half months will fly by. Marcus will hold him in his arms and then, there—all the doubt and hesitation and everything else will disappear. They will be parents, at last. Anthony will coo and gurgle and charm them. A baby! A boy! Look! Marcus's diapering skills will improve. The adjustment will be hard but worth it, so, so satisfying. Baby Anthony will crawl then walk. Sounds then words will fill his beautiful mouth. They will tell him things, teach him things. Their house will become what it's never been: a home. They will, however, eventually move to a bigger house, a better neighborhood with better schools and better malls, better everything. Marcus's back will heal and he'll be able to work again. Anthony will grow, grow: the miracle of childhood. He will start school and excel. *My,* his teachers will say, *what a smart boy, what a bright boy, you've got a very special child there,* *Mr. and Mrs. Morris.* Good things will happen. Promotions at work. Investments paying off. Time at the gym and regular doctor checkups and clean bills of health. Anthony a boy that will hug freely and without restraint, that will be warm and loving, and that also will like sports. Baseball. That will be his game, and he will excel here as well, and they will attend all his games, support him and love him, always love him. Then it will be junior high already and the girls will call on the phone, naturally, Anthony sweet and a little shy, Marcus having started his own business, following his dream, and it will take off and there will be another house and an even better school, life amazes, and Anthony will make all-stars for the second year in a row, plus they'll take vacations to Hawaii and Europe. Then high school will be upon them, Anthony joining clubs and of course the baseball team. They'll purchase a new car for Mavis, a Mercedes, even though she rarely drives, hates driving and yet lives in L.A. (funny, right?), and pretty soon Anthony himself will be driving, applying to colleges and thinking he wants to be either a scientist or a lawyer. And through it all, as the years accumulate and yield better and better things, Mavis will every now and then think of the girl, think of their old neighbor, how on that day she touched Anabelle and then touched her own stomach, how something must have passed from the girl to Mavis, and everything thereafter was blessed, everything thereafter was changed, and you could argue it was the girl or Mavis's own positive thinking or that's just how things would have worked out anyway, it didn't matter, because it all happened, her life finally happened the way it was supposed to happen, and it was all beautiful and just like she'd always pictured it.

"I'm telling you, Marcus," she calls out to him. "I can feel it."

"Why don't you just take one of those tests you can buy at Sav-ons and be done with it?" Marcus answers from the bathroom.

"I don't need a test to tell me what I already know," Mavis says. "I know what's happening with my body. We got a baby on the way, so get ready, husband. Get ready for the adventure of your life."

* * *

Bryce Resnick hands out the last of the T-shirts—red, short sleeves, ANABELLE'S ANGELS blazed across the back, a pair of angel wings hovering above the words, his own design, only Smalls and XXLs left. He's also trying to keep things as orderly as possible now that the procession has commenced; he's running from the stage to the designated start of the line, people coming forward, hungry for their time with Anabelle. It's only just begun and already he's exhausted, having been going-going-going since five this morning, making phone calls, setting up, coordinating, checking the p.a. system, tracking down extra trash cans and duct tape and markers for signs. After Karen spoke, he went to the mic and explained to the crowd how it would work: from the viewing line that's been formed here between the two sections of chairs on the field, we'll start letting in small groups, then you can come up onto the stage, walk past the tent, and see Anabelle inside, feel free to pause, take a moment, but please try to keep moving along as much as possible, because, as you can see, we have a lot of folks here today, then keep walking and exit down the stairs on the side of the stage, I'll be at the front of the line helping out, like a traffic cop directing traffic and answering any questions you may have, and if you're sitting in one of the chairs, please consider that there are others waiting for your seat, and when you pass by Anabelle pictures are fine, video is all right, too, but again try to remember to keep it brief, I'm sorry, but we want to accommodate everyone, this has been an amazing journey and the spirit of Anabelle will always be with us, and if you think about it this isn't an ending if we keep Anabelle and what she represents in our hearts, thank you.

He doesn't know what will happen after today. The arrival of the husband—John—sealed his fate. Even though, sure, he'd fucked things up before that with that kiss. His communication with Karen has been minimal as of late, mostly details and logistics related to the day, but at some point he'd need to talk to her. There was still the website, all the e-mails, the reaching out from all over the country and the world. Maybe Karen was ready for it to stop, but he wasn't.

"Can I go yet?" asks the woman who's next in line, her forehead beaded with sweat, shifting her purse to her other shoulder, switching the bouquet of flowers to her other hand.

Bryce checks his watch, looks up at the sky, gaping and alive with clouds and color and complicated light. It was a year ago today that his mother died. After a long illness, as they say, and after he had moved back home to take care of her, putting his life on hold—not that it was much of a life, living in West Hollywood working odd jobs and going to acting auditions and being told things like his face was too asymmetrical. Besides the cancer (specifically, lymphoma; more specifically, non-Hodgkin's lymphoma), there were strokes, broken bones, pneumonia, neuropathy, depression, dementia. A total betrayal of the body and mind, and he was witness to it all, his father long dead and his brother long gone. At the end it was just him and the hospice nurse, a

Filipina woman named Donna with whom he primarily com-
municated via hand gestures and degrees of eyebrow arching.

A year ago today, as he watched men with suits and gloves
carry his body-bagged mother out of the house, the accident also
occurred. The very same day. Almost simultaneously. Coinci-
dence? He thinks not. He no longer believes in coincidences. He
now believes in fate, destiny, the inevitability of things. Just look
at how Anabelle came into his life when he needed her, needed
something to turn him inside out, after too many years of floating inconsequence. Anabelle gave him hope. Anabelle gave him
something that previously did not exist within him.

"Is it my turn yet?" the woman asks again.

"Not quite yet," Bryce says. "Almost."

* * *

Kellee Clifton is not working today, not officially. She's not covering the event, but she's here anyway, flashing her press creden-
tials to bypass the lines. She's here to give thanks, wanting to see
Anabelle one last time, because she got the call from the network
and she's moving on, bound for New York and the real big time,
ABC headquarters, a national gig, and it's because of the girl.
The Powers That Be had followed her series of stories about the
Miracle Girl, and they were impressed, they made an offer, and
now she's in the midst of packing up her apartment in Los Feliz,
saying good-bye to friends and colleagues, breaking up with her
boyfriend (poor Dalton, he wasn't taking it so well), and it was
so amazing to think—Kellee Clifton from a small town in West
Virginia no one has ever heard of, and for good reason, growing
up poor and invisible, a stutter, a glasses-wearer, a bark-eater, a
talker to trees, a girl that didn't get invited to birthday parties

because everyone in town knew her family couldn't afford a gift, and now look at her, just look, the transformation, and if it wasn't a miracle then it sure sometimes felt like it, how your life can surprise you and surpass your expectations. She wants to touch the girl's hand one more time, feel her skin, and give thanks.

* * *

The earth shakes briefly, then stops.

* * *

He purposefully left his clerical collar at home, opting instead for a T-shirt he received after running the annual Marina del Rey 5K Turkey Trot N Fun Run last month. Meaning he's here covertly, like he's undercover, and he's here to absorb, not make conclusions, part of his ongoing, neverending research. Actually, he should probably be in his office, combing through his findings and deciphering all his notes and preparing for the upcoming presentation to Archbishop McAdams. The calls from the media, the pressure from his superiors. Building, building. Poor Nancy about to crack. Everyone wants to know: what's the church's official position on the matter of Anabelle Vincent and her supposed miracles?

Good question, agrees Father Jim Hinshaw, who's currently standing on the five-yard line, about three or so people away from the front of the line leading to the girl, also now calming the jittery woman behind him who'd started hyperventilating when the ground shook with a fierce jump and then ceased just as suddenly, causing a wave of exclamations and *whoooooa*s among the steadfast, heat-dazed crowd. She's not from California, the woman explains. She's from Tennessee. She's not used to earth-quakes. In fact, it's her first.

"They're not all so short and brief," says Father Jim. "Espe-cially the ones we've been having lately. They go on and on. This one was minor compared."

Talking like a long-time resident, Father Jim recently celebrat-ing his two-year anniversary in Los Angeles, an occasion marked by a phone call to his parents and a pint of Ben & Jerry's.

"Guess I've been baptized then," the woman tells him. "I'm officially in Southern California."

Father Jim laughs. Baptized. If she only knew who she was talking to.

He'd arrived early this morning, his bus getting stuck in the swell of traffic, although he was more than happy to hop off and walk the two miles to the high school. Now it's past one, the day sweltering along (December! Winter! When would it ever cool down? It was snowing back in Ohio), and the line moves swiftly, efficiently, they're doing a pretty good job of maintaining the flow of traffic, and soon enough he's next, and a young man in a red T-shirt tells him to wait here until it's time, then it's time, and then he's walking toward the stage, rehearsing his prayer for and to the girl. The mother, Karen, sees him, waves him over to the front of the stage and steps down to talk to him.

"Father Hinshaw," says Karen. "Were you waiting all this time? You could have come right up here. I didn't see you."

"That's OK. I was fine waiting in line. I just wanted to see Anabelle again. Like everyone else."

"This is my husband, John."

A man on the stage approaches the edge, leans down, extends a hand.

"John, nice to meet you."

Father Jim shakes hands with the husband. There's never been a husband before.

"Hi," says John, a tallish, uncertain-looking guy. "You're a . . . priest?"

"Well, I left the collar at home today. We're allowed to do that sometimes. Plus the heat. I'm better off."

"Father Hinshaw has been working on the investigation," Karen explains to John. "By the Catholic Church. They putting together a report. How's it coming along, Father?"

"Oh, we're plugging along. A lot of people to interview. A lot of information and stories to sift through. But we're making progress. Slow but steady. We'll get there. All your cooperation has been a big help."

And as he says all this, he's picturing all the documents and articles and testimonials piled up and waiting for him on his desk. All the data gathered so far. And yet what it will come down to—for him, personally, not the report—is a gut feeling, a sensation of knowing/not knowing. Like a cop with a hunch. It is, ultimately, a leap of faith. He knows his Kierkegaard. Faith and belief—these supposed occurrences, these purported miracles were not based on evidence, could never be. You make the commitment of belief because that's what you know to be true in your heart. It was that simple. Doubt still exists, still descends like a dark cloud from time to time. But you make the leap. Again and again. Just because you believe doesn't mean you don't have to cross that river repeatedly. You do.

"How are you holding up, Karen?"

"It's been a long day. But we"—looking back at her husband—"we felt like it was the right thing to do. We just didn't want it to end with shutting and locking our door. It seemed necessary. Some kind of a final send-off. *Closure* is what people have been saying."

"It's very kind," Father Jim says. "This and everything before. Not a lot of people would have done what you did."

"Thank you, Father. That's nice to hear."

Father Jim turns and looks behind him, at the line he'd been standing in, a river of souls waiting in the sun. This is what amazes him, even more than the girl: the people who came, the people who need something, the people seeking their own individual solaces, some named, some not named. They had the faces of angels.

"Why don't you go inside," says Karen.

"Thank you," he says.

He climbs the stairs to the stage, ducks into the tent, nods to the doctor and stern-looking nurse who are monitoring everything. The girl appears the same as on his previous visits to the house, except sweat rims her forehead and face. She remains hooked up to various machines, the portable air conditioner chugs away, and additional fans have been brought in as well. Yet it's still balmy inside, rain forest-y. Father Jim quickly catalogs the small mountain of items that have been placed at the foot of the stretcher/bed throughout the day: flowers, balloons, cards, candy, photographs, handwritten notes, stuffed animals. It's like a minishrine, one of those memorials that spontaneously spring up in the wake of tragedy and death; Anabelle, however, is alive; or rather her own unique version of alive; somewhere in between life and death, hovering in a kind of spiritual and physical limbo, which is perhaps what bestows this apparent holiness upon her. Perhaps.

Father Jim makes his prayers, says what he has to say. His

time is up, and he departs the tent, getting envious stares from those filing by—who is he to receive such special treatment; they are just the masses, and there are so many of them on this long, last, almost-end-of-the-millennium day.

* * *

It wasn't meant to be a funeral, but it kind of feels that way, what with everyone shuffling by, as if paying their final respects, though it's certainly an ending—or is it, John wonders, really a beginning? For him it is. It's his chance. His second chance. And he's not going to fuck things up this time.

Of course he'd seen it on TV—the people, Anabelle, Karen, the reporters, the spectacle, the women fainting, the men crying—back when he was in Henderson, and then, in person, at the house after his return. Now this, now today. A high school football stadium—his old high school, in fact—brimming with activity. Helicopters flying overhead. Cameras everywhere. If it wasn't his daughter he'd probably scoff, make jokes, dismiss the whole thing. But he's inside it, part of it, sort of. So it's different. He's experienced firsthand the scores of people who seek out his daughter, and whether or not anything actually happens (a cure, a healing, a prayer answered) it doesn't really matter. They are better. They have hope. Something that previously did not exist. And it's the same with him: now he has hope, too.

They've been sitting on the stage for hours, next to each other, side by side, not saying much, occasionally commenting on the size of the crowd and the growing mountain of flowers and gifts at the foot of the stage, crossing and recrossing their legs, sipping bottled water, thankfully shaded by the canopy, marveling at the sight before them, witnesses to countless visitors coming and

going, Karen at times checking in with Dr. Patel and the nurse to
see how Anabelle is holding up (so far so good). Somebody said
the estimate was now over ten thousand. More police were on
the way to help out.

"Do you want to go for a walk?" John asks.

"God yes."

They hop off the stage without telling anyone, roam around
like teenagers playing hooky (something, in fact, they did together while she was still in high school, driving to the beach and
disappearing for the day, everything a possibility and adventure),
and everywhere they go people approach Karen like she's the
Pope, wanting to talk to her, shake her hand, give her a hug,
touch her if only briefly, commenting on the earlier earthquake
and asking her what she thought it meant. It's like being with a
celebrity. And that's what Karen has become while he was gone:
someone that people recognize, that they think they know even
if they don't, a face that elicits an automatic response, warm and
welcomed. There's one guy—kind of pushy, glasses, wearing a
backpack, hair greasy, neglected—who says he has a website
and could he ask her some questions, but John intervenes, tells
the guy Karen needs to clear her head and get some food, sorry
man, and then just like that someone else hands them two giant
sub sandwiches wrapped in foil, and they peel away from the
crowd, munching their food and settling on an empty wooden
bench next to the gym, named for a long-ago alumni who played
in the NFL for two seasons.

"Any big plans for New Year's Eve?"

Karen smiles. The sandwiches are almost finished. They'd
both forgotten to eat, too immersed in the proceedings to note

their hunger, which had been unleashed now that food was en route to their stomachs.

"I don't know," she says. "Probably just stay in. I'll be lucky if I make it past eleven."

"Come on. Dick Clark is counting on you."

There are full-blown conversations now, even some of their old banter. Each day, then, he proves his worthiness a little more. Progress. Because when trust has been broken like this—well, there are no quick fixes. He knows this. The only cure is time. Proof that he's staying, will stay. He also knows there have been phone calls and conversations on the subject of his return. Warnings to Karen from family and friends and people he doesn't know. Some overt and some not so overt. If he left once he'll leave again. Men are men. People don't change, only the seasons change (unless of course you live in Los Angeles).

During those awkward times, he'll slink toward Anabelle's room and check on her and the current visitor, who usually will thank him and confess his or her story to him in a few hurried sentences. He's heard a lot of stories since he's been back. He already understood how fragile life can be, how quickly things can change and turn tragic (the accident had taught him all that, and more), but he receives further affirmation of this from these brand-new tales of woe and despair and misfortune. How people can be shattered yet still manage to wake up in the morning, do what they need to do. Then the visitor will leave (again thanking him) and he'll be alone. Just him. His daughter. The room. The first time he saw her after his return: her face looked essentially the same, a bit older perhaps, motionless and mysterious as ever, but he discerned a sparkle of recognition there, a sense that she, too, knew he was back. And she was happy about this. And wanted to throw her arms around him and say she loved him still. Welcome home, Daddy. These were the people of his life: his wife, his daughter. This was where he should be. Daddy. Husband. John. Life could resume now. He was lucky. He was sleeping on the couch. And that was fine. This low-level kindling he hoped to coax into a full-on flame.

They've finished their sandwiches. Could have eaten another one, both of them famished. The bench filled with chipped paint and splinters, carved initials and cryptic slang. Whatever happened to all those people he went to high school with? Was twelve, thirteen years really so long ago? Maybe they'll go searching for the sandwich person on their way back. That could have been the best sandwich of his life. The most nourishing, most needed, certainly.

Karen says, "How long do we let it go on?"

Her smell. God. He had missed her smell. Not her perfume-y smell. Her life smell.

"However long it takes, I think," he says.

"We could be here well into the night."

"Will the lights go on?"

"I don't know."

"I guess we'll find out."

He wonders: What did he himself really believe? What did he make of what had happened to his daughter and wife? What did he make of anything? All his life this vague sense of adolescent drift, of moving from one thing to the next without seeing the connections, without fully understanding the deeper implications. Other people—friends, adults—had advanced in a way he hadn't. There'd been a general stalling. When would that end?

Maybe now. Maybe now that he was here. Back. Redeeming himself. Making it right. Yes. Maybe now there was the chance, the possibility. His true life would begin.

"Are you ready to go back?" she asks.

"No," he says.

"Me neither."

"Then let's not."

* * *

After a while you get really, really tired of people asking if you're tired. Karen can't count how many times she's been asked that question or flat-out been told "You look tired" or "My, you look like you need some sleep, dear" throughout this very long, very draining day. But she *is* tired, so fuck it, who cares—she's beat like she's never been beat (which is saying something), the sun finally sinking down, the SoCal sunset blazing red and orange and purple, like one of those Laserium light shows she and John used to go see at Griffith Park (minus the soundtrack of Pink Floyd's *Dark Side of the Moon*), and still there are more people waiting, always more people, always more faces. The only dreams she remembers now are the dreams of faces. Nothing else but faces. One after another, a neverending movie reel, each different and new and wanting something from her. It's hard to imagine ever being alone again. Or just her and John. And Anabelle. Always Anabelle. They need to get back to that core: the three of them, a family. But not like they were before. Different. Transformed. Again, that word.

The football stadium lights do come on, in a sudden, surprising burst, flooding the field with an influx of manufactured brightness. The crowd spontaneously applauds. It's a pause, a

breath that everyone seems to need. She senses their energy sagging, true, yet they remain dedicated, alert, collectively yearning.
It takes a while for Karen's eyes to adjust to the new light, like
when an eye doctor dilates your pupils. Everything temporarily
sensitive and blurry. It would be nice to have a margarita. Her
left ass-cheek burns. These folding chairs they've been sitting on
all day truly suck, probably dating back to before she was born.
She blinks repeatedly until there's focus again.

Not long after the lights switch on, Dr. Patel stops by for his
hourly update, informing them that Anabelle is a trooper, she's
doing fine, asking how much longer they want to keep going. She
glances at John, sitting next to her, leaning forward and tapping
his thigh to prevent his leg from falling asleep again. He sips a
Snapple lemonade, looks extremely tired as well. But he nods.
So does Linda, who's next to John, who's also in it for the long
haul, prepared to see this through, giving Anabelle mini massages every other hour. Seems like days ago when the ambulance
pulled into the driveway at the house, the three of them, plus Dr.
Patel, watching the mustache paramedic guys transport Anabelle
to the vehicle, then climbing in themselves, backing up with the
lights flashing and the brakes squeaking. Her neighbor, Mavis,
waving at them from across the street, calling out something they
couldn't hear.

"There's people still waiting," Karen tells Dr. Patel, motion-
ing to the line, trying to suppress a noticeable yawn. "Let's keep
going for a little while longer if we can. Let's see how many more
can get through. I don't want to have to turn anyone away."

Plus she's also given like ten, twelve, twenty interviews today,
saying the same things over and over, reminding her of professional athletes and their stock locker-room phrases: *we're taking*

it one day at a time, we're trying to stay focused and positive, one game doesn't make a season, we know what we need to do and now we just need to go out there and do it.

"I'll tell the nurse and Bryce," says Dr. Patel. "But I'd recommend no more than an hour longer, Karen. It's been quite a day. She's doing fine but we don't want to overdo it."

Dr. Patel wears a white long-sleeved shirt and patterned tie yet he doesn't sweat. He's short, heavyset, always glancing at his watch. Probably not much older than her sister Tammy, who surprised her by coming today ("I need to be around more," she told Karen), along with Dom of course (another piercing, this time her lip), along with her friends Marnie and Meredith, who had been there since the beginning, when the house first smelled of roses. Karen's always astonished by people around her own age, like Dr. Patel, who have made it in the world. The confidence required. The lack of self-doubt. Not caring what others think. Some people were like that. She wondered how they lived, how they came to be that way, so far from her own hushed existence.

"All right," she says. "One more hour then."

"And I think we're going to need a truck for all the gifts. You could open your own store."

After he speaks briefly with Bryce, Dr. Patel returns to the tent, and the procession continues.

One more hour then. John now taps his other thigh, and she thinks of how she's glad she convinced her mother not to come, who otherwise would be here on the stage, how she would second-guess everything, from the clothes Anabelle was wearing to the music playing over the loudspeakers, always putting in her two told-you-so cents, asking if it was all right to smoke even though prominent NO SMOKING signs were posted everywhere, all of which would have made for an entirely different day. For the best.

It feels strange to be on a stage, elevated like this. Reminds her of high school graduation, of walking across the makeshift platform to receive her diploma. She'd hurried along, kept her eyes down, almost tripped. She's never liked the spotlight. Her own locker-room phrases include: *I have mixed feelings about all this ending, and but I can't help but wonder if it is ending, I still have my daughter, I still have Anabelle, that is never going to change, you're a parent forever.*

But she's learned how to present herself, even though she knows she still blushes, her neck and chest blooming an embarrassing red. When a reporter asks John a question, he just shakes his head, says he'd rather not, it's not his thing.

True, John was never much of a talker, a man of few words, fewer monologues. Hates talking on the phone, too. He did call her, once, during his time away. It was fairly early on and she was halfway through a bottle of wine, Dom spending the night to help with Anabelle and give Karen a little break. The "break" consisted of folding laundry while watching a *Designing Women* rerun (and the wine). His voice sounded distant, like he was calling from somewhere far away that he'd never actually be— Europe, China, Australia. She started to cry. She tried not to, but she did. He apologized. Said he needed to figure some things out. He'd take care of them. He'd send money. Every week. Whatever he had. To help with Anabelle's mounting medical bills. To tide them over until the money from the lawsuit finally came through. He'd figure things out and then. She kept crying. She said you let me know, you let me know when you figure things out because I'd like to know, too. The conversation ended at some point and the dial tone morphed into that annoying beeping/squawking, which she didn't realize until Dom was there and hung up the phone for her.

Bryce's voice booms through the p.a. system: "Hi everyone. Me again. Bryce. How's it going out there? Just a little update. We weren't planning to go this long, but we really want everyone to be able to see Anabelle today, so we're extending for one more hour. That's one more hour. It would be helpful if you could speed up the pace and then hopefully everyone who's still here will get their turn. Hang in there. And thanks again for your patience today."

Bryce, who's a different person now that John is back. Bryce, who she wants to take aside and say something reassuring and life-affirming and original and not a stock letting-you-down-easy-type phrase *(it's not you, it's me, things happen for a reason, you're a great guy, you'll find someone else, love comes when you least expect it)*, but she's not sure what words to use. He's already moved away from her, and she understands.

One more hour then. She wants to be home. She wants it to be over. The past six months are like a dream, a fiction that is also true. She realizes that, more than anything else, she believes in her daughter. Not all the religion and God and miracle stuff. She simply believes in her daughter. She reaches over and touches John's hand, skin against skin, hers, his. She finds herself doing this often now: touching him, verifying. He touches back.

While he was gone, she often asked herself: What if he never comes home? What if this is permanent? Would she survive? She came to the conclusion, after several months, that yes she would survive. Damaged, yes; lessened, sure; but she'd survive.

She realized she possessed a strength that she previously did not know existed. She would survive either way. But this way was the preferred way. This way was better. And it would continue to get better, if she believed, if he believed. She wanted to tell him things right away, right now, before they escaped her. It was hard not to give in to this electric urgency. But there was no rush. Because now there was time. The better way—

A woman screams. Who? Everyone sitting on the stage turns. It's a woman passing by Anabelle and who has now stopped moving, as has everyone else. The woman looks around, panicked, like a shoplifter who gets a tap on the shoulder, guilty, caught. She screams: "The girl! The girl! She moved! I swear, she moved!"

Karen and John rush over to the tent, followed by others onstage, plus the passersby surging forward to take a look, a general jockeying and rubbernecking for position to see what's going on.

"Are we filming?" someone yells. Cameras point, aim, click, focus.

The woman who screamed moves aside so that Karen and John can go in and check on their daughter. They trade alarmed looks, gaze down at Anabelle. Nothing. The tent's plastic is clear but could the woman have seen anything from outside? Or is she crazy? Is it another tall tale? Another story that will be passed down no matter if it's been proven true or false? Karen tries to calm the insistence of her rapidly beating heart, working its way up higher and higher to the bottom of her throat, rising, a motherly alarm now all too familiar. They wait.

"I swear," the woman repeats outside. "I swear."

They wait and nothing happens and they wait some more and then yes something happens: Anabelle, their daughter, opens her mouth; opens it farther, that is, since it's already ajar; blinks her eyes, once, twice, several times; curls her fingers; lifts her arm; tilts her head; yes, it's true, she moved, is moving; and it looks like she's about to speak, to say something, a declaration, her jaw finding its way, and everything changes, again.

* * *

Technically, scientifically, rationally, Captain Dave knows the Cessna is heavy, something like 1,500 pounds, yet he's always felt his beloved plane was weightless, capable of a feathery, beautiful drift, and piloting it was like a piloting a cloud or dream. You just have to keep it up in the air. You have to keep it going. You have to have the balls to believe you can fly. Then the magic will happen.

He's exhausted, having done two shifts back to back, taken his two breaks, fixed a faulty headset, filed his last traffic report of the day, and cleared his flight path back to Fullerton Municipal Airport. This one might make his Top 10—his own personal list of the L.A. traffic-related incidents he remembers most. There's something humbling, something privileged, about seeing all this activity from above. He never gets used to it. Yes. Perspective. Plus his back is killing him. The pills he takes don't work. His wife takes pills, too, for other ailments, the number always increasing: another doctor's appointment, more pills. They now keep them all in a rectangular plastic container, each day of the week with its own specified slot so they don't mess up the dosages and frequency. They'd never had kids. It's the kind of thing you think about when you're an old man and there is only the simple fact of flight, when you're up here among the clouds, aloft and distinct.

The back-and-forth with KTZ's Layton and Peck, drive time's top-ranked morning program in the über-competitive Los Angeles market, was a little off today, the Captain reflects, always immediately critiquing his shift once it's over, how he could have done better, how he can improve the next day, it's what makes the Captain the Captain. Might have been because he was thinking about the girl, all those antlike believers down below, lost in his whirly thoughts as the day progressed. You have the stop-and-go nature of life in L.A., but then something—something besides the traffic—really makes you stop. Of course it could also be that he's just too critical of himself, which is why his wife puts little notes in his lunch bag or briefcase, her elegant, schoolgirl handwriting telling him to have a nice day and be nicer to himself. He tries. We can always do better. And we better hurry. Tomorrow night the world was supposed to blow up, after all.

He swoops and accelerates the Cessna for a final flyover of El Dorado High, invisibly waves good-bye to the still large flood of people gathered at the football stadium and scattered throughout the school grounds, as well as those hiking back to their cars, parked (and double-parked) far away, all over the neighborhood and beyond, what a day; Captain Dave wishes them well, salutes them with an official Captain tip of the hat; he hopes they are able to find whatever it is they're looking for; and ahead of him the sky is open, calm, gentle—a familiar embrace.

PRESS RELEASE

ISSUED BY THE ARCHDIOESE

OF LOS ANGELES

CONCERNING THE MATTER OF

ANABELLE VINCENT

(AKA "THE MIRACLE GIRL")

ARCHDIOCESE OF LOS ANGELES

NEWS

Office of Communications

3424 Wilshire Blvd., Los Angeles, CA 90010

Phone/Fax 213 791-7172

Contact: Father Jim Hinshaw

213-791-7172

email: jhinshaw@laarchdiocese.org

**ARCHDIOCESE ISSUES PRELIMINARY FINDINGS
ON MIRACULOUS CLAIMS REGARDING
"THE MIRACLE GIRL" ANABELLE VINCENT
STATEMENT BY MOST REV. LAWRENCE P. MCADAMS,
ARCHBISHOP OF LOS ANGELES**

MARCH 24, 2000—During the past approximate 9 months, many miraculous claims and various unexplainable cir-cumstances have occurred in the proximity of a bed-ridden 8-year-old girl named Anabelle Vincent. As the notoriety and fame of Anabelle grew, I asked a team of medical and theological professionals to review the matter to determine its possible impact, negative or positive, on the Catholic faithful, the family, and the people who sought out Anabelle in such growing numbers.

Just as the commission was about to report its prelimi-nary findings to me, Anabelle came out of her "coma" during a much publicized "farewell viewing event" held at a local high school on December 30th of the year past. Since this time the claims of miracles and heal-ing have significantly curtailed (the Vincent home, it should be noted, is no longer "open" to the public), and Anabelle has been interviewed by several commission members, including myself.

The girl has no recollection of being in the previously mentioned coma state ("akinetic mutism"), or of any of the "other than normal" experiences supposedly occur-ring in her home, or of all the media attention she and her family received. She is also at present being exam-ined by multiple doctors (specialists) to determine if the coma, and the concomitant trauma from the accident that caused it, as well as a subsequent mishandling of medication doses (resulting in a lawsuit), have led to any long-term brain damage or mental capacity reduc-tion of any kind. The doctors additionally point out that recovery of consciousness in cases such as Ana-belle's is rare, usually brought on by a regimen of drugs and therapy over time, not by the patient simply and suddenly "waking up". It is therefore hoped that

Anabelle's case will provide them with great insight into better understanding this condition.

The commission has now issued a revised preliminary report to me, concluding that, while further study is recommended in some instances, no manifestations of chicanery were found regarding the claims reviewed. This does not, however, mean that the commission endorses the verity of the claims. According to the fundamental rules of logic, one cannot presume that the inability to explain something automatically makes it miraculous. This simply means that thus far no instances of fraud or deception have been discovered.

One area of further study is regarding the composition and source of the oils and other substances found in the Vincent home. In doing this, I want to strongly emphasize that any "paranormal" occurrences are not miraculous in and of themselves. In the hundreds of years since Pope Benedict XIV (1740–1758), the consistent practice of the Catholic Church has been not to use such occurrences as verifications of miraculous claims.

Lastly, more systematic study needs to be done before the Church can even begin to evaluate the concept of "victim soul." This label, unfortunately, has been troublingly applied to Anabelle. This term is not one that's commonly used by the Church except for Christ himself who became the victim for our sins and transgressions on the cross.

Much remains mysterious about the case of Anabelle Vincent and these extraordinary claims. I urge continued prayers _for_ Anabelle, her ongoing recovery, and her family. But praying _to_ Anabelle is not acceptable in Catholic teaching. As matters move forward, one might do well to revisit this quote from English cleric Jeremy Taylor (1613—1667): "A religion without mystery must be a religion without God."

A more in-depth summary of the commission's findings can be obtained by contacting Father Jim Hinshaw, who is also available for interviews with the media.

THE MIRACLE GIRL

THE BABY IS crying. The baby is always crying, one of those prickly newborns who constantly fusses and squirms and is never right with the world. She was the same way, according to her mother and father, who never tire of telling her the war stories of the sleepless nights, the neverending frustrations, the tactics and remedies tried and failed (swaddling, not swaddling, giving antigas drops, tummy massages, rocking her in a rocking chair, driving her around in the middle of the night, putting her in her car seat on top of the dryer while it was running, and so on), and plus their overall inability to soothe and console, and how this made them feel like the shittiest parents ever. You weren't the easiest baby in the world, that's for sure, they recount, sometimes we didn't know how we'd make it. And Anabelle listens, nods, even smiles, but it hurts to hear all this, she'd like to take it all back. She was just a baby, she didn't know. She promises herself she won't say these kinds of things to her baby when she gets older. She'll only talk about the good.

It's now the day after the day the world was supposed to end. Some Internet preacher guy had predicted yesterday would be it, the end, the reckoning, Judgment Day. In recent weeks, billboards had popped up all over the country, warning of the coming devastation. The preacher's followers were leaving their jobs, giving up their homes and their life savings, abandoning everything to prepare for the end times. Videos of the preacher, who looked exactly the way you imagined he would (gray shock of hair, grizzled beard, intense animal eyes), were released online and went viral. He was everywhere: CNN, Fox, *The View*. Then, when it didn't happen and the sun still rose on May 22, 2016, he backtracked and said he'd screwed up the math, quickly revising his prediction and claiming the Rapture was now set to occur five months later. She'd been watching the news all morning, drifting in and out, thinking about the preacher and his crazed face and how all those people believed in him and could give up everything like that, while she also cleaned and scrubbed and got the house ready. Because it's also the day her parents are visiting to see the baby for the first time, three weeks after the birth. The sky outside gray and dim, like it always is here. The sun a distant, druggy memory. That perennial Pacific Northwest drizzle.

And the baby is crying.

Her parents' flight from Los Angeles had already landed, and they were now likely nearing the end of their short rental car drive from Sea-Tac to Evergreen, where she lives in base housing, Joint Base Lewis-McChord, with her husband, Marc, who'd fulfilled his boyhood dream of joining the Air Force. She wishes Marc was here—for support, for everything—but he's somewhere way across the world, deployed again, in a country she previously hadn't heard of: Qatar, which was right next to Saudi Arabia and located on the Persian Gulf, a Muslim country, and yet, according to Marc and his e-mails and letters, they have Walmart and Applebee's and Chili's. He'd been there when the baby was born. And he'd be there for another five months. It was bad enough missing him and needing his help with the baby, but she also worried about being alone so much and forgetting (because she forgot things, her brain was sucky, wasn't all it could be) and doing something that could harm the baby.

To combat her chronic absentmindedness, she makes lists, puts up notes, bright pink Post-its all over the house. Things like CHANGE DIAPERS!!! and PAY PHONE BILL TODAY!!! and TRASH/RECYCLING ON TUESDAYS!!! But she still forgets, she gets lost easily when driving, she has headaches and spells, she gets tired, she can't always follow the plots of movies or TV shows, it's like she's on a different speed than everyone else, or it's like she's drunk but she hasn't been drinking, just a little off—all because her brain wasn't right because of the accident and the coma and all that happened to her when she was a little girl. She didn't remember anything of that time (her knowledge consisting only of her parents' stories and the cable TV movie that had been made; the guy who'd played her dad was later in a doctor show that ran for several years, and whenever they'd watch TV and see the actor her dad would joke "There I am" or "Damn, I'm looking pretty good these days"), but it had altered her, made her forgetful and slow, like an old lady, and she tried, tried, tried to keep up and be normal and someone who was just like anyone else. Her neighbor, Michelle, whose husband is also deployed, comes by in the mornings and after she gets off work to check on her and the baby. If something happened to the baby because of her—well, she doesn't know what. It's one thing to get lost and spend the afternoon driving around. But a baby. Her baby. Brianna. Bri. The baby who was never even supposed to be born. Marc says he isn't worried. "You'll be fine. You'll be a great mom. I can tell. And hell, I forget stuff all the time. You'll remember the important things."

It became a mental battle to see how long she could hold out, how long she could go before she yielded and picked up the baby. She was inconsistent, she knew. Sometimes picking her up right away, sometimes waiting a short time, sometimes waiting a long time. This was not good. Being inconsistent turned out to be a highly suspect trait as a parent, a sign of your doom. All the books and websites said so. Consistency was key. She tried. She tried to make her actions and reactions the same, but are people really like that? And she should have written a Post-it for MOM AND DAD ARRIVE THURSDAY AT NOON!!!!!! She had forgotten to do this, though, and it was now noon, and it had almost slipped her mind that they were coming.

Deployed: it's such a strange word, it feels funny in your mouth when you say it out loud and when you think it, too. *Deployed.*

And so finally she picks up the baby from the crib next to her bed and starts walking with her throughout the house, singing, making up words and melodies. The crying does not stop, however, and when the doorbell rings, she jumps. She's still surprised, even though she's been expecting them, telling herself to remember, to focus and remember. Did she have a girlhood dream, the equivalent of Marc's boyhood dream? And if so, what was it? Nothing immediately comes to mind.

"There she is!" her mother exclaims as she enters the house

and shakes off the damp and wet, and it's not clear if she's referring to her or the baby or both of them, followed closely by her father, wheeling luggage and carrying a box of diapers and flowers. The last time she saw them was Christmas, half a year ago, and they look the same basically: middle-aged, graying, rounder, saggier, slower. You always see your parents as you saw them when you were a child, and she's still getting used to the concept of parents that age and do not stay the same, vulnerable to time after all.

Hugs, embraces, passing of the baby, whose crying has escalated further ever since the arrival of her parents. Everyone ignores this.

"You look good," her father tells her, holding her hands and examining her. "Motherhood agrees with you."

She guides them from the small entryway into the adjoining living room, where the TV is going and she has put out crackers and cheese (she remembered!) on the chest/trunk that serves as a coffee table, and where she and Marc spend the majority of their time when he's home. They've lived here for two years and still the walls remain bare, no plant life or photos or cozy knickknacks, everything feeling temporary, most of their belongings in storage, "military spare," as Marc jokingly calls the decor. And they have hardly any furniture anyway, so there's just a red, bumpy couch (left by the previous occupants) and two nonmatching folding chairs, and next to the TV there's a shelf lined with DVDs, mostly Marc's, and a few books (hers), though it's hard for her to read, the headaches start up after about ten minutes. The room has always smelled, mysteriously, of mushrooms. The baby's Pack 'n Play sits in the corner and now dominates the room.

"I still don't know why you didn't want us to come earlier, for the birth," her mother says, sitting down, sinking into the couch. "We would have come. It would have been all right."

"Mom, let's not, OK?"

It had been hard to explain—to her parents, to Marc even— but she'd wanted to have that initial time to be alone with the baby, to get used to just the two of them, before the rest of the world joined in.

"Well, we're here now," her father says.

But she could have put out the cheese and crackers two hours ago instead of two minutes ago. When cheese is left out too long it starts to sweat, you can tell, right? She stares at the cubes of sharp cheddar and they look fine, freshly cut, not sweaty. Her father will stay a week then return home; her mother will stay another two weeks. Sweaty cheese. Deployed. Sometimes words were like glue in her mind. They got stuck there, and she repeated them over and over. One of the many things she doesn't remember is how she supposedly made up her own language as a child. Went days speaking nothing but this nonsensical language, driving her parents crazy.

"There's cheese," she says. "Help yourself."

"Thanks."

"We had peanuts on the plane. I thought they stopped doing that but I guess not."

"The air. Just the air here is so different. From when you first walk off the plane."

"Do you miss Southern California?"

"Sometimes. But I like it here, too. It's different."

"I could stay longer, you know. They can get someone else to cover at work, for another week probably."

"Three weeks is plenty, Mom. I really appreciate it. Thanks. We can maybe go up to Seattle, see the Space Needle."

"You've got a lot of notes here."

"It helps me. It helps me remember."

And the other thing is noise. Loud TVs, loud restaurants, loud music. Her brain can't filter out sound. All there is is the blaring sound. It's not background noise to her; it's all foreground noise and she can't work her way around it. The louder it gets, the tenser she becomes, the more likely her temper will kick in. Many times she and Marc have left a restaurant mid-meal because she couldn't take the noise anymore, Marc patient, Marc boxing the food and paying the bill while she sat in the car and put in her earplugs and practiced taking deep, rejuvenating breaths. A good man in your life makes all the difference.

"We miss you, Sweetheart. It's only a couple of hours away, to fly, I know, but it still feels so far away. Marc, is he doing OK? We worry about him."

And she gives them the Marc update: the computer systems he runs and repairs, how Qatar is different from what you'd think, the Walmarts, the Applebee's, and how he writes a lot, tons, misses the baby, feels bad about not being there, says not to worry, and in eight more years he'll be done and he'll retire early and they'll be all set, he'll retire from the Air Force and then get an IT job somewhere (probably Seattle or Redmond) and they'll buy a house with the money they've been saving plus what was in the special Miracle Girl savings account created by her parents (including the money from the hospital lawsuit, which dragged on for years, and which, once all the lawyers' fees had been taken out, wasn't as much as they thought it would be) and then they'll be all set, life will be good.

"Look at this girl," her mother says, lifting the baby, whose limbs dangle as if they were made of rubber. "Look at this little baby girl. Hello Baby Brianna. Hello Baby Bri."

Without noticing it, she realizes the baby has stopped crying. The baby who wasn't supposed to have been born. They'd tried before, unsuccessful, prior to Marc's first deployment. They visited their respective doctors and were told she wouldn't be able to have children; whether it had anything to do with the accident and the coma and all that, her doctor couldn't say. But then it happened. She didn't get her period. She tested and retested and then went to the doctor, the same doctor who'd said it wasn't possible, and he confirmed. "It's a miracle, I guess," said the doctor, who didn't know who he was talking to. Yes. A miracle baby. A Miracle Baby for the Miracle Girl. These things happen. They happen every day.

She watches her parents watch the baby. They are grand-parents. They are happy, she can tell, having found something over the years. A familiarity, yes, but also something more than that, a permanence and a peace that you don't always see in couples. She knows there were troubles, from both before and after the accident. He left for a while. Doubts and uncertainties. Before she married Marc, her mother told her, "For a long time I worried. Your father wasn't always there. There was a part of him that was somewhere else." "What happened?" she asked. "He changed," her mother said. "People change. Sometimes you'll hear people say that it isn't possible. But he changed. We both did. We both got lucky."

And she had been lucky, too, of course, waking up all those years ago, that day at the high school football stadium, all those people there, all that they needed and she was somehow able

to give, resuming her life after being sick, recovering from akinetic mutism, a rare occurrence according to her doctors, who
were never able to fully explain why she woke up. Just last year,
for the first time, she met someone who'd had the same condition and also recovered, though not as well, still needing super-
vised care and help every day. The woman's doctor thought a
visit from Anabelle might be inspiring, so the woman's family
flew her down to Houston, where they lived. It was right after
Anabelle found out that she was pregnant. The woman cried
when she heard this. Her name was Ellen Smith. She said she just
wanted one thought to flow to the next. She wanted speaking to
not seem like such a chore. She wanted to remember names. She
wanted to remember TV shows from when she was a little girl.
When it was time for Anabelle to leave, the woman cried again.

Her parents switch, her father now holding the baby, who remains still and calm, who doesn't fuss or cry or try to escape. It's
a good sign. And it's hard for her to always appreciate the baby
because of all the crying, but she does so now, admiring her tiny
fingers and tiny eyelashes and the pure beauty of her mouth, her
skin, her lips. She will grow and continue to grow and become
something else, a person, a full-sized adult, and it was her job to
prepare her daughter for all that. Sounded simple, sure, but she
could already tell it wouldn't be so simple.

"Last month someone came to the house," her mother says.

Which happens every so often. Someone will show up at the
house where she grew up, now owned by her cousin Dominique
and her husband, who have two sons. Someone will knock on
the door and Dom will answer and the person will say "Is this
the house? Is this where the Miracle Girl lived?" and depending on Dom's mood she will either let them in or not, she will,

if inclined, show them around and even lead them to the room, allow them some time alone in there so they can make their prayer or whatever. And after they're done, the person will begin to talk and start to tell their story.

"After all these years, still," Anabelle says.

Yes. These things happen. Call them miracles or call them life. They happen every day.

Acknowledgments

Writing is often a solitary pursuit, but no book and no writer is an island. I've been fortunate enough to have had many people believe in me and *The Miracle Girl* over the years, and it's a true pleasure to thank them here.

First of all, there's my agent Michelle Brower. Her patience, her wisdom, her enduring belief in me even when I wasn't so sure—she is one of the true "miracles" behind this book. Big thanks, too, to all the fine folks at Folio Literary, especially Melissa White and Annie Hwang.

I can't think of a better editor and advocate than Andra Miller. Her passion for this book has been inspiring. I'm eternally grateful. And I'm happy to have gained a new friend. It's also been a pleasure and honor to work with everyone at Algonquin: Elisabeth Scharlatt, Ina Stern, Craig Popelars, Debra Linn, Emma Boyer, Kelly Bowen, Brooke Csuka, Lauren Moseley, Brunson Hoole, Anne Winslow, Chris Stamey, Kelly Clark Policelli.

As I wrote *The Miracle Girl,* I was lucky enough to publish a few excerpts, providing me with much-needed encouragement along the way. Shout-outs to those who helped usher these previews into the world: Andrew Scott and Kevin Morgan Watson;

Scott Garson; and Colleen Donfield, Andrew Snee, Tim McKee, Sy Safransky, and everyone at *The Sun*.

For reading, encouragement, advice, friendship, commiseration, and more: Carol Keeley, Bonnie ZoBell, Heather Fowler, Peter Rock, Hannah Tinti, Will Allison, Rob Spillman, Jon Raymond, Roy Parvin, Alicia Gifford, Taryn Thomas, Doug Dorst, Amy Wallen, Linda Swanson-Davies, Michael Krasny, Jim Ruland, Justin Hudnall, Richard Lange.

And my parents. Strangely, wonderfully, they never dissuaded me from becoming a writer. Their love and support fuel these pages (and everything else I will ever write). Growing up, I didn't realize how lucky I was to have such a supportive mother and father. Now I do. And I miss you, Dad. Really miss you.

Biggest, hugest, most heartfelt thanks of all to my wife, Maria, and our three children, Ethan, Henry, and Celia. Thank you for making me a better person. Thank you for making me a better writer. And thank you for inspiring me each and every day. The adventure continues.

THE MIRACLE GIRL

A Note from the Author

*

Questions for Discussion

A Note from the Author

We started taking shifts—my mother, my wife, and I. Caring for my dying father as the days and nights somehow passed. Spoon-feeding him applesauce and chocolate pudding. Dropping morphine drops on his tongue, which he stuck out like a baby bird. This had been going on for weeks, ever since we'd had a hospital bed delivered to the house and converted the extra room downstairs into his bedroom. We were all so tired. My father had been sick for years (cancer, strokes, a series of countless lesser ailments), and now that it was getting close to the end, we were numb, ghostly. As it turned out, my wife, three months pregnant with our first child, was the one in the room with him when he finally died.

At that moment, I was sitting in the nearby living room, writing in a journal that I had been keeping. Here's what I had written earlier in the day:

Today, Saturday (10-30-04), it's a shock the first time I see him. He's so dark. Ashen. His face is transformed now, extracted of color and life. His stubble clings to his jaw, chin, neck. It's like the last living thing.

Death—haunted now, fully.

M. comes in room w/ a sandwich, asks if I want to split it. Food?

"Look at his face."

She does and she's shocked too. She starts to cry. I should have warned her. It's that much of a change from yesterday. Sitting there, sense th—

When my wife cried out, I ran to the room. There he was, mouth open. There my wife was, her belly now slightly rounded. And there I was, the living in-between link. And I had the uncanny sense of something having passed from my father to my unborn son. It was the most powerful moment of my life and I knew right then that nothing would ever eclipse it. Three generations in this room—one gestating, one alive, one dead, but all connected—part of the same story, the same shared history, together for the very last time.

* * *

I've never been a religious person, unless you count my brief preteen infatuation with the miniseries *Jesus of Nazareth*. But when you experience one of those big life moments—like losing a parent or becoming a parent, which, in my case, both happened within a matter of months—you inevitably question your beliefs and your place in the universe and whether or not there's more to this life than, well, this life. And if you don't have religion to turn to at such moments, you come to admire how it can be a comfort and consolation for so many people. You find yourself with an acute case of spiritual envy (to quote the title of a book by Michael Krasny, a former professor of mine).

I'd already been thinking about the power of religion and belief for a few years, having started writing what would eventually become *The Miracle Girl*. The initial spark was seeing an episode of ABC's news program *20/20* in the mid- to late nineties. It featured the story of a Massachusetts girl named Audrey Santo. Young Audrey had been in a swimming pool accident that put her in a comalike state called akinetic mutism. She could not speak and she could not move. According to her doctors, it was unknown whether Audrey was conscious and aware of her surroundings. Her day-to-day care required great effort and sacrifice, a deep, vast love. And she was also the object of a growing fame because of the miraculous events that supposedly occurred around her.

There were the usual stories of statues weeping and bleeding, of illnesses and ailments cured. People came to the Santo house in droves, a stream of the hopeful and devout and curious, lining up as if it were a theme park. The Catholic Church was investigating. Believers and skeptics alike were interviewed. Audrey's mother was very religious, certain of what was behind her daughter's reputed powers, while her husband was estranged from the family. The garage was turned into a chapel/bedroom for Audrey, and the family even replaced the garage door with a glass partition so more people could "view" her. Most haunting of all: the young girl's eyes were open, making her seem both alive and dead at the same time, trapped in that transitional moment.

I immediately knew this was something I wanted to write about, leading me to a series of "what if" questions: What if the mother wasn't religious and was trying to make sense of what was happening around her, while also struggling with the burden of caring for a child in such a consuming way? What if the estranged father came back and had to deal with the guilt of his abandonment? What if the backdrop was the approaching millennium, with all its buzz about reckoning and doom? What if, instead of Massachusetts, the story took place in suburban eastern Los Angeles (where I'm from)? And what if, besides the family, I also told the story of the people who came to visit the girl, seeking her help, her guidance, her healing—and not just for physical ailments or spiritual direction, but also for things like heartbreak and other commonplace disappointments we all face?

I've always been drawn to stories of miracles and the pilgrims they attract, both in real life and in fiction—from Chaucer's *The Canterbury Tales* to, more recently, Don DeLillo's short story "The Angel Esmeralda," in which the apparition of a murdered young girl purportedly appears on a billboard, drawing scores of onlookers to a street in the Bronx. Why do they come? What do they hope to find? I wanted to explore this collective (and ancient) yearning for the miraculous to be true, to impart meaning and purpose, particularly in a day and age when such certainty seems to increasingly elude us. And I wanted to write a novel not only about the power and mysteries of faith and how the possibility of miracles can sustain so many but also about how a different kind of miracle can be found all around us in our everyday lives—like when you hold your child for the first time, or when you say good-bye to your father for the last time and you tell him, *This child is going to know all about you. He's going to know how excited you were when you heard he was on the way. He's going to know how funny you were, how you liked to play tennis, how you liked to tell stories about when you were in the*

Merchant Marines during the war. He's going to know all these
things. I promise.

*   *   *

We chartered a boat to scatter my father's ashes off the coast of
Dana Point, California. The day was emphatically sunny, bright,
clear. My mother and I had some trouble with the ashes. They
were in a box, a very nice box, but there was also a plastic bag in
there holding the ashes. When we tipped the box upside-down to
scatter my father's remains in the sea, the plastic bag came out,
too, even though we'd been warned about this. I guess we should
have rehearsed it a little bit more.

Then this happened: After the ashes had been put in the ocean
and we witnessed their slow descent, a school of dolphins appeared, as if on cue. About twenty feet in front of us, beautiful
and otherworldly, rising up and out of the water and then back
down in an effortless glide. We stood and watched and marveled.
It was another moment when you just wanted to believe.

Questions for Discussion

1. *The Miracle Girl* is a story largely about faith and belief. How did your own faith and belief affect how you read the novel?

2. Some readers have said they believed the miracles described in the book were real; some have said they didn't think they were real; and others have said it didn't matter to them either way. Did you feel like you had to make that decision as a reader? Which category did you fall into and why?

3. The author has said in interviews and in the essay that follows the novel that he's not religious. Does this surprise you? Does it change the way you view the novel?

4. The hunger for miracles to be real is timeless. But do you find that this hunger is even more pronounced in today's world?

5. People from different walks of life are drawn to Anabelle. Besides those who were ill and sought actual physical healing, what void do you think Anabelle was filling in people's lives? How was she able to help the various visitors? Do you think the author was also questioning a larger cultural void?

6. As word about Anabelle's miracles spread, more and more people showed up at the Vincent house, "all with their reasons, all with their doubts and certainties and everything in between" (page 134). Would you have visited Anabelle? If yes, what would be the reason for the visit?

7. *The Miracle Girl* takes place in the latter half of 1999, as the millennium approaches, amid the buzz and chatter of Y2K, computer crashes, and the end of the world. How does having the book set in this time period reflect its themes?

8. After the car accident, John leaves his family and embarks on a period of exile, wanting "to become a monk, and if not that, then at least be able to classify himself as monklike" (page 95). Throughout the course of the novel, do you feel like he was able to redeem himself? Can he ever redeem himself after abandoning his wife and child? Is he ultimately a sympathetic character or not?

9. Compare Anabelle before and after the accident. In what ways was she already different and isolated and set apart before she became "the Miracle Girl"?

10. Did Karen do the right thing by letting people into her house to see her daughter and spend time with her? Was she right to share her with the world? What would you have done?

11. Peter Ustinov once said, "Love is an act of endless forgiveness." How does this quote and sentiment relate to the book, and in particular to Anabelle's parents, Karen and John? Why do you think Karen took John back? Were you surprised?

12. Discuss the role that the media and the Internet play in the telling of Anabelle's story. In what way is the book a commentary on how the media and the Internet pervade and even define our lives? With so much white noise out there, and with so much information and data coming at us and requiring our constant deciphering, how difficult is it to find something that you can truly believe in?

13. *The Miracle Girl* has a large cast of characters. Why do you think Roe decided to tell this story from multiple points of view? What does this add to the story? Would the novel have had the same impact if it was told from a singular point of view?

14. Most depictions of Los Angeles in books, TV shows, and movies feature the stereotypical L.A. of celebrities and airbrushed beaches. The part of L.A. in which this novel is set is a very different place. Roe has stated that he chose to set the book in suburban eastern Los Angeles not only because it's where he was born and raised, but also to give readers a more complete picture of L.A., which is such a diverse and varied area. Do you feel he succeeded? How did the setting contribute to the story?

15. The book certainly has some heavy and difficult subject matter, as well as plenty of tragedy and despair. But do you ultimately consider it a hopeful book? If so, why?

16. Were you surprised by the epilogue and getting to see Anabelle as an adult? Why do you think Roe chose to end the novel this way?

DAMIEN O'MALLEY

Andrew Roe's fiction has appeared in *Tin House, One Story,* the *Sun, Glimmer Train,* the *Cincinnati Review,* and other publications. His nonfiction has appeared in the *New York Times,* the *San Francisco Chronicle, Salon,* and elsewhere. He lives in Oceanside, California, with his wife and three children.

Other Algonquin Readers Round Table Novels

Running the Rift, a novel by Naomi Benaron

A stunning award-winning novel that—through the eyes of one unforgettable boy—explores a country's unraveling, its tentative new beginning, and the love that binds its people together. The story follows the life and progress of Jean Patrick Nkuba, a young runner who dreams of becoming Rwanda's first Olympic track medalist.

"Benaron writes like Jean Patrick runs, with the heart of a lion."
—*The Dallas Morning News*

"A culturally rich and unflinching story of resilience and resistance."
—*Chicago Tribune*, Editor's Choice

"Audacious and compelling . . . An authentic and richly textured portrait of African life." —*The Washington Post*

Winner of the Bellwether Prize for Socially Engaged Fiction

AN ALGONQUIN READERS ROUND TABLE EDITION WITH READING GROUP GUIDE AND OTHER SPECIAL FEATURES • FICTION • ISBN 978-1-61620-194-4

The Girl Who Fell from the Sky, a novel by Heidi W. Durrow

In the aftermath of a family tragedy, a biracial girl must cope with society's ideas of race and class in this acclaimed novel, winner of the Bellwether Prize for fiction addressing issues of social justice.

"Affecting, exquisite . . . Durrow's powerful novel is poised to find a place among classic stories of the American experience."
—*The Miami Herald*

"Durrow manages that remarkable achievement of telling a subtle, complex story that speaks in equal volumes to children and adults. Like *Catcher in the Rye* or *To Kill a Mockingbird*, Durrow's debut features voices that will ring in the ears long after the book is closed . . . It's a captivating and original tale that shouldn't be missed." —*The Denver Post*

Winner of the Bellwether Prize for Socially Engaged Fiction

AN ALGONQUIN READERS ROUND TABLE EDITION WITH READING GROUP GUIDE AND OTHER SPECIAL FEATURES • FICTION • ISBN 978-1-61620-015-2

Mudbound, a novel by Hillary Jordan

Mudbound is the saga of the McAllan family, who struggle to survive on a remote ramshackle farm, and the Jacksons, their black sharecroppers. When two men return from World War II to work the land, the unlikely friendship between these brothers-in-arms— one white, one black—arouses the passions of their neighbors. In this award-winning portrait of two families caught up in the blind hatred of a small Southern town, prejudice takes many forms, both subtle and ruthless.

"This is storytelling at the height of its powers . . . Hillary Jordan writes with the force of a Delta storm." —Barbara Kingsolver

Winner of the Bellwether Prize for Socially Engaged Fiction

AN ALGONQUIN READERS ROUND TABLE EDITION WITH READING GROUP GUIDE AND OTHER SPECIAL FEATURES • FICTION • ISBN 978-1-56512-677-0

A Friend of the Family, a novel by Lauren Grodstein

Pete Dizinoff has a thriving medical practice in suburban New Jersey, a devoted wife, a network of close friends, an impressive house, and a son, Alec, now nineteen, on whom he's pinned all his hopes. But Pete never counted on Laura, his best friend's daughter, setting her sights on his only son. Lauren Grodstein's riveting novel charts a father's fall from grace as he struggles to save his family, his reputation, and himself.

"Suspense worthy of Hitchcock . . . [Grodstein] is a terrific storyteller." —*The New York Times Book Review*

"A gripping portrayal of a suburban family in free-fall." —*Minneapolis Star Tribune*

AN ALGONQUIN READERS ROUND TABLE EDITION WITH READING GROUP GUIDE AND OTHER SPECIAL FEATURES • FICTION • ISBN 978-1-61620-017-6

Pictures of You, a novel by Caroline Leavitt

Two women running away from their marriages collide on a foggy highway. The survivor of the fatal accident is left to pick up the pieces not only of her own life but of the lives of the devastated husband and fragile son that the other woman left behind. As these three lives intersect, the book asks, How well do we really know those we love, and how do we open our hearts to forgive the unforgivable?

"An expert storyteller . . . Leavitt teases suspense out of the greatest mystery of all—the workings of the human heart." —*Booklist*

"Magically written, heartbreakingly honest . . . Caroline Leavitt is one of those fabulous, incisive writers you read and then ask yourself, Where has she been all my life?" —Jodi Picoult

AN ALGONQUIN READERS ROUND TABLE EDITION WITH READING GROUP GUIDE AND OTHER SPECIAL FEATURES • FICTION • ISBN 978-1-56512-631-2

In the Time of the Butterflies, a novel by Julia Alvarez

In this extraordinary novel, the voices of Las Mariposas (The Butterflies), Minerva, Patria, María Teresa, and Dedé, speak across the decades to tell their stories about life in the Dominican Republic under General Rafael Leonidas Trujillo's dictatorship. Through the art and magic of Julia Alvarez's imagination, the martyred butterflies live again in this novel of valor, love, and the human cost of political oppression.

"A gorgeous and sensitive novel . . . A compelling story of courage, patriotism, and familial devotion." —*People*

"A magnificent treasure for all cultures and all time."
—*St. Petersburg Times*

A National Endowment for the Arts Big Read Selection

AN ALGONQUIN READERS ROUND TABLE EDITION WITH READING GROUP GUIDE AND OTHER SPECIAL FEATURES • FICTION • ISBN 978-1-56512-976-4

A Reliable Wife, a novel by Robert Goolrick

Rural Wisconsin, 1907. In the bitter cold, Ralph Truitt stands alone on a train platform anxiously awaiting the arrival of the woman who answered his newspaper ad for "a reliable wife." The woman who arrives is not the one he expects in this *New York Times* #1 bestseller about love and madness, longing and murder.

"[A] chillingly engrossing plot . . . Good to the riveting end."
—*USA Today*

"Deliciously wicked and tense . . . Intoxicating."
—*The Washington Post*

"A rousing historical potboiler." —*The Boston Globe*

AN ALGONQUIN READERS ROUND TABLE EDITION WITH READING GROUP GUIDE AND OTHER SPECIAL FEATURES • FICTION • ISBN 978-1-56512-977-1

West of Here, a novel by Jonathan Evison

Spanning more than hundred years—from the ragged mudflats of a belching and bawdy Western frontier in the 1890s to the rusting remains of a strip-mall cornucopia in 2006—*West of Here* chronicles the life of one small town. It's a saga of destiny and greed, adventure and passion, hope and hilarity, that turns America's history into myth and myth into a nation's shared experience.

"[A] booming, bighearted epic." —*Vanity Fair*

"[A] voracious story . . . Brisk, often comic, always deeply sympathetic." —*The Washington Post*

AN ALGONQUIN READERS ROUND TABLE EDITION WITH READING GROUP GUIDE AND OTHER SPECIAL FEATURES • FICTION • ISBN 978-1-61620-082-4